ESITIMA

GREGORY EFFIONG

authorHOUSE®

AuthorHouse™ UK
1663 Liberty Drive
Bloomington, IN 47403 USA
www.authorhouse.co.uk
Phone: UK TFN: 0800 0148641 (Toll Free inside the UK)
*   UK Local: 02036 956322 (+44 20 3695 6322 from outside the UK)*

Published by AuthorHouse 03/17/2021

ISBN: 978-1-5462-8109-2 (sc)
ISBN: 978-1-5462-8108-5 (e)

For my Late Parents, Mr Michael Effiong and Mrs Maria Michael Effiong.
and
Veronica, my beloved wife; Anietie, Elisha, Emediong-THE BOYS, my real bundle of joy.

CHAPTER 1

I MET HER FLIPPING THROUGH PAGES of a file she had brought home from work. Feverishly worried with a reduced energy level of the body and puckered countenance, Aritie buried her head down in the process thinking intently. At the screeching sound of my opening the door, she lifted her eyes to my direction. I could see her beautiful rosy face wrinkled out of form; and my presence then meant absolutely nothing to her.

The usual emotion of excitement with our meeting together frizzled away. And now, those sentiments were no longer at ease with her disturbed state of mind as she bowed her head down in sadness. Nearly a year of our courtship, I've never seen her in that mood before. This worried me seriously.

And as I clicked the door back to close; Aritie dropped her head down low sadly; sighing and moaning in pains of her present problem. Although she didn't pay attention to her fingers on the file as it appeared-she flipped through the document just to relieve her worries. The exercise seemed soothing to her pains.

"Hello sweetie, what's up" I said assessing her carefully.

"Is anything the matter; come on … are you alright?"

I quickened my steps in her direction.

Aritie didn't answer a word instead, closed the file and continued displaying her sad disposition. I stood beholding her with the expectation she would say something to me, instead Aritie rested her chin in her left palm dropping it on her thigh and shaking unconsciously. I was in awe observing her body language, I wondered what might have gone wrong with her.

Quickly, I dropped the gifts I held on the centre table in a bit of consoling her with comfort.

"Come on honey, talk to me. What's the matter … are you alright?"

She remained in the limbo of lost hope. I kissed her cheek trying to excite her to see if this would raise her mood for her to respond to my queries. Aritie responded angrily.

"No, leave me alone." Pushing me away from her.

Voice sounded undertone; unlike orotund cadence I've known her with. She let off my grasp, tears trickling down her cheeks. I was in awe as Aritie started sobbing with heavy emotion.

"Darling stop blubbering please, tell me what's wrong. I am here for you, okay?"

I was confused about her tears as she held the problem in abeyance much longer than was necessary.

'Did she meet with some problems at work?' was my thoughts. 'Or have I done something to annoy her?'

I started assessing myself for a possible clue to my behaviour that could annoy the love of my life yet, I found none.

Aritie was a woman I wouldn't like to see in any form of distress. We were passionately in love which had grown to a point that I wouldn't hurt her feeling for a second. Her musical voice evoked a compelling sense of passion. Literary, I would identify Aritie's voice within a loud noise in the crowd. Honestly, she was a very special person after my own heart.

"Come on, talk to me honey, what's the matter? I am here for you darling"

I continued appealing to her passion.

Then she lifted her eyes slowly regarding me with misery written all over her. And I could feel the pangs of her pains piecing like arrows through my own heart. Bending forward, I picked the tissue paper on the table and handed over to her. She collected and wiped her tearful reddened eyes.

"Meaning you've been crying for hours now, what's wrong. Talk to me, please."

She turned around wiping her eyes again and hissed heavily with emotion of pain and grieve.

"I witnessed a terrifying scene that set up tremendous motion of anxiety and pain in me."

She had finally ventilated in a cracked voice still sobbing. With diligence, I grabbed drawing her closer to myself and patted her back. Then waited for her to elaborate, but she lifted her eyes regarding me gently without saying anything further.

In a calmer and modulated voice, I sorted for some clarification.

"What scene love, at work?"

She adjusted herself from the bed she sat facing me and nodding her head.

"Yes,"

she added her voice.

"...when I tell you that that woman is evil incarnate you say I shouldn't speak that way Etido."

Aritie held up observing me slowly. A feeling of despondency hovered around her.

"Today is the day that her atrocities have reached the biting point...it has been blown open, and sadly, I am the victim of that dross."

She continued sobbing.

"Honestly honey, I don't understand. Could you let me have the full story please?"

She held onto my left palm breathing heavily.

"I discovered, to my chagrin, that Esitima killed my uncle at The Tavern so that she could have the freedom to go around satisfying her desires"

That information caught me like bolt from the blue. And I looked at Aritie dismayed.

"You don't mean it, unbelievable! Who told you that? Oh my God?" I expressed overt surprise.

"I knew you wouldn't believe me for a thousand years"

She dropped my palm and turned away from me.

"Not that I wouldn't believe sweetie, but the thought of the act is absolutely too scary. It's a thing most unimaginable to believe for a lady of that calibre. Obnoxious!"

"Obnoxious, there you are. When will you ever believe me, Etido...Is Esitima more honourable to you than I, obnoxious?"

That answer was chilling. We remained quiet looking at one another slowly for a second.

I held her right hand caressing slowly.

There were ongoing family feuds since the demise of that erudite Professor, Bassey Mbede, her uncle. Many believed the adulterous spirit of his wife, Esitima had killed him, while others blamed his sudden death on the University community he headed. They alluded to someone killing him to take his place.

Mkpasang people had a strong belief that a person shouldn't die young. Everyone should live out their years to old age. As such anyone that died young, his death would be attributed to some superstitious beliefs-ill health and disease or internal malfunctioning of the body organs notwithstanding.

As a young person, individuals should live out God's given number of years on earth. Anyone that die premature death would be blamed on bewitchment by significant members of his family whom they strongly believed to be a witch or wizard.

This pronounced superstition had held its presence so firmly in Mkpasang. The people regarded invisible power of witchcraft and sorcery as preying on their lives.

Weaker members of the community were seen as subjects of possible elimination by those they thought to be members of the occult groups. Such accusers may be the ones holding significant economic power and living above the standards of an average member of Mkpasang community.

The belief of linking wealth with something diabolical made it difficult trying to convince an average member of Mkpasang community to think outside the box. Anything they couldn't give logical or objective explanation will be attributed to esoteric illusion and they give spiritual meanings to it. And as such, relying on superstition to explain Professor Mbede's death became inevitable.

Therefore, Esitima and her father-in-law came into the picture as the accused. They also accused senior management cadre in the University community they strongly believed killed him to take his place of leadership.

Aritie told me that she stumbled over her information by accident during the review of the Closed-Circuit Television (CCTV) footage installed in The Tavern, her new place of employment. She told me that this happened as she prepared to take charge of running the establishment. She needed to familiarise herself with the workings of every department in the establishment.

"I brought my eyeballs closer and closer to the computer screen, browsing through every page closely." She had said

"One page after another revealed the veil and identity of the perpetrator's action. The scene that enveloped and surrounded the death, the death of my uncle. The scene that had clouded Mkpasang community for so long was finally blown open. It's a heart-breaking thing to watch the real genesis of uncle Bassey's gruesome murder. Tears and fears overtook my entire existence."

Aritie sobbed as she recounted her experience. And I expressed my sympathy for reminding her of the death she had seemed to forget. I held her tight to my Bosom, consoling her with the empathy of love.

"I saw my uncle lying on the floor twitching and foaming from his mouth, and pieces of food he had just eaten in his mouth and some on the table with an empty bottle of beer rolling towards his head. No one was there to help him, instead Esitima, his wife stood shedding crocodile tears…"

"Wait a minute" I interrupted her "…you mean his wife was unwilling to help her husband even to remove pieces of foodstuff stocked in his mouth knowing that he might be chocked?… oh my God"

I was furious.

"That tells you how diabolical she is… that bitch is a witch, all she knows is wickedness and lewdness. Should I have any respect for her anymore? No, not at all"

I could feel the weight of bitter jealousy she had for Esitima in the tone of her voice.

Aritie went on to say that earlier on, Esitima was telling her husband tales of lies and funny stories about her unfaithfulness. She claimed that she was kidnapped and raped by some strangers.

"Would you believe such cook and bull stories, Etido?"

"Well, you can never tell, the onus of proof lies on her. None of us was there as a witness, honey."

"Who would drug an old strumpet like her then carried into the hotel for sex? That is a cooked lie made up to cover her infidelity. And she thought that anybody who hears such crab would clap hands for her, isn't it?"

Aritie said.

Aritie had loved her late uncle so dearly that she still cuddled his memory with engaging passion. The reason she continued living in his property long after his death. She stayed there to assist in the upbringing of his children in the face of Esitima's lack of mothering skills. This had denied her children her adequate motherhood care and affection.

Esitima had no touch with family dynamics, she concentrated all her attention in managing her boutique. The responsibility for the upbringing of the kids and running the family had fallen solely on Aritie. She was a mother surrogate to the family. And for these reasons, she couldn't bear to put away the current reminder of his death in a hurry, and bringing it back was quite a distressing thing to her.

"Cheeei, Esitima! you have done your worse. Biting the finger that fed you? I can't believe it."

She was distraught recalling the scene of that incident on the CCTV.

Series of emotions she displayed, including physical reactions like worries, anxiety, fear and being on edge as we talked. Inadvertently, if her vital signs were taken then, blood pressure would have arisen significantly. And as I hugged her, could feel labouring breath as though she had just finished 100 metres race. The distress that this event had brought to the woman I loved no doubt, was unbearable not only to her but to me too.

Aritie was compelled by the agony of the moment not to discuss how she intended to handle the situation. But I suggested keeping it confidential until we could work out suitable strategies on how to deal with the matter. She continued from time to time to evidence flashbacks into the situation as we remained together.

"Darling you need rest else you'll have a breakdown. This is how Post Traumatic Stress Disorder starts. Come on, have a bath and rest. I can't afford to miss you."

"Heeeei." she screamed louder again "…could this be true?"

Her mind was loaded with grief and tears trickling from her eyes "What on earth is this? Oh my God!"

She was hysterical trying to walk away from me, but I prevented her. Her heart pounded and fluttered to breaking point. Filled with agony, Aritie's grief and anger were towards Esitima whom she accused of deliberately killing her husband.

"Poor uncle Bassey, all education acquired; fame and influence, all ended in a ditch."

Aritie was distraught by the death of Bassey, her uncle, and she felt disappointed that such a good gentleman could die so young too soon. And that reminder brought once again, an avalanche of pains, anxiety and grieve to her very existence.

After taking shower and resting I went home with her that night as I wouldn't leave her alone in that situation. All through the night, Aritie was brooding with the traumatic pains. She had woken several times in the night frightened with nightmares and flashbacks that had deprived her of adequate sleep.

"Darling I told you if you go on this way the likelihood of visiting a psychologist is there. I just don't want this to happen to you, please. Cheer up and wind-down your thoughts. Things done can't be undone, especially death for that matter."

I continued cuddling and petting her throughout the night.

In the morning I persuaded her to call in sick, but she refused thinking she had just started work and taken charge of the office the previous day, wouldn't be ideal for her to be absent so soon. I then drove her to The Tavern with the plea that she doesn't view that CCTV again as this will worsen her condition.

"And remember to keep the information confidential let's see what will come out of it, okay?"

She had nodded in agreement.

"See you later"

I had kissed her, and she bade me well on the journey which I had undertaken that day.

Hurrying down to an important office assignment which I had to go away for two days. During this period, I kept calling and texting her several times for reassurance. However, leaving Aritie behind was the most agonising experiences that I had ever had.

CHAPTER 2

ARITIE SAT DISTURBED AND OVERWHELMED with fear and unbelief. She kept asking herself why Esitima would do such a terrible thing. Why on earth would make her kill her husband! Such a nice and generous gentleman of rear stock! Lost for word, she sat down ruminating and overburdening her mind with the thoughts of how to avenge Esitima for her shameful action.

In the donning twilight of the evening, Aritie sat tensed in her bedroom. Her window curtains had been folded slightly to one side providing little rays of sunlight into the almost darkened room.

Her right leg crossed over the left, with the right hand stocked to her chin and elbow resting on the right thigh shaking repeatedly. Aritie's eyes roved side to side, staring blankly on the wall with grimaced face and thoughts that appeared distant miles away.

She stared bizarrely with a little movement of her mouth as though whispering to someone. With twisted facial expressions and blank stares of the wall, Aritie appeared distraught.

Gazing without seeing anything and listened yet heard not the footsteps that had stealthily entered the room and taken a position by the doorpost. The fellow had observed her appearance outside from the windows then stealthily, positioned himself just by the doorpost to know what was happening.

Although initially, he thought to play a prank on her but held up as he saw the seriousness of her appearance. He stood at the doorpost casting a grotesque dark shadow on the wall just in front of her. Aritie was still absorbed in her thought and imaginations without seeing the fellow or his shadow. She seemed too deep and too far away in her contemplation.

And for several minutes, the figure stood there silently observing her gestures and wandering what had become of her. All along, his shadow kept making some movement without her awareness. Eager to gain attention, the fellow jostled his feet on the floor synchronising with screeching noise produced by the chair which he dragged along on the floor.

The combination of those sounds, together with the sudden jerky ghostly movement of the dark shadow on the wall startled Aritie with fear! She sprang up suddenly from the chair screaming on top of her voice.

"Eh ewooh! Jesus Christ!"

She screamed, stepping back and looking scared! Aritie's voice echoed and re-echoed through the obscurity of her mind. Then, she turned around and beheld Etimbuk at the direction of the noise.

Her heartbeat pounded as though she had just finished 100 metres Olympic run, she looked quite scared and breathless.

"Etimbuk!"

Aritie called out

"You've scared the breath out of me"

She brought her left hand over on her chest staring at him in awe! But Etimbuk stood fixing his gaze on her squarely without blinking or saying a word.

"What's up?"

She regarded him with a glance of suspicious thinking about his mother and the atrocities that she had committed.

"That wasn't funny, was it?"

But he remained mute without a word.

Trying to organise herself, Aritie pulled the four-yard piece of the wrapper which she had wound around her armpits hastily; in that instance, she would have exposed her nakedness!

"Shh!"

She cautioned bringing one finger on her lips and with a bittersweet smile.

"Look the other way, small boy."

Giggling, as she did so again her mind was yearning and flowing with the bitter thoughts, utter disgust and hatred for Esitima, his mother.

Etimbuk with childish innocence turned his attention away from her.

"I was wondering what has come over you, Aritie"

Etimbuk intoned, taking slow steps into the room with much effort.

"I've never seen you in that mood before, is anything the matter?"

But Aritie observed him with a note of caution and sudden urge to divulge the information, but stronger inner compulsions held her back. She sensed the danger of telling Etimbuk before she could properly digest it, much more so Etido's instruction to her not to tell anybody. She obeyed those intuitions.

'It mustn't be told to anyone else for now' She had reasoned. 'Especially to Etimbuk.' Then stammered.

"N... o thing! There's isn't a...n issue Etimbuk... I'm just tired after staying in the office that late."

Aritie struggled to voice out her words, sounding quite unconvincing.

Etimbuk regarded her in silence as he was bewildered of her attitude; 'don't I have the right to know her worries?' He had turned it over on his mind.

"Are you sure, Aritie?"

he called her again

"The picture you presented looked more like a worried person than tiredness. I've waited at the doorpost for a couple of minutes"

Again, he asked bringing down the tempo of his voice

"Is anything the matter, Aritie? Tell me, I am your cousin, I might be of help."

Etimbuk insisted but Aritie just regarded him without a word but with the worrying gestures of 'I hate your mother, she's the problem. She supposed to die. If I have my own way, I'll nip life out of her'

Etimbuk waited briefly then intoned

"However, keep it to yourself if you may. Remember I am a psychologist and I know it."

He was trying to pull her legs to see if she might eventually let him into the subject matter of her worries. But Aritie had resolved not to open that problem to his knowledge.

"Oh! Ah ah! You know what; my mind?" She cackled in a burst of high-pitched bittersweet laughter. "You must be joking or have been reading clairvoyance if that ever does exist in real life"

"Of course, it does exist. A quick, intuitive knowledge of things and people. The soundness of judgement of projecting yourself into someone else's point of view to understand his own side of the problem. It's called, invasion of the mindset, or sagacity if you like" Etimbuk said. "And that's in existence, Aritie"

"That's interesting. Etimbuk, the telepathist!-But you wouldn't practice that art on me" she giggled.

"Well, it's an art that could be applied in any given situation of needs, and I know this wouldn't be an exception"

Etimbuk asseverated sitting on the only empty cushion available in the room.

"I know anything that threatens the peace of one member of this family, threatens the cooperate existence of all. We supposed to tackle the threat together as a family, Aritie"

"That's true but…"

Aritie ceased to maintain complete eye contact with Etimbuk due to the level of bitterness and jealousy on her mind for Esitima, his mother. And pretentiously, the word stuck to her throat. Aritie pretentiously began searching for an appropriate word to fill the blank space and then, started coughing and writhing about in the room.

"But what, …are you alright?" Etimbuk queried, assessing her carefully.

But she shielded the fear billowing on her mind by continuous coughing and writhing in the pretence of chocking reflexes in her throat. Etimbuk continued looking at her in awe and bewilderment.

"I've told you there…is nothing wrong, Etimbuk; I am only tired…" coughing again "after staying…in the office that late." …in a cracked voice.

Etimbuk laughed in unbelief while handing her a glass of water.

"Thanks" she responded.

"You're welcome."

His eyes were still on her, he laughed and shook his head.

"Ah! I can see…worker!" Nodded his head like a woodpecker

"That mood celebrates the beginning of a working career eh! Isn't it?"

Observed her carefully without a word for a second, and then added. "If things are going to be this way for you Aritie, think again, that isn't the right place for you, okay"

He was quite uncomfortable that Aritie was hiding what he thought a piece of very sensitive information away from him, he was disturbed.

However, Aritie continued gazing at him with a feeling of discontentment and contempt towards his mother.

CHAPTER 3

ETIMBUK REMAINED ON HIS SEAT examining the room for any possible clue into Aritie's problem. Why would she be so preoccupied with her problem and yet refused to share it with him, he thought. After a while, he put out Today's Newspaper he was holding in his hand and continued.

"Anyway, I called in to share my own worries and predicament with you, the threat that further delves mighty blow on my destiny and security"

He did this simply because Aritie was privy to his plan, other than that, Etimbuk wouldn't dare as he won't, telling anyone. He considered it inappropriate to talk about his personal problem with people. He doesn't like people seeing him as vulnerable in any situation.

Etimbuk had always remained strong and uncomplaining in the face of disturbing problems. Never wanted people to judge him as weak, negative and unable to face up to life's challenges with an open mind.

For him, rocking the boat and killing the moods and wellbeing of others with his complaints may have negative impacts on his health. This could weaken his immune system, raise his blood pressure and increase other risks and negative effects on his health.

To prevent these, he wouldn't want to sabotage or whine his ego before anybody with unnecessary complaints.

Aritie with her present predicament was quick to assert.

"Yes, what is it?"

She responded adjusting her position in the chair to be more comfortable. Focusing all her attention on him with complete eye contact and urgent desire to be told the problem immediately. She initially misconstrued to be related to her current situation. Quite nervous.

"How would you feel seeing your world collapsed before your very eyes. You would feel bad, won't you?"

"What is it? Tell me"

She pressed on hard in desperation to know. But Etimbuk continued moaning and lamenting his loss.

"Seen the advert on page eight of Today's Newspaper?"

He thrust the paper over to her. And Aritie quickly collected it from him. Hurriedly she flipped opened page eight and took a hard look on the displayed list, then exclaimed in frustration.

"Ah!... I can see"
nodded her head like a woodpecker.

"Eh! this is absolutely ridiculous. I never expected this would happen this week" she was indignant "Who could have done this Etimbuk?"

Etimbuk remained silent for a while contemplating about the implications of his unsuccessful scholarship award. This was the only hope that had remained for him. And now that hope was crushed. Etimbuk thought of the effects of this betrayed trust on him and the sneaky ordeal hovering around his educational pursuit, then responded in frustration wryly.

"It's the way our society is structured, the powerful are always out to silence the weak making them voiceless. Although it might be too early to make assumptions, make no mistakes, this might be a well-orchestrated handiwork from some unscrupulous elements in the University community."

Alarmed, Aritie exclaimed.

"Don't be sarcastic. Who in the University community would do such an unworthy thing; don't they care? Would such a fellow not understand the predicament this family has gone through? Maybe the person is deranged."

Etimbuk in his sophomore was nominated for a State Government scholarship to enable him to complete his studies at the University, and Aritie was privy to it. They were so confident of the publication of his name soon. But as part of ongoing corruption in Idiaimah, an officer in the University community betrayed the vision by substituting the name of Etimbuk with that of his son's.

"I'm finished; absolutely pissed off. I think someone should tell me what to do. Where do I go from here? I know my enemy has pulled a fast one on me"

Etimbuk lamented bitterly with tears trickling from his eyes.

"Calm down Etimbuk,"

Aritie rose up to offer some consolations. She cuddled his hands for a while and patted his back

"Calm down" she said again "this has become more of a challenge. Come what may, you'll finish University education and becomes a graduate. Be a man and comport yourself, opportunity lost might be regained with another trial."

Aritie knew that the past doesn't always predict the future. That one failed yesterday or today or will fail tomorrow don't necessarily mean that he is a failure in life. All that is needed to be done is persistence and staying focussed on pursuit of a goal.

She reassured him of her desire to help. If it would mean sacrificing her meagre wages in pursuance of this pressing goal, she wouldn't mind.

After all, she had benefited immensely from the largesse of Bassey even after his death, she still drew from that boundless source daily. Besides, Aritie was a cousin to Etimbuk and confidant. And aside from her present problem with his mother, her determination to helping Etimbuk was resolute and it grew profoundly.

With this, Etimbuk had a little consolation seeing her offer as magnanimous and thanked her for the show of such altruistic gesture.

Aritie resolution to help her cousins was inevitable. Over the years she had been instrumental to their growing and robust confidence. Whatever social skills Etimbuk and his brother Patrick possessed, could be attributed to her tutelage. For when their mother would leave them alone trotting the world, Aritie would be there guiding and guarding them in life's paths. Therefore, she had to finish the good works she had started on them.

They were so close together. Both remained in the room thinking of the misfortune and imagining the dogged nature of Bassey who wouldn't negate but hold on to his integrity in matters of this nature.

After some soul searching and reflective assessment, sluggishly, Etimbuk moved away though not from the problem which tucked on him like the very hair that grew on his skin, refusing to let go. He went down to his room, but his mind was loaded with the pain and shame of having to remain unlettered the rest of his life.

For Aritie, anger was a milder word to describe her entire being she was overwhelmed with a big dose of bitterness and acrimony toward Esitima. She thought of an urgent plan that would destroy Esitima completely, if not actually kill her. Indeed, she must pay for the shame of her atrocities, she thought.

Aritie spent the whole night dissecting the possibility of confronting Esitima with her discovery. Thought that pitched on the difficulties such an affront would cause her in the family especially with her cordial relationship with her children. Therefore, she settled on playing it covertly by involving those she considered professionals. Those who can execute the plan perfectly well without any iota of suspicion. And with Enobong and Uyai her friends, that task would be done.

Aritie wasn't certain her fiancée, Etido could handle the situation with professional adeptness and satisfaction going by his attitude towards Esitima. There's that tendency to be lenient with her on certain strategies.

She had honestly hoped that with the help of her two friends, she would be able to find the appropriate way of avenging Esitima as a tribute she must pay to the memory of Bassey, her beloved uncle.

CHAPTER
4

I CAME BACK FROM MY ASSIGNMENT visiting Aritie in her office to how she was coping with the situation. There, I discovered to my astonishment that Enobong her erewhile friend, at least that's what I thought, was with her. As a gentleman, I tried to reorder my thought and behaviour, hiding away the disappointment and grievance under my sleeve.

"Hello beauties am thrilled to see you both together" I greeted, Aritie stood up to offer a bigger hug and a kiss. She had guessed what I meant by that greeting.

"You're welcome darling" staring down at me.

"Hope you're okay?" I responded. I realised she could radiate a few warm smiles after all.

"You're welcome Etido, fine boy" Enobong greeted rising for a hug which I accepted with reservation.

I sat on the chair assessing both with their eyes fixed on me.

"How are you, is everything alright?"

I asked holding her hand and rubbing it continuously.

"I am alright darling, how was the trip; any success?"

She asseverated.

"It was alright. You look good. I am pleased"

"Thanks"

"It's been long I don't see you in town, did you travel?" Enobong added with a smile.

"No, am very much around, not going anywhere from Mkpasang in the last six months except for the last two days I went to Ariaria on an official trip. Are you alright... how's your boutique; anywhere?

Enobong chortled with delight keeping the strands of her long wig backwards from occluding her eyes.

"Thanks for asking. My boutique is in progress, in fact, what I came to discuss some detail with your fiancée about the possibility of assisting in any way. We're set for a relaunch in two weeks times. That's why I've been very busy the last few weeks trying to fix a few decorations to update its status in preparation for the big day"

"Oh, that's fantastic" I retorted "I see the whole place wears a new appearance now, and with that, you'll be getting quite a lot of clients, especially from the university community. That seems possible"

"Well, we'll see what will happen after the relaunch coming soon. We'll swing into full action" she responded "You're invited as a very special guest, Etido"

"Wow! thanks for the honour, I do appreciate it, thanks. Your friend shall keep me updated… Oh! Wait a minute…but I intend going on a business trip within the coming weeks. But if I am available, we'll get cracking"

"The event is slated for 28th August" She searched her handbag for invitation card, then handed over a well-grafted card to me. I collected.

"Thanks, the card is so beautiful, thanks"

Aritie brought bottles of lager to the table, filled the glasses and handed over mine to me. I collected. The foamy and the effervesce coming from the carbonation sparked my taste buds giving real satisfaction as I gulped the juicy contents.

"I watched The Vine; it's an exciting piece of work, you were brilliantly wonderful, Enobong." I added just to impress her. "It's a lifeline story that catches the imagination of the people. And tells the story of modern Idiaimah"

She crackled with excitement "Thanks, we do all we can to educate and inform the society helping her to yield to acceptable moral standards."

"Wow, indeed!?"

I was startled for Enobong to become a behaviour moulder in Mkpasang. Is that not ironical? It left me with absolute disappointment hearing Enobong express such incongruity in her words, quite contrary to the horrible things she had done in Polywood.

"Morale! Hope it'll not like the proverbial 'do as I say, not as I do' concept that can't change the behaviour of the people." I added.

She was a bit uncomfortable with that comment; at least the sudden change in her expression did say so. And Aritie regarded me with the note of surprise in her gesture.

Enobong was a seasoned actress in Idiaimah. Her early contact with the industry brought her incredible fame and recognition. It sharpened her skills and ingenuity with a clear sense of direction. And most of her works had been widely accepted by the majority of her Idiaimahi followers. But Enobong wouldn't rest on her oases until she would achieve much more.

A six-footer actress, elegant in fame and strong will that matched her height. The display of these qualities had been her pride propelling her into Idiaimahi hall of fame and drawing many to the big screen. She had been always very captivating with astounding sense of purpose and ability to hold her audience spellbound with her storytelling skills. Very efficacious perspectives causing the public to feel the heat of her stories.

Upon all that, Enobong still had a passion and hunger for playing bigger and much more challenging roles in her carrier. Such was possible through her intelligence. As an avid reader, social researcher and a creator of stories relevant to Idiaimah society, she stood ahead over her contemporaries. This made Aritie see in her a formidable force with the potential to execute her envisaged monstrous plans of vengeance. Of course, added to with her knowledge that Enobong was Esitima's adversary.

She featured in most of Idiaimah Home Movies which Esitima had refused to watch. Esitima considered Idiaimah home movie inferior to foreign ones because of pronounced displays of diabolical and fetish contents in almost all its production.

She loathed unrealistic parade of wealth and unprofessional nature of their film productions; this had been one of those elements which added to sway her away from the patronage of the delectable piece of work many in Idiaimahi enjoyed.

Enobong was an actress with a purpose, she was very glamorous and with a distinctive personality whose presence in Home Movies always evoked passion and delight among her followers.

Erudite, strong and knowledgeable with an addictive sense of humour added to showcase typical mannerism that drew her audience spellbound. These delicate skills she developed and mastered as an actress added to project her as an enigma in the industry by all standard, indeed she was in a class of her own.

Although a talented actress, Enobong also was full of bitter jealousy in her heart for anyone who might threaten her sense of security and success. And one of such persons happened to be Esitima and her boutique, Ndiokko de Vogue. These stood on the way of prosperity for Asurua Galore, her fashion brand.

All along, she had been searching for any available avenue to do something about this. And Aritie's project provided her with that opportunity.

As a prolific actress, Enobong's confidence in conveying emotions that had tremendous positive effects on her actions and behaviour was staggering. Attributes which no doubt, had presented her as the master in her own class. An excellent actress in Pollywood.

I was boiling inside talking with Enobong about morality considering numerous atrocities that had permeated the landscape of Pollywood in recent time. Some which were attributed to her greed and self-aggrandisement.

No doubt those who knew her beyond Pollywood like me, were disgusted of these unspeakable actions and behaviour. For me too, she doesn't deserve to comment on morality. Her criminal behaviour was too appalling and stinking like rotten eggs.

Given our kind of environment with tolerance for virtually any illegality, Enobong should have been in jail by now. She should have been arrested for long but left to walk around causing disaffection among the people. But then, she was left to go roam the streets to accomplish her malicious intent no matter whose ox is gored.

The incident that occurred during the shooting of the movie in Idundu is still very fresh in memory. That unfortunate occurrence consumed the life of one of her finest colleagues in the profession leaving the other with life-changing injury and disability. Initially, people thought it was an accident, but it later revealed, she initiated the act in order that she'll be the only one recognised playing major roles in the industry.

Her role in Governor Akpan of Itunde State sacking a commissioner is still very fresh in memory. Enobong engineered this action for her nominee to be appointed into State Executive Council as a commissioner. And the State House of Assembly corruptly endorsed her wish without asking questions.

Once Enobong set her venomous fangs on her prey, she would follow through tearing her victim to pieces. She's the most ferocious human beast I've ever known.

This is not the kind of friend I'll want my fiancée to keep. And this, I discussed thoroughly with Aritie. Therefore, I excused myself and left their midst without causing any suspicion to Enobong. Although Aritie did suspect as she had been quite uncomfortable throughout my stay with them.

CHAPTER
5

I MADE MY WAY HOME BOILING in the inside of me. How could she allow that brat into her office? So Aritie wouldn't listen to my counsel. I have spent time discussing what she's like and capable of achieving, but she completely ignored me. Is this the kind of wife I want to marry? Maybe she's waiting for Enobong to strike her before she could learn some lessons.

I do know one should learn from the mistakes of others without necessarily waiting to make the same mistake. I had to get into the bottom of this sooner than later.

Not quite a while after I left them, Aritie bombarded my phone with calls. But I ignored her. After she received no answer, she called home in person. As she walked into the room, I refused to talk to her upon all what she had to say, I remained unyielding.

"What's up; Etido, are you blaming me?"

She stared at me cunningly. And I wasn't moved.

As she moved in to sit on the cushion next to me, I flared up.

"Don't try me."

Asking her to stay far away from me.

"And don't touch me" I stretched forward my hands to stop hers reaching mine.

"Go ahead and register at Pollywood, you'll make a good actress, isn't it?"

Aritie regarded me cautiously for some minutes.

"How could you say that it wasn't I who invited her, she came on her own just a few minutes before your arrival, Etido. She told you she came to talk about the relaunch of her boutique"

Aritie put up her defence. She reluctantly pulled a chair and sat down still looking at me. But I ignored her gestures remaining quiet.

"That criminal doesn't wouldn't cross my path," I said "I hate her actions with every drop of blood in me. I was just talking to that villain for her not to suspect that I don't like her actions"

"Each time I think about this Etido, it makes me quite nervous. Breaking up long time relationship with someone is not so easy, even for the right reason as it is, in my best interest, but it's still very painfully hurting. Give me time to reflect on the best way forward, please"

Aritie appeared very remorseful.

And I can understand her relationship with Enobong was there before we met. But as it was, that relationship was no more tenable going by the information made available to me.

"Time! You need time, isn't it? Then go ahead and have all the time in the world. For me, from this time onward I'll watch from the side-lines."

"Darling, if you really love me please understand my plight. Exercise patience for my sake.

Give me another chance to work out better strategies for gradual disengagement without much pain, please?"

She was sober and began to cry.

During her tears, I remained still examining her carefully. I mustn't be cowed into a situation that would potentially damage my wellbeing and progress in the future. I know that lady is wicked. And the best way to deal with her is staying apart.

"She is a woman that will pretend to love you, she'll disguise in order to torment your life making you miserable at the end. That your friend obviously is a very toxic brand, you need to stay off or you will stay in with her evil deeds forever. Once she stings you with the toxin of a scorpion. Aritie, you might regret ever knowing Enobong…don't be caught off guard. Be on your watch."

I reiterated my earlier warning to her.

"Now tell me, those of my friends who're aware of her atrocities seeing you my fiancée relating with her, what do you think they will be thinking? Wouldn't they raise some questions? Proverbial bird of the same feathers flogging together. No, I never will allow this to happen to me"

No, Aritie must disentangle else I'll throw in the towel. I kept repeating this within me.

"You'll need to confront her face to face with the fact of the case that you don't want her friendship anymore. Aritie, this must be explained to her in a precise language. And that, you must do urgently too"

"Don't be so hard on this, darling. Consider our emotions, no matter the situation, it hurts, and that counts seriously. I'll need to deal with the feeling once the whole problem is over. Like you know, our friendship is as old as we're. I need time to handle the aftermath of this breakup"

"Think seriously about this matter at hand, I can't emphasise it hard enough,"

I told Aritie.

As Aritie left my house that evening, our relationship became threatened. No doubt, she had been a significant woman in my life the past ten months and plans were already underway to seal our relationship with a nuptial tie. But now I was ambivalent about the union. My fears heightened each week I reflected on my future relationship with Aritie.

This affected my mood seriously and friends and family members insinuated on the reason for my behaviour. The situation also had a tremendous bearing on my work. And for the first time in two years, I stayed off sick.

I lost the momentum of visiting Aritie. Although she became more frequent to woo back my love, but I was waiting on the side-lines to see what this would turn out to be. Certainly, the fire of that love had started to dim in my heart.

It was interesting to watch Aritie from a distance most of my engagement with her. I discovered, to my chagrin, Enobong frequent engagement with her in the office and once, she drove her out of The Tavern to Asurua Galore. They spent quite a remarkable time together leaving her work to suffer.

Ordinarily, at first, I thought Aritie was working on strategies of gradual disengagement, but as things turned out, their relationship soared much more by frequent coming together. It enraged me, and I took further steps back.

Aritie engaged with Enobong, her partner in crime with the aim of destroying Esitima. I wasn't aware of this. Her strategy had been kept in secret to me all these years even before she came to The Tavern, she had been antagonistic with Esitima because of her friend.

She was not in terms with that noble lady, and now they were looking for a possible avenue to stifle life out of her. And knowing that I wasn't in agreement with Enobong's attitude, Aritie wouldn't discuss anything pertaining to her with me.

Although I had warned her seriously to allow me to work out the best way forward in dealing with her worries, Aritie ditched that suggestion, depending solely on her malicious friend to fix her concern.

Enobong had been quite aversive of Esitima's continuous progress in the fashion business. In her mind, that stood tall on her way of success. She cashed in on that knowledge to bring Esitima down. Her current frequent consultation with Enobong suggested she trusted her to handle her concerns better than I would do. And that really irritated me, and I gave her further arm's length.

CHAPTER 6

ARITIE HAD A MEETING WITH Enobong to formulate workable plans to bring Esitima down. Having been versed with the knowledge that Enobong had been aversive towards Esitima's continued success in her fashion business-Enobong had been complaining about this as a potential threat to the current lean finances of Asurua Galore.

Having also known that Enobong wasn't comfortable with that development, therefore, if she got to know her story, may be interested in finding a solution to her pressing problem. Hopefully, she considered this a veritable avenue for Enobong to settle her long-standing scores with Esitima.

Enobong and Esitima were from Ibattai village, their families were arch enemy, by all standard. Given that Esitima's family was empowered with some level of financial strength, and that of Enobong was struggling under the weight of economic depression. And as it's said, 'the rich and the poor have nothing in common.'

Esitima's family had the bubbly spirit of being the people that held the economic power of the community, and that of Enobong was prejudiced against. This led to frequent wrangling and feuds between them. Enobong being who she was, carried the torch of this shared family discriminatory behaviour over with her in her mind for many years.

Therefore, if Enobong got to hear Aritie's story, Aritie was certain, she might be very pleased, and glad in putting the whammy on Esitima and stopping her on her voyage.

Aritie had earlier thought about the possibility of confronting Esitima with her plans which I would bring up but found that outrageous going by my resistive attitude with Esitima. She wasn't trusting me again in anything, not even my marriage proposal to her. Therefore, she thought most appropriate to approach her malicious friends to fix her worries.

In Asurua Galore they met, and she narrated the story of how she came to her knowledge about Esitima's story. The intended working out adequate strategies devoid of any doubt in the accomplishment of her envious and callous goal. Possibly, Aritie had wished Enobong could make the whole saga into a movie for Idiaimah audience.

"Enobong, something happened a week ago that has a serious impact on my very existence." She took a sip from her cup and then continued. "The incident has savaged my mind turning it upside down to the extent, I can hardly think right. It's a big concern for me. For one week now, I am not myself"

"What is it?" Aritie held onto her glass looking at Enobong carefully.

"It's about that bitch, that witch, called Esitima, the usual suspect."

"What about her, what has she done this time?" Enobong was loaded with bitter jealousy and acrimony for Esitima.

"My dear, she has done her worst by destabilising the life of our family with her salacious lust. And that leaves me with no other option than the desires to stop her ego. And that, I am determined to do. I'll not forgive her this time"

"Not forgive her, how do you mean, has it come to that?" Enobong examined Aritie "Gracious. What has the noble lady, my kinslady done? No sin is unforgivable, Aritie."

Enobong was very excited hearing Aritie talked about unforgiveness of Esitima for what she had done. For her, that was a strong positive statement coming from Aritie concerning her arch enemy. She was very eager to be told the whole story straight away. However, before Aritie could continue, she had noticed Uyai's car approaching the car park.

"Kinslady my foot, you better take her away to Ibattai else that house wouldn't contain both of us. Afterall the man she married died, she has no right to continue staying there."

"Come on babe, serve me the story while it's still hot"

"Wait a minute, Uyai is here. The happening babe is in the house! She needs to hear it from the beginning. I'll better serve the hottest part for her ears to share."

The arrival of Uyai in her new BMW 1 series car changed the dynamic of the conversation. With the air of optimism, Uyai stepped out swaggering toward them with pride.

Lately, the threesome had been doing their mischievous business together. One wouldn't do without the other. The mission of Abadi Gabriel Akpanang, as the code-named AGA was carried out by the trio.

In that highly secretive missions, they succeeded installing their nominees as a Commissioner in government at the expense of democratic process and good practice. Both were delighted to see the arrival of Uyai as expected to complete the equation. Uyai on her part was pleased to be just on time.

Uyai sat in an empty cushion in front of them crossing her long elegant legs and blustering in her tumultuous voice.

"What's smoking here girls? Aritie babe, take five." she presented left palm forward to Aritie who responded in the same gestures, they met palm to palm with excitement "Enobong give me something to cool down, the room is quite warm. Eh! Aritie, you're bubbling and exuding in styles. Can l join the fun? Enobong, what's up?" At the same time, she picked a hand fan on the table and started fanning herself.

Opening her soft velutinous brown handbag, she brought up lipstick and a mirror. With care, applied this on her lips rubbing and pressing the lips together in a series of smoothing motions.

"Not good at all, babe" Enobong responded, "It's seems we're heading for the Waterloo, unfortunately."

"Waterloo! Why, what's the matter?" She suddenly stopped surprised, looking at Enobong.

"Oh yes, and a big one too, Uyai babe" Enobong added.

Aritie who had been particularly expecting Uyai responded. "You're welcome, happening babe. Calm down your temperature although a big problem, I know we can handle this. Feel free to explore or even explode your ingenuity here. I always cherish your insight, baby cheers"

"Oh yes oh, once the glistening one is in the house we can ride on the lion's back, no qualms. Yeah, let's crack baby." Enobong held her breathe examining Uyai for a brief moment.

"Uyai, the news is quite disturbing. I am so concerned." She intoned popping open a chilled wine to inaugurate their talks.

"What's the news? Please break it immediately" Uyai was quite disturbed about the imminent danger she thought was awaiting them. Her immediate thought was their last mission which she had had some reservations about and to which Enobong insisted they mustn't delay, even when the end seemed defeated.

It was the mission to halt implementation of the plan to build the recreational centre in Mkpasang, and take it to Ibattai, Enobong's village. They had met with the people concerned and it still appeared the plan may not be visible. Last they tried to negotiate with someone in the state government as usual, but they met with a brick wall. Enobong was determined to push it one more time with some steering committee members or at most, delay the project. Although they had succeeded in hijacking the project, it had remained inconclusive. That was the immediate worry of Uyai.

"Good news and bad, which one do you want first? May not be what you're thinking about"

"Good and nothing but good news, I abhor bad news in its entirety, you know that... Oh, Aritie! Are you announcing, 'I do'? This is serious, what are you up to; when is it?" Uyai asked wondering if Aritie will finally break away sooner from their midst.

"This is a prelude to my wedding, Uyai" Aritie crackled with encompassing laughter dropping the glasses on the table. "And you'll be my chief's bridesmaid while Enobong leads the train. Hooray!!! Job done. How do you see that?"

"That's perfect for me. But have your hired confetti and bunting yet, what about toastmaster and pin-up girls? Wedding collections for you, Aritie, is knowing the key essentials to choose from and making it simple, sweet and elegant. That doesn't depend much on the price. I will choose the easiest and affordable wedding dress without compromising the beauty and elegance. And of course, credible groomsmen too."

Her friends stared at her, joining in the laughter.

"Organiser extraordinaire!" Aritie said mockingly "I admire your verdict, ride on my babe".

"Party jockey!" Enobong chided harshly "I know you're expecting it, is it?" Enobong turned her back on Uyai.

Uyai was so excited to be part of her friend wedding feast. She had always cherished gathering of that nature as a possible avenue for forming friendship and possibly, meeting with her heartthrob. All the men Uyai had so far involved with, none qualified in her concept of husband material. The man of her dream should be tall, handsome, intelligent and rich. Not minding the source of his wealth.

Like most girls and single ladies in Idiaimah, Uyai wouldn't attach importance to a man with a sense of adventure, appreciate her quirks-accepts her the way she truly was, not trying to change her to his will. Above all, has good plans for her life. Provided her type of man is financially buoyant-usually, riches may be acquired fraudulently through illegitimate means, she wouldn't mind.

Young girls and single ladies threw morality into the trash can when it came to romance. And the acquisition of wealth, money and riches was far more important to them than good qualities of leadership, moral etiquettes, honesty, accountability and integrity.

Enobong responded "Hold your breath Uyai baby, you've made your wishes known" looking at Uyai who was filled with outright excitement "and jumped to a joyful and scintillating wedding feast arrangements. Ideally, this gathering may not be for the fun of the wedding. But some intrigues and overtures that threatens our cooperate happiness and existence. And on that note, Aritie has exciting news for you"

"Come on, this is becoming interesting! Unwrap it quickly please, am anxiously waiting, are we safe?" Uyai intoned.

Aritie got up from where she sat moving cunningly towards Uyai. She rested herself directly in front of her before presenting her preconceived and malicious blueprint.

"Uyai babe, on a very serious note, what does your happiness tastes like?" Aritie tempted her with that question.

"Tastes? How do you mean?" She held up observing them succinctly. "Of course, you know what I love Aritie"

"No, I don't know."

Uyai hesitated … scanning the environment again her eyes roving between her two friends, both friends fixed their eyes on her.

"Okay, Sweet-delicious. Ecstatic!" She sounded thrilled, over the moon.

"That's fantastic. Mind's fruity, low-fat, low-calorie that pop with flavour. I wouldn't mind mingling it with a bit of saltiness."

"Wow! That sounds the Mediterranean." Uyai added with good-natured laughter.

"Certainly, I love Mediterranean foods, they're mouth-watering tarts" Aritie emphasised. And then turned around looking at Enobong expecting some answers from her. "And Enobong?"

"Mmm" she murmured "You know I am not a fan of veggies; I love something meaty… Umami"

"Oh, that's sensational, savoury broth. I like it too?" Aritie said, "My taste falls in between veggie and meaty."

"Yes, certainly good for everyone. It raises the protein content of the body and repair cell and makes the tissues more viable" Enobong replied.

"Mediterranean food also provides excellent dietary intake that meets five-a-day fruits and vegetables nutritional requirement. Girls, you know we may not have fruits and verges daily, but intake of this can augment for it." Uyai said. "Delicious cuisine that sticks out when you add fish or poultry to it or colourful veggies and beans, most importantly, nuts as a substitute. As you settle down to it with red wine, Wow! Enobong, the yummy flavour will blow your taste buds."

"Oh, master chef" she laughed with the air of congeniality "When did you turn a culinary artist cuddling tastes with passion?"

Enobong was interested on the recipe, although her mind was on the urgency of getting that information from Aritie about Esitima, however, she dodged the subject for now putting it over for another time. Uyai's recipe aroused some degree of interest in her. She looked very subtle, an indication of interest in the subject. "Anywhere, let's leave lecture on food, for now, we have an urgent task at hand"

"I know! This is an excellent diet that costs relatively less. Do you know the intake of fruits and vegetables, wholegrain and fibre add to longevity, girls? And we live by what we eat."

"Wow! Thanks for the lecture, master chef." Enobong replied. "I said let us leave food lesson now and be prepared to eat real food and get the gist from Aritie, please."

Their order arrived. They sat down the do justice to it. Aritie continued with the narration of her story.

"Girls, life depends on these tastes for survival. But the real substance of living is the test of freedom we all yearn for. Ability to live and manage your affair at ease without someone monitoring you. Freedom from all espionages, chaos and oppositions. When your freedom is threatened hell is let loose, Uyai."

"We all seek a sustainable base to stand and express our emotions with the taste of satisfaction and freedom from all interferences. This is the essence of this meeting and the reason I have a proposal to make. The fantasy and euphoria of food fads and weddings can wait for now, okay?"

She waited to allow this sink down.

"You're speaking in coded language; I don't have a glue at all, come out of it and let me in, please."

"Hold your peace Uyai, you'll understand," Aritie assured her.

Uyai remained silent and reflected carefully on what Aritie had said. She remained quite uncomfortable never understood where she was coming from. Then, Aritie began unfolding her contemptuous plans with Esitima. She led Uyai and Enobong into her inflated world of machinations fashioned to inflict Esitima with pains and discomfort-a world of brutal evil and nefarious plot issued from the mouth of a traitor herself.

"Girls, would you believe Esitima killed Bassey, my uncle?"

She asked, her friends received the news with astonishment. Enobong surprised and Uyai confounded. They all left the food and sat for some minutes without a word. All eyes were directed on Aritie.

"Tell me something, hope is not a joke, well I know today isn't 1st of April? Unbelievable!" Enobong looked at Aritie agape. "Really?"

"What do you mean, Aritie, Esitima killed Prof, sure? What are you talking about?" Uyai questioned her.

"I was so stunned with fear when I came into this incredible information myself at The Tavern a week ago."

Enobong and Uyai sat overwhelmed with shock. Enobong in particular was curious to know more. Cautiously, she looked at Aritie with a sense of vindictive intent in her heart.

"Do you know she poisoned my uncle at The Tavern just to get him off the scene so that she can be free to go about her lecherous acts with pride?"

Aritie provided what she thought might arouse her friend's interest to the possible reason for Esitima's murderous act of her husband. Her two friends remained silent and Enobong tapped her feet on the floor, working out the appropriate response to her submission.

"I've always said it, this is the real story, I'm glad someone has eventually discovered the missing link in the story of the death of Prof. Please tell me more, Aritie." Enobong glowed her mind on Aritie with excitement. She harboured revenge for all those years she had struggled in her shop without success. But Uyai, was rather overtaken with doubt and unbelief, she strongly questioned the validity of Aritie's information.

"Are you serious?" Enobong responded in a calmer reflective tone that never indicated any specific dictate of her mind.

"Esitima can't do that; such a noble lady can't possibly be a murderer, the killer of her husband. No, she's so meek and mild in her actions and behaviour, none can question. Oh no! Esitima can't possibly be a murderer, let alone kill her husband."

Enobong ridiculed Esitima with what she termed good-natured laughter which she rattled out. But Uyai remained adamant, unyielding in their smear despite their excitement. In fact, she needed more explanations from Aritie, such that would make her really believe in her and her story.

"Wait a minute" Uyai redirected Aritie "…are you insinuating that Lady Mbede definitely killed Prof, her husband?... Unbelievable! This could be the biggest news of the century for such a respectable figure in society to meddle herself in such an unspeakable act of evil. No, it might be a mistake Aritie, Esitima can't possibly do such a demeaning thing"

Aritie fought on "If you could allow me to finish at the end, you take a stand and judge by yourself if she did it or not, Uyaiobong"

"O yeah, carry on" Enobong urged her on. "Uyai babe, take it easy it's always hard to believe any evil committed by a known 'righteous' individual. She lifted both hands and brought her second fingers to indicate the word 'righteous' "Aritie, my love, crack on, this is becoming quite interesting."

Enobong urged them to rush and finish their food before they can continue. She considered this a very important part of their meeting that evening, as such, demands attention. In fact, she quickly put aware of her food without finishing. And she hurriedly cleared the table asking Aritie to give her narration of the event.

"You don't know her Uyai, do you? I guess you only see Esitima from a distance. Should I that spend the majority of my time with her evidence what I know about her?" She held her breath regarding Uyai.

"Ordinarily, Esitima is arrogant and manipulative in nature. A woman who always displays some levels of aggression in behaviour and attitudes towards everyone in her home including her late husband. She's noted with coercive controlling behaviour toward everyone. Threatening and arrogant and proud to be the owner of Ńdiokko de Vogue, the business that had generated billions of dollars for her."

"Esitima will repeatedly make you feel isolated, humiliated and scared. She'll be proud to put you down and call you nasty names to your shame. A very mean woman by nature."

"Earnestly, you need to be around her to witness numerous wroth of her hostilities, happening babe"

Aritie lied in her bit to tarnish the reputation of Esitima just to get her way.

On the contrary, Esitima had chosen the life of kindness in character as a noble lady. She was courageous, patience and honest, treating everyone with the highest form of respect and integrity.

The virtues of compassion, loyalty and sincerity were in the character of Ñdiokko to which she imbibed. The emotional resilience strong mental character she demonstrated towards people even in the face of difficulties. Esitima cultivated and mastered these delicate virtues overtime right from her youth.

Honestly, Esitima was one of the noblest woman in character, quite unlike prejudicial assessment Aritie had made of her.

"I need to get her down" Aritie insisted "she must be termed of that surpassing arrogance and impulsive ego she parades around with pride"

"But then, it sounds odd anywhere Aritie. Remember it's your words against many. And you're a lone voice in this case" Uyai argued.

"Could this be really true?" Enobong was sarcastic laughing and clapping her hands exceedingly. She was flooded with a wild sense of euphoria and hatred long inherited from her family for Esitima.

Happy, she had finally come into what may be the magic wand of revenge that could solve the backlog of the financial struggle facing her boutique and paid for generational family hatred "…unbelievable Aritie, how do you come into such provocative information anyway, who told you?" she added.

Aritie gave bitter laughter of resentment before replying.

"Technology! The ultimate fact you all need to know. The Closed-Circuit Television (CCTV) installed at The Tavern gives evidence that will blow your mind. It authenticates my evidence Uyai which stands tall and strong against those of many witnesses, Uyai.

"Very staggering revelation, it broke my heart into pieces as I watched the display of the bruising images on the screen, so frightening" She ended up with cracked voice as though she would cry.

Enobong watched her carefully, "Take it easy, Aritie. Hold your peace. I know it's difficult to do away with such scenes, especially when it reminds you of a loved one like uncle Bassey." Suddenly, she became more sarcastic. "Will it be possible we view the CCTV? Just be convinced that a woman of all people could dabble herself into shedding innocent blood, the blood of her husband?... Astonishing!"

"I hope you know they're doubters, Aritie. Those who must see before believing, l am one of those doubting Thomases. Only seeing the evidence would convince me." Uyai was very sceptical of the whole story.

"With all pleasure, you're welcome to my office any day, any time. I'm always available, take a bite." Aritie was filled with the wild sense of renewed courage.

Enobong took a sip of her wine with satisfaction that she had finally come to revenge not only for her business but for many lost years when her family suffered shame and ridicule from the hands of the Ñdiokkos. She assessed Uyai carefully before letting Aritie realise the enormity of envisaged plans in her sleeve.

CHAPTER 7

Asurua Galore wasn't a business built with success in mind, it was shambolic. Conceived from day one to fail. Many attributes culminated into its shame and failure.

First, Enobong never considered the link between Asurua Galore's location and customers' relation which is crucial in any business in financial terms. Her store was located at the back of another property and hidden significantly away from sight of potential first-time customers. And customers found it difficult to access its location even when told by words of mouth.

Considering the difficulties associated with house numbering in Mkpasang. For this reason, Enobong struggled for years to attract many newbies, who could be crucial in sales to her business. In business, first impression counts, and location speaks much louder than words about Asurua Galore in this regard.

As a newbie into fashion industry, choosing such a hidden location propelled Asurua Galore into disadvantage position with the like of Ńdiokko de Vogue and others, that were situated on the high streets and with constant offering of lower prices. Asurua Galore hadn't taken these issues into consideration.

Enobong never considered stock from global market as important factor the reason why Esitima was having an edge over many competitors. While Ńdiokko de Vogue had renewed stock worldwide, but Asurua Galore dealt with local stuff and was very indigenous in its outlook. That was enough to cause setback for the company.

Moreover, Enobong was a novice in business. She had no adequate knowledge and sense of organisation as an entrepreneur. No ability to analyse the market and her competitors to know the delicate issues involved in management, let alone fashion business that demanded enormous time and attention. These left her seriously handicapped and eventually, starving her boutique with customers.

Instead of getting close to learn from her competitors, she rather developed hatred and animosity towards anyone found dealing in the same line of business with her. And this had a devastating impact on Asurua Galore.

Enobong never learned the language of branding which is key and most important aspect of building a successful fashion world. She failed to realise that brand identity made customers able to identify her and her products, making her business stay unique and relevant to them and the market.

She failed to realise that a large marketing budget is key to establishing a well-known fashion business. Ńdiokko de Vogue was a longstanding brand in Mkpasang and had reputation was great. She constantly offered discounts to meet the need of her teaming customer, coupled with aggressive advertisement networks.

Asurua Galore as a newbie, was struggling against price cut and meeting profit margin. We all know customers like to pay less, hence would stream to where the price is low.

As women clothing shop, seasonality and obsolescence are basic element of women clothing, but Asurua Galore never considered this as a factor of risk in her business. All what she knew was keeping outdated inventory in her shop. The changing fashion of women wear which swung with new season cannot be an oversight therefore, as a small business, trading with outdated stock diminished her profit margin leading to huge loss.

No doubt, she had had a successful career in acting and filmmaking, that knowledge wasn't transferable into business. Fashion business was a new kind of experience that demanded enormous time, another kind of creativity and consistency which she had none to offer.

Enobong felt having astute knowledge in one sector meant the same could be transferred to another. This naïve attitude made her not to subject herself to training and learning the trade or employing competent people to manage the business for her. And it summed up to the failure of Asurua Galore.

She spent most of her time either rehearsing scripts in preparation for shooting of new movies or on the road sourcing for characters to develop new plots. She wouldn't maintain her workers long enough to master the art and science of salesmanship and be beneficial to the business.

Hiring and firing at will was very much known with Asurua Galore. Inconsistencies in her outlook to business management made some of her friends and customers not to trust her business model. They subsequently turned away from visiting Asurua Galore.

Moreover, her boutique was stocked with mostly local fabrics as opposed to the like of Ñdiokko de Vogue-her major source of her headache, that experienced renewed stock from international big model every month. Ideally, Asurua Galore wasn't positioned for success going by her naïve attitude to business.

CHAPTER
8

"A RITIE"
Enobong called her while tapping her feet on the floor,
"are you prepared to sign up to the depth of what you're about to do?"

She asked, and Aritie without thinking about it answered with a sense of great expectations and pride not minding the repercussions that might follow.

"Bring out your plans, and I'll execute it to the later"

"Have you told Etido about this Aritie?"

Uyai asked, pre-emptive of actions which might be questionable to her fiancée. She thought, for Aritie to succeed, the knowledge of Etido would be a factor and inevitable as he might question some of her actions.

"Why? Must I tell him everything; who even cares? The two of us are different entities."

"I feel that's the most sensible thing to do, discuss with him, first…"

"Etido can wait, Uyai, if not, go to hell. I don't really care. I have gotten enough headache from him already."

"What do you mean?"

"Exactly what you've heard. Period!"

"Are you serious?"

Uyai was taken back with shock. She had thought her friend was preparing for the wedding all these while but not knowing, the relationship had hit the rock, she wasn't happy. Uyai looked at Aritie with open mouth wondering what went wrong.

"That's okay…" Uyai ventilated. She never wanted to probe further into the personal matter as she wasn't ready to hurt her friend's feelings.

"Aritie, as I was saying" Enobong interjected

"You may not understand the implication of your envisaged action. This could be a delicate business which might go either way, good or bad. But while we always desire this for good, we must consider the other side too, ok?…

"Never mind Uyai, she's just a distraction"

Enobong added further.

"This might be a lethal weapon that could explode; and the consequences mightn't be pleasant, Aritie."

Aritie was ambitious and bold in her will as she was in her actions always. Her aim had been to finish the business at hand. Seeing this as a veritable weapon, she put in her energy in full force as the key to unlock answers to her uncle's untimely death. She responded.

"Never mind her, she doesn't understand. I assure you that whatever it'll cost me, I am ready to pay double and go all out to succeed to show Esitima that mischievous deeds are outdone by mischievous mindset"

"Leave the details with me then" Enobong concluded "I'll be back, much of which of course will be concluded after we have viewed the video piece tomorrow"

"That settles it; my mind leapfrogs for Esitima. That fool continues with her arrogance even after killing that kind-hearted and loving gentleman of rare stock. His blood must certainly be paid for in full sooner or later!" Aritie was optimistic.

Uyai remained jittering, she was ambivalent, quite unable to accept or reject their views on Esitima. She was waiting to watch the video to believe that Esitima could indeed be the murderer of her husband.

Invariably, viewing the CCTV footage by the trio at The Tavern became the tinderbox that brought Esitima from the height of her glory down to canvass.

CHAPTER 9

U YAI ASSERTED HER FEET FIRMLY on the matter of bringing Esitima down. It was her duty to ensure Esitima was taught the hardest lesson of life. Although she had been a very successful actress like Enobong with a close relationship with Aritie in whatever project they set out to handle, this was the first assignment she would ever undertake alone on her own term.

Uyai was briefed on the role she had to play to ensure adequate safeguards and survival of Asurua Galore. And she knew that was a very delicate part to play as first-timer, therefore put enormous energy to outplay and succeed. The credit would be theirs at the end, but failure might cost them their jobs and positions in society.

Therefore, before setting out on the malicious mission two weeks after being commissioned by her friends, Uyai understudied Esitima for one full week ensuring that she made no mistakes. On several instances, she had gone into the Boutique for window shopping.

Taking time off to examine the environment appropriately and establish the Achilles feet of her mission. And when she had finished, excitement filled the air. She was overtly overjoyed for the mission accomplished!

No doubt, this was something Enobong was quite capable of doing herself, but she wanted Uyai to experience the real taste of their friendship.

Uyai had reservations at first for the deal but had been convinced by the antics of her friends. And she gruntingly tried her hands on the shoddy deal. After all, there is always the first time in every situation, they had reasoned, and her first time was now or never!

Esitima had gone to her boutique on that fateful day as usual, but two hours into the shop, a strange face walked in through the door. She presumed her for a customer, but that was a false judgment. Uyai had appeared so glamorous with the latest outfit and smiling at ease with herself. But there was something mysterious about her which Esitima was unable to fathom. Something that pricked her conscience immediately she had set her eyes on Uyai, therefore assessed her with a note of caution.

"Good morning Mrs Mbede."

The visitor had said with a sense of respect in her voice and a big smile moving closer to Esitima. Esitima smiled back, still regarding her with caution.

"This is a huge boutique, a lovely place in town" She added.

Esitima responded by the same gesture with a courteous glance. She dropped clothing materials she had on her hands on the nearby hanger moving gracefully closer toward the visitor.

This was the art Esitima had mastered over the years as a saleslady. She then directed her salesgirl nearby to attend to the merchandise.

"Eduek" she called out "arrange those dresses well on the mannequin; also attend to the shoe rags as well and properly display those ornaments and pieces of jewellery as you do always, okay?"

"Yes Mma."

Eduek was the most trusted of her workers. She had been working in Ńdiokko de Vogue for about five years and had known the company's policies well enough. As a good team player, Eduek had been flexible to her tasks, she was confident and full of stamina to get her work done. Every staff in Ńdiokko de Vogue including customers loved her because of her politeness and confident in giving adequate information about the company.

She had skills of recommending products, answering customers' questions and providing the necessary advice. In fact, Eduek stood as a customer relations officer for the company, qualities that drew her even closer to her boss.

"Oh, my dear gentle lady, sorry, I have to do this every day"

Still assessing the visitor with care.

"Oh, you look so gorgeous."

She moved closer with admiration of Uyai's outfit

"How can I help such a glamorous lady?"

"May I have a word with you, please?"

"Yes, my noble lady."

She smiled at ease and Uyai responded with infectious smiles that evoked love with care.

With that reassuring gesture, Esitima thought her initial opinion about her was false.

"How's business" Uyai began.

"My dear, we thank God for his mercies"

"So sorry dear, I am Mrs Uyai Akpan, my husband and yours attended the same school and were youthful acquaintances. Sorry, I hadn't had the opportunity of meeting with you before now because of the nature of our different schedules"

Uyai appeared calm.

"Honestly his death was very sad and painful indeed to bear. The whole family including Mkpasang had lost a rare gem"

"Mmh"

Esitima gave a mournful groan of sadness

"my dear, such is life, you know when you were born, but none of us can tell the day or hour when the messenger of death strikes. My dear, come this way."

She pointed the way to her expensive office chamber. Uyai followed her. Both walked side by side, Uyai took a detailed assessment of the boutique which ran into Millions of Dollars.

"Mrs Mbede, this is an awesome boutique in town"

She giggled with laughter trying to get palsy-walsy with Esitima

"You must have really invested fortunes in it"

"We do what we can to keep ourselves together in the face of our disappointments and sorrows"

Uyai took a quick step forward to admire a displayed dress.

"This frock is beautiful; I just love it. It's so inviting to the eye"

"I know, it'll feel awesome on your twisted figure too when you put it on. That's a perfect size for you"

"Thanks…the boutique is so awesome; it is breath taking to behold! I am completely blown away"

"We have them in stock all sizes and colours to fit everyone, and I know, it'll fit you too."

Esitima said with the expectation that she was a customer. But Uyai dropped the dress down following her into the office.

CHAPTER
10

WHEN ESITIMA LET UYAI INTO her tastily furnished office chamber, she thought the visitor was a customer and a potential friend. But little did she knew, behind those smiles lie a predator, a chameleon about to spit fire and vicious venom on her dynasty. Uyai came with the intention of racking terrible havoc on Ñdiokko de Vogue and to the very essence of Esitima existence.

Loaded with a significant dose of threats, Uyai was set to damage the power and influence which for many years, Esitima wielded in the business world in Idiaimah.

Her office chamber was breathtaking. The oak writing desk, marbled flooring and inserted flowering carpet ushered her into a hugely expensive oval office apartment. Other harmonic furnishing splendour spelt the essence of royalty which for over two decades, had been the distinctive identity of Mbede family this part of the world.

The visitor sniffed the air of opulence as she was ushered into an exquisite and imposing office edifice, enough to go for a presidential palace or residence of the Queen of England! What she had seen outside was only a toast of the iceberg. Uyai couldn't wait to sound her salvo.

"Congratulations Queen Elizabeth the second, I am not surprised; this does to confirm my investigations."

Esitima was surprised and she suddenly stopped to look at her in amazement. Uyai, however, took a step toward her with deviance. "Esitima, so you could be so dubious and malicious enough to kill such a lovely, learned gentleman. You killed him in other to give yourself enough room to hawk around, isn't it? Shameless woman."

Within a split of a second, Esitima's mind reeled with anger in the weight of such impertinence and absurdity in her office! She was taken aback with a sense of annoyance rolling and turning in her mind. Esitima wandered why Uyai came up with such unimaginable outrage of insults in her office.

But Uyai certainly didn't bulge. She wasn't in a hurry to leave and she had not yet done with her disparaging slur. Esitima was startled in heart; she beheld her in awe as Uyai moved around majestically taking details examination of the imposing and amazing furnishing splendour of the office and boutique...the edifice which had honestly amused her very sense of beauty.

The admiration she had for the boutique, impeccable furnishings and the quality of merchandise stock in the boutique had blown her mind. And she moved around majestically with ease of pride and aversion without regard to Esitima's presence. She roved her eyes on the features cunningly and wasn't in a hurry to leave.

"I beg your pardon?"

Esitima asked in awe with her heart pounding repeatedly.

"Madam, you heard me well"

Uyai answered sharply moving towards her threateningly in her direction and shaking her head.

"H-e-i, stop it."

Esitima stated in annoyance closing her eyes and lifting her right hand.

"How dare you? No matter who you are, you have no audacity to come into my boutique and insult me. F U C K off, Idiot."

Esitima pronounced the word with added emphasis

"What's the hell do you think you are a god or something? Look at the effrontery, the arrogance of insult right on my very nose."

...moving forward as she talked with the intention of locking the door and calling the Police.

"By the time I finished with you, you'll realise that you've crossed the red line. Bastard"

Uyai stepped forward with confidence and speed of an actress on the realisation of her intension. She moved forward beside her holding unto the door handle firmness and brushing Esitima aside.

In the ensuing squabble, Esitima lost balance falling to the floor.

Esitima couldn't believe her eyes! Her self-image which she had spent years to build had suffered a severe dislocation. Indeed, she was utterly humiliated.

That taunts of insult, scornful gibe and shame she couldn't imagine in her life had happened to her very eyes. It shook her to the foundation. Esitima couldn't believe her ears! It was like a scene out of a thriller, jet was real.

She remained there on the floor dumbfounded and overwhelmed with fear and aversion, quite unable to get up and help herself.

"Ah ah look at you, you don't have common stamina,"

She stretched forth her right hand towards Esitima, moving it up and down. Uyai continued

"A lair; an international whore. Life isn't always what you bargain for, madam. I'll finish with you first, old tart. The blood of that innocent gentleman shall hunt you for the rest of your life."

Esitima remained on the floor sobbing with pain, heartbreaks and grieve. She experienced defamation and rudeness she had never witnessed, and never hope could happen in her life. And she was absolutely devastated.

Loss of her husband was the most grievous thing to her, and she continued to treasure the memory of that devastating experience with unimaginable adoration. And she knew if he was still alive, she wouldn't be exposed to such evil of insult.

Esitima moaned for her self-respect which had nosedived to a point that a stranger could come into her office and pour such malicious accusations on her about something she was quite ignorant about. She remained there with overt embarrassment sobbing for quite a while.

After that chilling encounter, Uyai slammed the office door behind and walked out with boldness. Her mind had been filled with schadenfreude-the excitement of seeing Esitima's fall. And quite frankly, she had achieved her aim and was certain from then henceforth; Esitima was finished. Never to be the invincible lady, the untouchable sacred piece of jewellery which she always portrayed herself.

That fall had indeed the significant representation of a great fall about to come to the establishment. It marked the beginning of an end for Esitima and Ndiokkos de Vogue to the world.

She had indeed witnessed serious humiliation in mental, physical as well as psychological existence which she found very hard to take in.

When Esitima struggled and got up from the floor, quietly she locked the door behind her with great pain and sorrows in her heart. She sank deep down into the visitors' seat nearby sobbing.

With heavy compunctions, she hissed and grieved for letting Uyai into her office.

Luckily, none of her salesgirls was nearby. Her heart bled profusely and profound grief. Esitima was absolutely devastated beyond any consolation.

Remembering when she cried her heart out after the demise of her beloved husband, whose memories she still cuddled with profound adoration, Esitima's heart broke the more. She is crying differently-for her bruised pride and chequered self-image.

The prestige and honour long built up for years had suddenly evaporated into the thin air. Time is no longer on her side to wait. If she must think clearly, it shouldn't be here.

"Who is this woman."

She questioned herself.

"Definitely she must have been planted by someone close to Bassey" she had thought rightly.

"If not, why wouldn't I meet her long before now? Almost three decades I have been married, why shouldn't I set my eyes on her?"

A few moments later, Esitima got up and hurriedly, dried her tears and put a call to the Idiaimah Police to report the incident.

"Hello, is that Mr Akpanika, the commissioner of police?"

"He is, certainly."

"Hello, sir. I am Mrs Mbede of Ńdioko de Vogue. I have been attacked and seriously insulted in my office by a certain lady. Could you come immediately to 45 Udoro Way? It's a matter of death or life, please."

After long buzzes and noises at the background then came the reply.

"Madam, you need to come to the office and incident the report, right now there's no fuel for the police to respond immediately to your request"

"Come to my boutique sir, I'll reimburse you."

"Okay Madam, we'll be there shortly, bye"

"Bye-bye, sir."

The Police arrived hours after Esitima had waited endlessly and gone home. They sought to know the information from the salesgirls but unfortunately, none of them would know anything in relation to their queries.

The girls were surprised to hear the information from the law enforcement agency which they seriously doubted.

"Oh, did Madam keep anything for us?"

The police questioned but the girls knew absolutely nothing of such.

Esitima had closed office door behind her without a word to them. She dashed out into her car and into the endless space and sorrows awaiting her and her entire empire. She rushed home as soon as possible to begin what finally turned out to be the anti-climax ordeal for a celebrity figure.

But for Uyai, she found herself embattled in the middle of that bargaining. Her action turned out to be her last. Both her feet and hands were eventually consumed in the fire of that imbroglio.

Uyai regretted ever knowing the duo of Enobong and Aritie in her life. She became a hitwoman that accomplished the malicious plans of bringing Esitima and her fashion house, Ńdioko de Vogue down.

CHAPTER
11

"**A**RITIE, THE MISSION IS ACCOMPLISHED." Uyai boasted mocking Esitima as the threesome met inside Asurua Galore. "That bastard nearly got me nagging if not that I've done my homework enough for it" Uyai submitted her report.

"I trust you happening girl" Aritie acknowledged sarcastically laughing her heart out.

"I told you to leave it with me, I'll deliver on a clean slate. The bastard is completely demoralised now." Enobong chortled with laughter.

"And do you know she would have gotten me into trouble," Uyai said "if I wasn't observant and be smart enough to notice her action then responded swiftly? She attempted locking the door against me. That would have a mean disaster, I stepped forward immediately snatching the handle from her"

"That's why you're an actress, swiftness of responses is one of those delicate skills which define your goal" Aritie interjected.

"Come and see how the bastard rolled and rolled on the floor like a baby. I never knew she has got no stamina. Just one uppercut"

Uyai demonstrated this with a push of her right arm upward as in a boxing duel "from my hand sent the bitch overboard" She was verbally aggressive with her report.

Their mouths were filled with laughter as they mocked and shamed Esitima.

"Do you know when I first met with her, I was in suspense that she might know me? But after walking and talking with her I realised she didn't, then my confidence grew wild"

"Don't mind the bitch; she wouldn't for a thousand years. Does she stay at home; does she even watch Idiaimah movies? All her attention is with the foreign stuff that does not reflect our cultural heritage. She thinks her engagement with them would change the perception of the people toward her, bastard". Aritie responded with fury.

They settled down drank and had fun together. And with a toast, they clicked the glasses of Champaign celebrating Uyai's success and a job well done.

"Now what's the next step?" Uyai sought to know after a while.

"Let's wait and see if she'll still have the courage to go around her business in that boutique again or travel abroad. I think you've gotten her by the jugular. That's my aim, to frustrate her out of business. Make her life miserable and put her in the agony of life until she is down and out.

For now, I think, we've completed scene one if need be, wait to write a script on the next scene later, girls."

But Enobong wasn't comfortable with that submission, she reeled as she stood up suddenly from the sofa, she nearly fell over.

"Be careful" her friends chorused.

"Are you alright?" Aritie added.

"Yeah. That's stumble of a lifetime, you can't always predict the result"

Enobong replied looking at Aritie.

"We've never ever wanted to tumble over this matter, do we?"

"No"

Aritie shook her head.

"Then, we have to put up plan B. Some kind of insurance to safeguard us from insurgent that may arise from this, girls."

Enobong cautioned.

"That's reminding me of her fall. A calamitous bang for a pompous ladybug fuzzed up on the floor with her emotional nonsense"

Uyai joked and they went into a hearty laugh.

"But I suspect we mightn't have too much time to wait, Aritie, I agree with Enobong. It's good we go with full force while it's still hot else she regained strength and resilience to do anything funny"

Uyai stated her feelings.

"Don't worry, I know Esitima better than you do. That single act has sent her down, it might take a long while to reconnect with her real-world again"

Aritie was confident Esitima had suffered a big psychological blow from that attack.

"But we still need plan B, robust enough to our advantage. Something to pin her down a bit more in case of an emergency." Enobong opined.

And Enobong formulated subtle and cunning plans debunked of any manner of suspicion. She used her skills, social media and personal contact to mount a campaign of calumny and slender against Esitima with the pronounced force of hatred.

Her main aim had been to instigate Esitima and turn the people of Mkpasang against her and her boutique so that Asurua Galore, her brand, could flourish becoming a trend to reckon with in town.

Enobong had struggled for years to develop her fashion hub without standard of success. She had had the notion that competitors like Ńdiokko de Vogue and others in Mkpasang were hindrances to her growth, and know that this opportunity had risen, she couldn't wait.

Enobong played with an utmost sense of animosity and bitterness with every inch of her breath. They engaged with the public from outside and within Mkpasang community spreading such unfounded, derogatory and defamatory rumours about Esitima. Esitima was unable to safeguard herself from the public glare. She became completely isolated and alienated from Mkpasang community.

"You mean Esitima was the ghost behind the plot that actually killed our Doctor, her husband? I can't believe my ears. Such a nice gentleman could become a victim in his own house?" Usoro intoned filling his calabash-a local drinking jar, with palm wine in the local bamboo bar.

Ekom was quick to add "My brother, I am not surprised. The only worrying thing for me is that people didn't believe when I spoke loud and clear that Dr Mbede was murdered by the forces within. They blame me for being a bully and lunatic. Do you see now, a wife can kill her husband, what does she really want?"

"What does she want?"

They chorused.

"Mmmh" Essien gave a low mournful moan. "That is the question on everyone's lip. Maybe" He brought his voice to a near whisper

"To satisfy her sexual escapades. You see what I mean? That woman is like a Casanova, never satisfied" He laughed open-mouthed.

"Wait a minute," another man said, "…are you insinuating that the young man was incapable of handling her concupiscence?"

"That's not the point. The eagerness and fantasy in some people could be unimaginable, I suppose hers is, the reason she can't control the urge."

Essien responded with a hiss that resulted in whiplashing laughter of all present.

"Ekom, people were only being overwhelmed with shock and sorrow that the death of Dr Mbede brought to the community. Quite unbelievably, it got the whole community of Mkpasang sorrowful. But even before he died, there were rumours flying around that she slept with numerous men like Eteakamba."

Essien finally finished his assertion taking a sip of the juicy wine. He was giving a burst of good-natured laughter while listening to Etisang who had been waiting patiently to air his views on the issue. All that he knows is that women indulge in immorality as if it's the only thing now on earth.

"Gentlemen are men saints, when did we start to play The Pope? Who had played hide and seek games for ages, is it not men?" He asked rhetorically with his eyes examining all present.

"Gone are the days when misogyny was the order of the day and men treated women with contempt, seeing moral breakdown as perpetrated by them although men were the main culprits. A man either covertly or openly indulges in sexual activities in marriage leaving his wife severely demoralised.

"But now, misandry and misogyny are growing hand in hand not only in the lexicon of modern-day Idiaimah but most especially, in practice. The husband would turn left while the wife goes into right in search of bed mates.

"They will come back together without the knowledge of the other. Of course, a woman may suspect a man, but men hardly imagined women could indulge in such an atrocious act of evil. What a debased generation is ours?!"

"It is time we start addressing this anomaly else, we may be confronted with deviant behaviour and many more domestic deaths in the near future"

"You're right, Etisang." Enam observed

"But are you in any way insinuating that our doctor was promiscuous? No, I think he was very noble in character. As we see, this is quite unacceptable! I know our society feel promiscuity is a good alternative to decency, the reason you witness odd, deviance and negative behaviour around us"

Enam was saddened by the level of moral breakdown in the society which was gaining ground in a greater dimension. He felt particularly concerned that the growth of these social problems, no doubt, was more pronounced among the educated class.

Another man Akpan, said it wasn't Akpambang alone who was involved in lecherous activities with Esitima, many other men do too. He said he was fortunate to witness Ntafiong, about three weeks prior to Bassey's death, coming out of The Tavern together with Esitima in his car.

But he wasn't aware that Ntafiong was a business partner with Esitima. And that too was something Bassey knew about. On the day he had seen them together, they were having business dinner with guests at The Tavern.

But Edet remained calm and collective without saying a word. He wasn't quite sure of the truth of the rumours, and as such, much of what was flying around about Dr Mbede's death was still a puzzle to him. Edet's mind was still not made up with the wake of such unfounded gossips spreading in the community. Therefore, he sat down looking at them and wondering where the thick cloud ceiling the community and tearing the integrity and reputation of Esitima and her business apart came from.

This had severed the community the past two months and nearly all were engaged with the rumour. Therefore, Edet played a waiting game and wished to see where this smokescreen would have their origin. As they say, he thought, there is no cause without effect-no smoke without fire!

Nevertheless, the gossips and the rumours kept wrangling along intensely within the community. It changed the direction and dynamic of the conversation to the extent that it wasn't impossible to ignore.

People engaged freely demonstrating love for Bassey, to the extent that the reputation and confidence that Esitima wielded with passion and enthusiasm faded away swiftly.

She started having nightmares with evidence of depressive thoughts. Ultimately, the rumours did depict the characters and nature of those who brewed it.

And like wildfire, it continued burning on with intensity among the rumourmongers-those feebleminded people who related to it far beyond boundaries until Etimbuk became ashamed of his mother.

CHAPTER
12

Esitima's big dose of ambition shrank. Those around her could easily perceive her lack of zeal and enthusiasm in things that were so dear to her which she had previously treated with an enormous sense of urgency and pride. And Joyce, her friend was very saddened.

Esitima lost confidence in keeping her business enterprise alive with stock from global markets. She lost her fashion life and her determination to always ensure that she hits the highest bar nosedived within a year following her husband's death. Indeed Esitima, was not in tune with herself anymore. She counted her losses on every step along the way.

Even the culture of mediocrity she hated previously with passion and wouldn't give into playing the second fiddle eroded away sharply. Esitima started getting goods to her boutique from local markets like Aba, Lagos, Ibadan etcetera instead of Dubai, London, Paris or New York which had been her marketplaces. Esitima's dream of excellence waned, she had resigned herself to mere imagination. And daily watched those ambitious heights diminished into oblivion.

She was no more a lover of excellence and beauty. Her fascination with clothing and general wears, unfortunately, became a thing of the past. The only one in Mkpasang whose majority of her customers easily followed her ideas of fashion and was easily connected with her and her boutique through engagement in new fashion trends that came in regularly. Above all her likeable personality that was so connected and communicated well with her ever-increasing customers suffered major landmark dislocation and failure.

Although Esitima, like most people, was not an all-round best, her determination and pursuit of distinction did pay off. The reason she succeeded in building her business enterprise, Ńdiokko de Vogue, to an enviable height.

This became a beacon of fashion hub in the local fashion industry. Unfortunately, this too experienced massive deterioration in scope and capacity through dwindling finances.

Esitima started experiencing loneliness with death wish lurking around her. She, therefore, locked herself up in her house engaging with intense thought of how she came to be in such a terrible situation. The thought of how on one occasion,

Mkpasang village organised a reception ceremony for her husband, Bassey, one of their illustrious sons who had accomplished academic excellence crept into her mind suddenly.

For her, that was an occasion for a business showcase that she wouldn't want to miss out: it was an opportunity to exhibit her merchandise and to gain more customers.

Esitima thought of how she was sensational, stunning and spectacular on that special occasion as a darling of fashion expressions! She presented a classic appearance that matched not only her business life but also sent messages across to everyone as an invitation to seek to know her and her business.

And true to her dream, she epitomised the glamour, grandeur and flavour of Ñdiokko de Vogue to the extent of crashing Bassey's reception ceremony!

Among the distinguished guests at the ceremony, she was one of the most dazzling and gorgeously dressed ladies presents. Everything about her was perfect and unique. Her elegance and beauty shone like a glistening galaxy of blazing stars emanating from the radiant evening sun. Her glimmering hat, purple dotted skirt with a blouse to match, gave her classic appearance she desired. And she was beautiful to behold.

Esitima's height of about 1.87 metres, her gazelle neck and limbs, athletic physique, and above all her infectious smiles sent shivering sensations down the spine of the gentlemen present.

Bassey, an eminent scholar and the guest of honour, was duped by the charm exuded by her elegance. Even female folks watched her with admiration, not to talk of men, her presence became a source of distractions for many.

Brilliance and innovation in the fashion industry were simply stupendous making her the most fashion aficionado of all time in her community. A fashion geek, an enthusiast that kept the dress and dressing industry aglow. She would always refresh her look and wardrobe with fine attires of 'A' hit list from her global stock, exclusive of any malfunctioning.

In her business, Esitima combined her superb delicate skills with her classic shape, which made her a perfect model of all times. All her life, the talented designer stockpiled seasonal embellishments, enough to go for the signature tune of her couture business. She was always well-packaged and had amazing confidence in wearing and displaying her merchandise to her ever-increasing chain of customers.

Esitima was indeed one among her equals and she engendered Bassey's romantic life and an adventure into the Ñdiokkos. He couldn't get over the embarrassment of losing self-confidence at the reception ceremony organised in his honour.

Esitima was the singular reason Bassey couldn't arrange his line of thought to give a vote of thanks at the end of the grand reception ceremony. Thank goodness; his father stood in for him.

Bassey found his adventure into the Ndiokkos family interesting. Esitima, the second daughter of Öböñ Felix Ndiokkos, won the admiration of her father one day when she appeared before him with flatteringly designed attire.

The Dad was enamoured by her daughter's curvy and twisty looks. He saw in her an upcoming model for the family business. And Bassey was consoled that if Esitima's father could be wooed by the daughter's elegance, his experience of falling head over heels with Esitima was not out of place.

For Öböñ Felix, Esitima was a paragon of beauty, an enigma of some sought and a potential asset and entrepreneur for Ñdiokko de Vogue, the family business. She was dexterously created for the advancement of Ñdiokko empire, Öböñ Felix thought to himself.

Bassey discovered even more stunning revelation that for years it was very difficult to separate fashion from the bloodline of Ñdiokko. The gene that carried the ace, as the most dressed, most fashionable and of course, the most famous with a difference in Ibattai village, was still very dominant and found spectacular expression in Esitima.

Her great grandmother, Mama Ubakka Ñdiokko was a pioneer seamstress in Ibattai village in the early 1960s. She had the stupendous skills and dexterity of designing various clothing and costumes for the local population.

Many from far and near patronised her ingenuity in clothe making business. Her skill and dexterity as a seamstress took Mama Ubakka Ñdiokko to various markets in many towns for purchases of fabrics and accessories for her emerging couture enterprise. And she conscientiously committed her time, resources and talent into developing an emerging fashion enterprise which in contemporary time, had transformed into a family business; Ñdiokko de Vogue.

Therefore, when Esitima eventually emerged as a fashion guru, many who knew her background well enough only gave credit to her materfamilias granny, Mama Ñdiokko.

It wasn't quite long into his adventure when Bassey started hearing about the Ñdiokko' ingenuity in everyday conversations:

"Yes, it's a genetic attribute and you can't help it."

Bessie remarked as she strolls with her friends Mandu and Ememöbön.

"How do you mean?"

Her friend Mandu queried.

"My mother told me that her great grandmother was a fashion geek. Do you know the fashion house at Akwa Efak, Ibattai? Ñdiokko de Vogue is their family business"

Bessie chipped in.

"Ah-e-eh, you can't be serious!"

Ememöbön interjected.

"Ñdiokko de Vogue! You don't mean it?"

"Do you mean that Americana Arena?"

She inquired, placing her two hands on her waist. With her head tilted a little forward, she continued:

"I've been there but could hardly afford a single item in that boutique. Does she want to milk Mkpasang dry with her expensive stuff?"

Bessie regarded her with a gesture of caution and then interrupted "Actually, their products are inexpensive when you consider where they came from, the quality and a current exchange rate of Idiaimah currency."

"My dear, you need a year's earnings if you must be a customer of Ñdiokko de Vogue, and of course, you'll look special," said Ememöbön.

"Let's see it this way. Their products displayed on the shelves for sale are not meant for all. You must have the buying power in order to lay your hands on them, except you're out there just to feed your eyes only" Basie lectured. "You'll not be able to get it because it's too expensive for you, but others will.

"Girls, every fashion do cost financial stress especially for young women desiring to look fabulous, who don't have the means of reaching it. For me," she said this with excitement on her face, she held her beautiful skirt by the sides and admiring it. She bought this from Ñdiokko de Vogue and was so proud to wear it.

"I've gotten something I needed so badly, and I know it looks epic on me"

Her friends were stunned in admiration of her new outfit.

"Wow," they said, "this is beautiful" They admired the dress.

"Yes, I've been wondering immediately I saw it. I wanted to ask where you got such a beautiful frog from" Mandu said.

"Don't be brainwashed by the euphoria of the situation to do something stupid that you might regret, girls" Bassie warned.

"Never mind, I shall size them up soon,"

said Mandu whose wildest expectation grew further:

"My new boyfriend is loaded. His political connection is very promising. Once he lands, we shall first download the package at Ñdiokko de Vogue."

All went into intractable laughter.

"Congratulations! That's my baby,"

Bessie asseverated.

"As we all know, trends do come and go, but good manners remained indelible for articulate ladies. There's nothing in fashion to necessitate flames of passion out of control" and Ememöböñ opined. "The dressing room questions, 'how do I look like or is this gorgeous?' are worth answering before one gets into choosing and changing fashion"

"Girls be yourselves. Okay?"

They all laughed equivocally walking away in opposite directions, Mandu and Bessie in one and Ememöböñ, the other.

"Bye!"

They chorused

CHAPTER
13

ESITIMA WAS A FASHION GENIUS, an addict to anything fashionable. She had a mind of a movie buff obsessed with every classic product. At Ňdiokko de Vogue, she was both an entrepreneur and a merchandiser with a vision, always seeking to galvanise the fortunes of Ňdiokko de Vogue to the wider world.

In her teenage years and during undergraduate days at the University, Esitima had investigated and validated trendy fashions of A-class hit list for her family company.

African and Western fashions were her haul catalogue collections which she made into beautiful memorabilia as a token of remembrance to her years of service to Ňdiokko de Vogue. This hung in her lounge at first sight to anyone that came into the home of Mbede.

Whatever was in vogue and trendy would first be identified with Ňdiokko de Vogue before anywhere else. Esitima supplied everything from delicate embellishments and sequins designs to folk wears of high qualities.

She established and maintained networks of an exquisite galaxy of stars in the couture industry worldwide. Every day, diverse locals flocked into her gorgeous boutique with welcoming boon. They came in to try on new arrivals, place order, purchase products or just sit there to flip through fashion catalogues for exotic models.

Always, there was something special at Ňdiokko de Vogue for everyone.

Merchandises from Aba, Eko, Dubai and Johannesburg; London, Paris, California and New York, Milan, and Naples. Ňdiokko de Vogue was the a-one-stop shop that had caused Esitima to write her name in the fashion hall of fame.

Keeping weekly entrants of trendy fashion for celebrities and A-hit list customers at Ňdiokko de Vogue, was a knack she created out of overwhelming demand for her designs. That of course, had lived with her for nearly two decades. And over the years, customers had scrambled to get their names enshrined on it.

Separate Esitima from Ňdiokko de Vogue, the company would go down the drain losing that glamour, grandeur and flavour that made it thick. She was indeed a perfect mix and match lifeline for the company.

The reason Bassey was enthralled by his adventure into Ňdiokkos ancestry. The discovery, to his amazement, that Esitima was the woman, the backbone and pillar behind the making of Ňdiokko de Vogue was awesome.

This soared his infatuation for her. But he wouldn't be on the silent exploration forever, thus he put his right foot forward to begin a courtship. After three months of courtship, Bassey invited

Esitima to their family house for a formal introduction to his parents as his bride-to-be. And his mother received the news with a note of melancholy.

Enenwan, Bassey's mother, knew the Ńdiokkos well enough. As an indigene of Ibattai herself, she as well versed with the Ńdiokkos family lifestyle. Their flirtation with fashion and stylish dressings was one too many and dangerous to contend with. Enenwan's contemplation of the marriage situation, at least, for her son would mean staying in a collision course with other suitable contenders in and around Mkpasang.

"Women from the famous Ńdiokko family are considered unsuitable for marriage. They've lost touch with the reality of life situation around them. While many in their neighbourhood are wallowing in abject poverty, they are there flowing and glowing in overwhelming affluence. Their insatiable appetite for wealth and opulence has caused much more trouble in society. And they know it,"

Enenwan had counselled.

Bassey was quite uncomfortable with his mother's assessment of the Ńdiokkos. But he kept quiet, listening as if all was well with him while at the same time making a critical analysis of the situation. After all, Bassey understood that life is not lived in isolation of problems. If one must live successfully, criticisms and disapprovals must form part of living. The more one is criticised, the more successful one might become if one could learn from those experiences.

The Ńdiokkos always took any criticism in good faith, it gave them an edge over their competitors! And they saw every criticism as feedback and appraisal of their business endeavours. This forced Ńdiokkos to rethink and be creative just to please and get more customers to like the boutique.

Perhaps that was why the Ńdiokkos were so successful. Each opinion meant an opportunity to learn more about how to satisfy their customers. Hence, they could easily improve on their services to their numerous of them.

"Eh-e-eh Mama, you never failed to amuse me. The family is wealthy, and so what stops the kith and kin from being identified as such. They worked hard to overcome poverty and got liberated from it. Is it their fault to be rich, Mama? Or when did being rich become a reason for discrimination?" Bassey shook his head with a nod of disappointment and disapproval.

For Bassey, poverty is a product of laziness, even though that's not the case always. He believed that if one worked hard and stayed focused, success is imminent. But those who sit down praying for manna to fall from heaven will forever remain poor. Thus, Bassey attributed hard work to the success of the Ńdiokko family and holds the view that they will continue to be rich if they keep working harder. Again, his mother gave her candid viewpoint:

"Bassey, you've been away from the village for so long and you're unaware of our contemporary norms and values this part of the world. I will suggest you search further away from Ńdiokko or we'll help find you a good wife if you will. There are dozens of women with good morals in Ibattai, Mkpasang and the environs, why get entangled with the Ńdiokko?"

After that, there was silence and calmness as when the music suddenly stopped from a disc player. Bassey turned to look at his father disappointingly and wondering if that had been their corroborative opinion.

Rather, his father was analysing the views of his wife, which he found too illogical to agree with. For him, his wife seemed to lost touch with the time and context of Bassey's marriage proposals. Gone are the days when parents would impose a woman or man on their children. Times have changed and Bassey, a well-educated gentleman, would not succumb to spousal arrangement against his will.

To Bassey's surprise, his father turned around clearing his throat and said. "Da Baa, for me I don't see anything wrong with good taste, decency and beauty; after all, God has made all things good and beautiful."

Deacon Mbede highly treasures his son's relationship with one of the daughters of the famous Ñdiokko family. It had boosted his status in Mkpasañg community and brought him a sense of pride in the village.

"I don't see why we should choose a wife for you, Baa." He emphasised his right hand up in the air. "With your exposure and knowledge, I am confident you have a good judgment to make the right choice. We shall not live with you, you know. It's you and your wife just like me and your mother. And your mother only has her axe to grind. Enjoy yourself my son. Go ahead! You have my full support and encouragement. Cheers!"

Bassey was surprised but delighted.

"Thank you, Papa."

He responded with a sense of emerging confidence and pride that his wish had prevailed. Bassey went ahead and married Esitima in the folk marriage ceremony. He wished that his wife would add more feathers to his hat by taking on advanced academic pursuit but Esitima had a different plan.

Thus, Bassey's marital challenges began when Esitima likeness for business over academics soared.

Although the decision went against his wish, Bassey had to put up with her because it was his conscious choice and willingness to marry her. After all, in the game of love one doesn't count gains all the time. He knew that when he chose Esitima as his wife, he had chosen everything in association with her: beauty, elegance, success, and above all, disappointments and failures.

Esitima could easily confide in Joyce, one of her favourite friends. She told Joyce about her preference for business over academic discipline, but Joyce couldn't hide her objection. When there was an opportunity for a conversation Joyce audaciously advised.

"Ima, your refusal to buy into your husband's dream for a teaching appointment at the University is the most annoying part of your stubbornness."

Joyce's comment took Esitima by surprise as they drove along towards her shop. And she suddenly slowed down the car and listened with attention.

"I request that you talk things over with him as soon as possible; he is absolutely piqued," Joyce advised.

Esitima was fuming with disgust at her friend's remarks and she found it quite uneasy to drive in that state of mind. Therefore, she slowly brought the car to a complete stop at a nearby parking space and waited for a while before responding to Joyce's comment.

"Joyce, you and I have been on this issue before. You know I don't like teaching. Let me be where my interest and passion lie, please. I know I shall be a very bad teacher if I ever tow that line. And above all, I'll never be happy as a teacher.

"Teaching will demand a lot from me and when I don't live up to expectation the students will suffer."

Esitima remained silent, letting her argument sink down and giving Joyce a look of friendship before she continued.

"The fact that I bagged a degree in economics doesn't translate into being a good lecturer. Does it, Joyce? But I can apply that knowledge excellently well in my business."

Esitima opined with emphasis.

Then Joyce interrogated.

"What about housekeeping and homemaking? That is another area which your husband has expressed deep concerns. Your attitude towards the upbringing of your children is the point in question."

"Da, don't exert your energy on those matters, please. Save your breath. We've talked extensively about those and other issues severally without arriving at any definite conclusions. Well, maybe, we'll be there someday. Okay?"

Esitima responded dismissively while starting her car to continue the journey to her shop.

"In all honesty, Ima, reconsider your stance on this matter urgently. Let go of your ego and pride, come to your senses. Remember no matter how educated you're as an African woman, homemaking is a culture we mustn't trample underfoot." Joyce cautioned.

"I hear you, madam lecturer. Thank you, I need a handout please." Esitima ridiculed and they both laughed as they stepped out of the car.

CHAPTER 14

Bassey met Esitima managing Ñdiokko de Vogue before he got engaged and eventually married her. His desire therefore for her to leave her business for a teaching job at the university had been a decision Esitima was so furious about. She was not at ease with that development. Fashion business had been the love of her life and she had made it a preferred choice of career above any other.

Esitima couldn't believe that her husband would expect her to give up her fashion business, but she understood his stance and needed time to consider if that could be possible. It's a lifetime decision that she would have to make by reflecting on her lifestyle and interests. She knew how to prioritise her values and would not be cowed easily out of her will.

As a thinker, Esitima wasn't stranger to mulling through her ideas over and over again before reaching a decision. Would she continue with her family business at Ñdiokko de Vogue or throw in the towel and take up a teaching career in a university? Time will tell.

Esitima wasn't actually in dilemma though, she stood on her decision and knew Ñdiokko de Vogue was her top priority, she wouldn't exchange that pride for something else, no matter how enticing that alternative might be.

Her self-awareness and managerial skills coupled with ingenuity allowed her to engage well with the wider world easily unlike the boring position of standing in the lecture hall, dishing out theories and concepts to students. She had made her mind known to him, but he was extremely annoyed and frustrated.

Bassey's family values and concerns were quite different. He couldn't understand why his wife would turn down a laudable plan which would give her ample time to be at home to raise their children with warmth and affection, for the pain, discomfort and hassle of managing a business enterprise. Does she really understand the implication of the decision she has made? Must she undermine the future of her family with the challenging choice of business venture?

Esitima's firm stand on various issues, especially, on her career choice had presented her as a stubborn and insensitive woman. But everyone has both strengths and weaknesses. Thus, her ingenuity in business may not mean that she is equally endowed with a teaching acumen.

And for the husband, Esitima is high headed, conceited and proud. This revealed the extent of differences in human relationships even in marriage. One is bound to encounter difficult decisions but the ability to manage through is what would make or mar the relationship.

Bassey and Esitima couldn't negotiate an open sharing relationship, that was beneficial to them. That's why their opinions and thoughts couldn't be respected amongst themselves. They always involve in irrational decisions making, opinions meant to be forced on the other.

The reason they experienced frequent chaos and anarchies in their relationship. They refused to acknowledge the obvious fact that decision making in marriage is a shared responsibility that must be talked though in an atmosphere of love and understanding.

But Bassey, no doubt had been really ready to do all he could to provide comfort and wellbeing for the family, but he had been frustrated and felt defeated by frequent failures from his wife.

His wife wouldn't like to review the important outcome of a decision with him, something necessary to come to a proper decision making and choice as the best way forward. The business was the first and the last thing on her mind, everything else was secondary. The reason Bassey had been left with no other choice than to force his choices on her most of the times.

CHAPTER 15

The death of Bassey brought serious untold emotional trauma to the life of the family members. His children faced the reality of the situation that their father's trademark of warm embrace, hugs and cuddling were no more tenable. Those skills that defined his fatherhood came to a sudden end, unfortunately.

Left with grief and continuous sadness, the family had to mourn his exit with grave fortitude. No more inspiration from those boisterous experiences of playing sports like scouting, skateboarding, football in the sand or anything else. Also, they missed watching their father's interaction with their mother and his relationship with people in society. The whole family, including Mkpasang community, were thrown onto deep sadness.

Setbacks and devastation continued holding sway within the family and the community at large, indication Bassey meant so much to the family and community. Children were suddenly confronted with the truth of what life is without their father. What life meant without their role model-that surpassing influence that shielded them away from many problems of life.

The incapacitated childbearing skills added greatly to the problems of Esitima. All that she knew was managing her business enterprise and this had taken so much of her attention away from the family. She hadn't time to listen to numerous concerns and aspirations of her children.

Bassey had been concerned about this development, the reason he had serious headaches in their relationships which invariably, resulted in Patrick forming relationships with the wrong people.

Esitima was too distant from her children, she lacked the strength and capacity to navigate through the family problems with ease. She had been struggling with building a meaningful family life as something that could keep the bond of unity together.

Aritie, Bassey's niece, had become the person responsible for all domestic affairs. She remained the rallying point for the family and the only one who got involved in the day-to-day running of the home. Aritie knew how to cook, clean and teach the children values of life and even help them in their homework too. Aritie was an indispensable source of hope for the whole family.

Lack of closeness, comfort and emotional support for the children had been what Esitima desperately needed. The reason Etimbuk always appeared withdrawn, sad and depressed. Although Patrick wasn't too concerned with family dynamics as he got numerous friends that kept him occupied.

But still, there was some element of loneliness around him. For Uduak, because of her age, there was nothing noticeable about her behaviour. And Etimbuk who was the hardest hit; had a daunted task contending these problems.

Prior to that devastating incident of the death of Bassey, their father, Etimbuk was a very social boy; his interactive skills among friends had been simply phenomenal. But after the death, Etimbuk retracted into his shell. He appeared pessimistic devoid of any interaction with people. He completely detached himself from everything that could bring him happiness and comfort.

CHAPTER 16

Onne of Etimbuk's Friends in the village, Enametti whom he had formed a strong affinity with left the village years earlier for studies in Ubandde-a city far away from home. Since then, Etimbuk had no one with whom he could trust and relate with.

Things were so bad that Etimbuk was left in the shadow of himself without friends of any kind. For Patrick, this lack of care drove him into forming bad companies with a phalanx of hooligans and lawless young men.

Therefore, with the news of the arrival of Enametti in the village, Etimbuk couldn't wait-he was so excited. The longing to see him sprang up alive with intensity urging him quickly to go and see Enametti, his good friend and confidant. But then, his recent problems were on his mind, and couldn't let go of him. His was entwined between his passion and his problems.

But then, he still found some courage for a stroll. And sluggishly, walked down a deserted country road humming a comforting tune along. Both hands stuck in the side pockets of his faded jeans trousers and eyes looked down his mind traversed three major lines of pressing thoughts: thoughts too intrusive for him to contend with.

"Should he ponder these thoughts over?" He questioned himself; "or should he let go of them?" But slowly, as he appeared knackered, he trudged on.

This had not been the first time Etimbuk had a cause to think seriously about his future. Oftentimes he had stopped to appraise and analyse the goings-on around him in the last two years. Those were the moments he felt the pulses of the present happenings, and their impacts on his future and those of his immediate family members.

There have been times when things seemed too difficult, almost impossible to scale through yet; he managed to forge ahead not minding the hassles involved. But on this very day and moment, his worries were quite incensed close to the breaking point.

Etimbuk was deeply tormented by the tripartite thoughts flooding his mind unceasingly and he wondered whether he should succumb to such mounting pressures or would he scale through to the end?

Interestingly, everything centred around his beloved mother. A woman whose sense of love and care was nonpareil. But now she was disconcerted and seriously threatened by lack of energy and drive. This was contrary to her impressive dispossession and focus in life which was her trademarks.

Top on the list of his worries was the possibility of completion of his university education in view of the current family dwindling fortunes. Also, his mother's deteriorating mental health in the last six months got him down and he had no energy to deal with other issues of concerns around him.

And most importantly, the wave of rumours and scandal swirling around and engulfing the personality of his dear mother as a fall-out from the sudden death of his father two years earlier.

These daunting challenges weighed Etimbuk down peevishly, sapping his mental, physical and psychological energy to the brink.

But his aim had been to see Enametti his only bosom friend who just arrived in the village and he couldn't wait. He wished to run away from the problems of life for a second.

But the ferocious rumours engulfing his mother's character and personality was a subject of his grave concern, and he put it always on the radar.

Etimbuk used to strongly reject such rumours, he tended to be on denial, but as he walked along thoughtfully, he vetted the veracity of the matter. He found it quite impossible to subscribe wholly to such an impetuous conclusion. He thought to explore all available avenues resolutely to either confirm or deny his frightening fear.

"Could Mummy have any connections with dad's death?"

The very thought alone was quite sickening. His mind kept saying. 'How can such a loving, caring and sharing wife of impeccable character be also callous enough to kill her beloved husband? Could her present predicament develop as the nemesis of her supposedly wicked action?'

I just have to think things through clearly." Etimbuk was battling with the most threatening of answers.

He and his brother Patrick were young adults of twenty-two and twenty years old respectively.

Etimbuk's bonhomie disposition of love and compassion were the endowments that eventually got him down with glut of life challenges enough to destabilise any person in such circumstance. His brother Patrick, on the other hand, was feeble-minded lacking the insight to keep up with Etimbuk. And that was quite appalling.

He was sick and tired of his brother, Patrick's braggadocios attitude to life challenges. Patrick's boastful and inflated talk and behaviours were out of order and Etimbuk felt his brother's grandiose behaviour betrayed the ideals which Mbedes stands for as kind-hearted and gentle people.

If Patrick hadn't said he was a billionaire now, he would concoct that he was one of the presidential aides the next moment. His ostentatious living caused serious trouble within the rank and file of the Mkpasang community to his disgrace.

Etimbuk was quite uncomfortable with this deceitful attitude and behaviour. He felt that Patrick was oblivious and careless about the enormous challenges facing the family. Patrick wouldn't want to be identified with any issue of concerns around him, except when he needed money that he squandered away at will. His mother's present ill health notwithstanding.

Therefore, Etimbuk found himself standing all alone and being the sole thinker and planner of day-to-day concerns within the family. He did this even while still grappling with his personal challenges and academic pursuit. He bore the enormous responsibilities entrusted on him by the circumstance of his birth with resilience and gracefully.

Two years earlier, Etimbuk and Patrick were two happy and outgoing lads, but things changed when they lost their father. Born into a family with a promising future, they had a lifestyle of comfort; getting what they wanted, and as a matter of fact, when they wanted them. And they proudly treasured their life of affluence which put them on the driver's seat amongst their peers and circle of friends.

This experience characterised their growing up years. There was enough money to burn around on any conceivable thing, just for the asking. Sadly, Etimbuk had to struggle and contend with a little of what he had now. For Patrick, the die had not jet cast. It would take him some time to come to terms with the reality of his new situation. Meanwhile, he could continue to delude himself with his magniloquence.

CHAPTER 17

ETIMBUK'S MISSION THAT MORNING HAD been to meet his most trusted friend, Enametti who came home after finishing his studies in another city, Ubandde. He was excited with the news of Enametti's arrival in Mkpasang, and this helped him to set aside his worries, at least for a while to enjoy a moment of joy and gladness with his good friend.

With all the turn of events in his family, Etimbuk felt he finally had someone whom he could trust, someone he can confide in.

Therefore, he walked along, his spirit was down, and he reflected on the troubling situations around him. He needed to regain his jolly moments and to enjoy his time with his friend, although he hadn't certain of the wellbeing of his family in future.

About twenty minutes after setting out, Etimbuk met with Enametti. Enametti was exceedingly excited but somewhat surprised to see him. He had barely settled down after a long trip and wondered how the news of his arrival in the village got to Etimbuk.

So, he hastened with eagerness towards Etimbuk, jumped and stretched forth his right hand for a handshake though with condescending mateyness. With the left, he caught Etimbuk with fascinating impulse, pulling him eagerly on the right shoulder close enough for a bosomy embrace.

"Oh boy, what a surprise! What a pleasant reception from you!"

Enametti exclaimed. "I never could expect you to be here so soon."

He looked at his hand watch. "It's barely an hour since my arrival. Oh boy, how has it been?" He giggled boisterously. "Thanks so much for this urgency, I am grateful. It's so good to see you again, Etimbuk."

He laughed with a glowing pleasure of seeing his friend after many years. And with great joy in his heart, he stopped to assess him.

"A sense of expectations filled my heart like streams of waters, and the urgency of this visit couldn't wait once the news got out to me," Etimbuk responded.

"Oh boy, see your moustache and goatee; so cute!"

"Thanks!"

Etimbuk said laughing with excitement. "You're not looking bad at all. Slim, tall, handsome, and spiffy. You're the cool man!"

Both friends cracked up each other repeatedly.

"My intention was to see you in the afternoon when I finish sorting out a few things with my parents. All the same, boy, you're highly welcome. You're a friend indeed."

The two friends continued to chat unabatedly, reminiscing on past experiences in their life and society. For a while, they were joking, laughing, and amusing themselves with tales of the past.

"Boy, the village has changed remarkably; if not for my sense of geography I would have missed our compound."

"Oh yes! This is called 'uncommon transformation', you haven't seen anything yet." Etimbuk said.

Indeed, things have changed tremendously since the last four years he was away. There were business centres and restaurants, new roads, new residential houses and visitors living and working in Mkpasang.

Expansion of the University which increased the population of Mkpasang. Phenomenal developmental projects had taken place within the years he was away from the community.

'A new heaven and new earth,' everything is new in Mkpasang. The atmosphere is pregnant and charged with many untold stories."

Enametti said with a sense of expectation.

"Take it easy Enametti; take a deep breath, you're in for good times. A four-year storyline is quite exciting." Etimbuk said. "It can't be told in a hurry, you're in for a treat."

"Really?"

Enametti replied.

"This homecoming is going to be quite amazing, exciting and full of memorabilia"

"Oh yes!"

"The joy of being together once again gives me great excitement, I hope all is well."

Enametti said with robust confidence and glowing sense of pride.

"Yes, of course, life is not without troubles, you know. We try to keep it simple all the time"

Etimbuk responded.

"No rush, no complexity. Life must continue inevitably."

As Etimbuk said so, he suddenly became a little bit withdrawn, lacking adequate zeal and drive to continue. With this incongruity of his affect, he was flooded with memories of the glorious years when his father was still alive. He had faced various challenges in the past two years and was still struggling with his mother's current situation.

Etimbuk then reclined at the seat on the foyer, thinking about his deceased father. Surely, if he were alive, he wouldn't be exposed to the negative trend of things that have denied him so many opportunities in life.

Perhaps, he wouldn't have been in Mkpasang but somewhere else in pursuit of his higher education like some of his contemporaries. He remained calm and quiet for a moment.

"Absolutely, keep on keeping on, the trouble got to be managed with expectations that tomorrow is pregnant with the future, isn't it?"

Enametti remarked again.

"And we have to be expectant knowing that we shall one day be liberated" Etimbuk grinned in acknowledgement of the complement and shook hands again as he awoke from his temporary meltdown.

"Thanks! How's school and studies in Mkpasang; I hope all is well?"

"Cool, I am trying by God's grace, everything seems Okay."

"Wow, Etimbuk please get up and come right inside. Such a good friend can't stay outside" Enametti led the way into the lounge and pointed to the upholstery.

"Sit down and relax, please uh! It's so exciting here." He said, "You're highly welcomed?"

"It's my pleasure to have you here with me."

Both regarded each other with a loving smile and affection. They appreciated and acknowledged the strong bond of unity that had existed between them, and they wished it continued.

Enametti sat with two legs crossed and arms spread out on the sofa in a noble way. His unbuttoned shirt was flying and dancing aggressively responding to the breeze from both the table and ceiling fans oscillating rapidly across the room. He was tapping his feet to the rhythm of reggae music booming from the speakers at the corner of the room, as he listened to Etimbuk with great eagerness.

"Oh boy! Bob Marley and the Wailers, even in the grave, the man still roars." Etimbuk observed. "His music shall play on for a long time after his demise."

"Yes oh, you can't overlook him, once he strikes the chord, party starts."

"Absolutely, though old in production, still remains contemporaneous in use. Boy, his music shall never die, it remains a bombshell any day anytime… It's Exodus, movement of Jah people." Etimbuk joined his voice to sing along, he rose up shaking his body at the same time.

"Do you know that reggae music is a concept through which most other rhythms evolve?" Enametti asked gyrating with the rhythm.

"Absolutely, it's music that will never die. Rastafarians!" Etimbuk concurred gyrating along.

Both danced around enjoying the rhythm and singing the lyrics alongside together.

"It has been really long, hope all is well?" Etimbuk interrupted the dance.

"Yes, distance neither diminishes the aura of true friendship nor lack of sight can break the authentic affection."

Enametti submitted.

"But disloyalty does and had done the worst for centuries. True friendship, nonetheless, endures forever. For when friends are far away and unable to communicate face to face, they draw strength from the past and savour their relationships with love."

Etimbuk looked at him with the utmost sense of appreciation and responded. "Absolutely, you're damn right Enametti. Even though four years seem forever, I always do have you in mind."

There was laughter between them.

"Me too Etimbuk. I've frequently thought about you…anywhere. What should I offer you, please? And what about Pat, your brother?" Enametti said.

"Oh, that little pompous brat is there. I hate to say anything about him."

"What about him?"

"The same old Patrick as ever before, no change. Sad. Isn't it?"

Enametti gave a peal of good-humoured laughter.

"He'll change, it's juvenile delinquency as he grows older, he'll change."

"Juvenile delinquency for a man of 20 years! It's ridiculous. I see this unchanged behaviour for him as a forgone conclusion. He will never change, but I honestly would wish this happens soon. I am fed up with this negative behaviour that brings shame and disgrace to himself and the family"

"Don't worry, change does take time with some people, I know."

Both friends continued celebrating their reunion. They resumed on their ballroom dance which had been pleasing to Etimbuk.

CHAPTER
18

Breaking into enviable mid-forties was a landmark development for Esitima. And she must celebrate it with pomp and pageantry. She thought through her birthday for a while then made long term plans to engrave the memories of this epic event on the sand of time.

Tellingly, keeping plans out of her husband's knowledge would be the best option for her. Esitima planned to celebrate this occasion as a very special gift of love with Bassey. Therefore, she thought it wise to surprise him with the invitation a few days to the celebration.

Her foreign trip this time wasn't really about stock for her boutique but shopping for her forthcoming forty fifth birthday Anniversary. "It mustn't only be a gorgeous and stylish celebration. The memory definitely has to last for a lifetime." Esitima had thought to herself.

She knew the age of 45 was the golden age, age of achievement in life where she can showcase her ingenuity and skills to the wider world. Yes, she had come of age of reckoning, therefore must tell it to whoever cared to listen.

Esitima continued roaming the world's capital cities with engaging passion, making friends with a good number of celebrities and peoples the world over. Some of her life decisions created serious rooms for her circle of friends to be a little uncomfortable with her choices.

A case in point was her failure to return on the day of her birthday which she arranged to be a special gift to her husband. This was adjudged an embarrassment to the invited guests. Esitima had planned her 45th birthday anniversary without the knowledge and consent of her husband and children except for few friends and business associates.

She had earnestly thought it to be a very special romantic gift to her husband, but lo, she didn't show up for the occasion.

"This is worrisome Prof. Do you know her where about right now; has she boarded a flight or not?" Dr Edemekong asked as he came in with the expectation of partaking in the birthday party.

"Edemekong, this remains a puzzle. I have no glue if she has indeed boarded any flight. She should have arrived two days ago but here we are, still expecting her. What is really happening?

In that instance, another of his colleague, Dr Okokon, walked in feeling anxious and carrying a beautiful bag of gift in his hand. He was followed by numerus university staff. "What has happened, Prof?" he queried.

Professor Bassey appeared rejected, sitting and talking with Prof Edemekong.

"Da Okokon, this is beyond my imagination, I lack the exact words to describe it. My wife was expected to return two days ago but up until now, she hasn't come back. I am so confused Okokon." Turning to Edemekong he asked. "Have you heard of any airline disaster recently, you're a journalist. Any report of bad news in the last 3 days or so?" Bassey's thoughts were fleeting; he could hardly think clearly.

"No, not any to the best of my knowledge, the Voice of America or BBC would be the first to report. I'm on a constant watch over world events and no such news has broken in the last 3 days." Edemekong gave him the assurance.

"Da Okokon, I am scared. What has happened to my wife?" Bassey appears agitated with no clear sense of direction. "This is out of character with her, quite unusual"

"Prof let's hope that all is well. Perhaps, some sort of remote situation had prevented her from coming back in time."

Bassey looked at him wondering and thinking if something outlandish could stand on the way of his wife's returning to honour her guests with her presence, particularly when she knew he was not involved in the plans and programmes of the birthday party.

"Did you say remote?" Bassey was perplexed. "Will you say that about a woman who planned to celebrate her birthday in a grand style? I think for her not to be at her own celebration, it's more than just some kind of remote situation. Some terrible incidents, perhaps one that has stopped her breath has definitely happened."

Okokon moved toward him with reassuring gestures tapping his shoulder to keep the tension down, while Edemekong reassured him of the safe return of his wife despite the present situation.

"I don't think so Prof, take it easy. I know it's heart breaking; I think she might be making her way home at the moment."

"Da Okokon, this is strange to her character, quite unusual. My wife is not a capricious individual so as to be so erratic when it comes to vital issues, especially in relation to others. This is a birthday party that I knew nothing about the plan, and for her to leave it for me to host is ridiculous. I think something is definitely wrong somewhere."

Bassey on his part had procured a birthday present for his wife in anticipation of her return and was anxiously waiting to see her, and now lost for words, his gift lay without arousing any desired interest after all.

"Prof, take it easy let's wait and see." Both men empathised with him again.

"Look at the crowd here present. Are you surprised that I've no iota of an idea why they're here and even the children haven't either?" Okokon, along with other invited guests remained silent wondering what the situation might be.

"Perhaps she planned to make it a surprise Prof." Edemekong proposed.

"Well, we were surprised to see guests drop in one by one, and I felt so scared. Even your presence stirred a sense of surprise to me. I never could expect to see you here even the rest of the quests Edemekong! If seams I am the only ignorant person to this gathering.

I never had the glue that this part was organised to this extent. A couple of her friends, including Joyce, came around to inform me this morning of the extent of the proposed birthday party." Bassey stated with pains in his heart.

"No, Prof. the invitation was sent to me by post may be the reason I had no time to mention it in the office. Of course, to know it's an annual event and wouldn't raise any eyebrow to talk about it in the office in the first place." Prof Edemekong spoke on behalf of them all.

"Can you imagine? Switching off her phone line is the most frightening part of the whole drama."

"Why would she make such an audacious plan without consultation with you, Prof?" Okokon observed.

Just then, Joyce and Emem alighted from the car and moved towards them, looking glooming. Both held their faces to the ground and minds seemed far from the rest of them all. Joyce in particular, appeared downcast, thinking what had gone wrong with her friend. They were really confused about what to do.

"Joyce," Bassey called out. "What are we into? Emem, any news?

Both moved closer.

"Prof," Joyce responded sarcastically. "We're waiting for the celebrant; and until she is here, we are never going to give up." Giving a bittersweet chuckling as she said so.

And Emem added.

"The good news is that your wife may be on her way to Idiaimah as we speak, Prof. We are here to assure you of her return; safe, healthy and sound."

But Bassey wasn't moved by their antics or disposition, he rather took a swipe on them with their supposed reassuring remarks dismissing these as mere gimmicks.

"That would be when she comes back from the grave, Emem"

"Come on, Prof, she's still alive and not dead, we can assure you that"

"Has anyone ever seen ghosts attending their birthdays, maybe what you wish to witness today, Joyce"

"Oh no, Prof, you've lost faith on her return already. Please be consoled, your wife is alive and expected home soon" Joyce asseverated.

She said this with a broken heart and moistened eyes. And wiped her eyes with handkerchief she held in her hand. Although she wasn't convinced by her statement.

Both really wished they knew answers to Esitima's whereabouts. And indeed, they had no glue where to locate her. They were only giving reassurances intended to douse tension, but these jokes appeared rhetoric here.

"Looks like we may have to wait for eternity," Bassey remarked.

"I don't think so Prof.," Joyce said, "I think she might be making her way home as Emem said."

"Really sure?" Bassey emphasised with his righthand fist up and down, making an aggressive gesture.

"Oh yes, Prof"

"Okay, let's wait and see"

"Prof, I have premonition she'll come back safe and sound, she's not dead, but alive," Joyce announced again, this time with the element of confidence.

They remained silent wondering where Esitima could be and Bassey groaned and mused thousand times over. He was completely devastated, couldn't know how to deal with the situation should something disastrous, as he thought, happened to his wife.

Bassey really wished his wife would be safe. Sincerely, he wished to be left alone for a moment to think things out properly.

But his colleagues disapproved of the wish. They couldn't afford to leave him alone in that situation therefore, Edemeköng and Okokon decided not to go away from him for a while.

Joyce and Emem too insisted waiting until the guests finally dispersed. So, they all attended him for some hours until they were assured that Bassey was safe with other family members before they left.

Invited guests were asked to go as the celebrant was unavoidably absent. They all dispersed with sympathy leaving their presents and gifts with the children.

Bassey's raging imagination wandered through their thirty years of marriage, even before then, Esitima had been very faithful.

'Could this be the first sign of things falling apart, could it be that Esitima has taken a dive with her destiny and become unfaithful? No, that is very unlikely' Bassey thought.

And for the very first time, Esitima could involve herself in a shoddy act of unfaithfulness since being married about three decades before. Even before marriage, with all her beauty and public attention she got from Ñdiokko de Vogue, Esitima remained modest and inviolate.

Right from her youth, she took pride in being undefiled because of her commitment to family values and religious convictions. She was chaste and free from all forms of obscenity and indecent behaviour.

Bassey was surprisingly caught by her chastity. And this strengthened his resolve and passion to walk the aisles of the church with her. Esitima had held her husband with unflinching love, high esteem and an inviolable loyalty. That bond must never be broken till death do them part.

Therefore, it would sweep Bassey's trust and confidence under the carpet if he would ever discover that his wife had cheated on him. That knowledge could fracture his marriage forever, and such discovery might not only kill his long years of cemented love and affection for her but could shock Bassey to death.

CHAPTER 19

Putting words together to convince her husband that it wasn't a deliberate attempt to appear disrespectful to him, but an unfortunate incident that happened out of her control which was quite regrettable, had been the biggest challenge to Esitima, and this, she determined assuredly to address. Therefore, she had decided to meet with her friend, Joyce, to cross-fertilise ideas as to what the best option might be. After all what are friends for if not to help ease one another's burden.

Esitima knew Joyce was more than just a friend to her, she had shared her values, and indeed Joyce was her soul mate. She stood out as an icon of trust amongst her circle of friends. Indeed, Joyce wouldn't fail to lessen the overbearing burden she was carrying. And she will be quite ready and willing to help find a lasting solution to this pressing problem plaguing her world without any hesitation, upon that too, maintain strict confidentiality. She had always cherished Joyce's perspicacious thoughts.

Esitima had arrived in Mkpasang the previous day from Las Vegas. She spent the night with Joyce brainstorming on the right way forward at keeping her marriage intact.

"Joyce, I am finished. I've lost everything I struggled to build in the last 20 years or so, and most importantly, my marriage."

Tears rolled down her cheeks in the local airport. The emotional build-up in her mind had been so heavy up to the breaking point. She brought out her handkerchief and wiped the tears from her eyes.

"Ima calm down; this is a public place, keep your anxiety, fear and whatever problems it is to yourself. Let's talk about it at home, okay?" Joyce consoled her.

She was watching all directions to ascertain that no familiar person saw them. Joyce collected her hand luggage, pulled Esitima to herself as they walked silently toward Joyce's waiting car. Quietly, they collected her luggage into the boot of the car zooming out of sight, heading for home.

Esitima had called Joyce the previous day while still in Las Vegas asking Joyce to pick her at the Airport because she intended spending the night in Joyce's house. Esitima needed to be in discussions on the very vital issue before going home the following day.

As a bosom friend, Joyce didn't object but had accepted the request with a note of reservation. Ideally, it's quite unusual for Esitima to come from such an important trip only to stop over directly in her house, this had never happened. The usual thing would be for her to give some information on arrival and Joyce would go over to the house or boutique for a gist.

However, in view of the delay in her coming back, and subsequent mess-up situation present in that much expected birthday party, Joyce had a hunch to handle a tough task. She had known her friend well enough, despite her frequent travels around the world occasioned by the nature of her couture business; Esitima would remain a faithful wife to her husband.

Her fidelity, although Joyce of recent had expressed some reservations, but had not outrightly doubted her devotion to the bound of their relationship. That apprehension was triggered by her repulsive attitude towards her husband's wish for her to take up the appointment in the University as a lecturer and her constant refusal to accept that offer.

Therefore, as a very good friend, Joyce was available and would like to listen and offer whatever assistance within her reach.

"Da, I've been bushwhacked" she sobbed and hissed, her mind went through many things "in one terrifying moment, my whole world comes tumbling down." Esitima began as they set to delve decisively into the crux of the matter.

"How do you mean?" Joyce probed.

Her eyes were wet with tears as she had sobbed with heaviness in her heart. Esitima trusted Joyce and considered their relationship with a guileless union. The inviolable relationship they had grown over the years with trust and faith in one another. Therefore, whatever she had to talk about would remain unassailable and fool proof-not to be heard outside.

Such superlative confidence could never in anywhere, be betrayed. Nonetheless, there had been hesitance in her voice at the start of the conversation. She attempted choosing her words with care to avoid her friend misjudging her. Esitima comported herself very well with remorse, despite the guilt of betrayal in her heart.

"There was this young man" she hissed "...who boarded the same flight with me from Chicago to Las Vegas; he is, to my assessment, what I might describe as an exceptionally handsome and intelligent man."

Esitima held up observing Joyce's countenance as Joyce pulled herself closer to her.

"His physique and facial appearance; height and sense of humour had been arousal-enough statistics to break the heart of a woman"

As she was talking, Joyce pulled her eyes so close and mind attentive, so that she might get the entire gist first-hand and avoid asking her to repeat. A situation she feared might not be with the exact words.

"At first, I dismissed my impression of him as a mere fantasy, but when he made advances-as he sat next to me, I realised I could go back to that schoolgirl gullibility and become instantaneously infatuated with a complete stranger in a foreign land!"

She gave a very heavy sigh and closed her eyes tight imagining herself engrossed in such brutal mural ruins. Esitima pitied herself and loathed ever indulgence in such unspeakable act of connubial betrayal again. The act that made her unable to gather herself together and move out of the hotel room days into the unspeakable ordeal.

The emotional scar was still very fresh, Esitima remained soaked in tears, crying out the woes and shame of her undoing continually while providing narration of her compulsive romantic entanglement with Jeremy Dandelion, an accomplished entrepreneur. This had been an affair which eventually victimised and diminished her robust self-elegance.

Feeling of a shattered dream, loss of self-esteem and outright humiliation punctuated her story. On her face were written lust, perfidy, cheat, and infidel. Utter loneliness and death wish prowled around Esitima and the sense of loss intimated her. As far as she was concerned, her marriage meant a whole world of goodness to her. But ultimately, she was emotionally unstable with a sense of disconnect to herself and her marriage.

"Ima, you mean you've brought yourself down to the level of sleeping with another man at the age of forty five? Oh my God, quite unbelievable!" Joyce was awestruck!

She always knew that adultery was a selfish and terrible act capable of destroying the fabric of the family. Therefore, her sense of disbelief rolled in her mind wildly for her friend to commit such a terrible abuse to her marriage.

Esitima became jittery overwhelmed with guilt and fear. She understood Joyce's harsh reprimand, as she indeed had felt extremely ashamed and saddened of her action.

Quite unacceptable for Joyce that Esitima had turned the birthday arrangement she planed into an arousal orgy. Extremely disappointed that such unimaginable overtures could stall something she spent many months to plan. This, she had hoped to be a very special gift to her husband. Joyce was furious and she made this known to Esitima.

How could she behave like a simpleton when it came to personal and family matters but very prudent in the way she handled her business? That had been quite unacceptable.

Family matters do not mean anything for Esitima? But Joyce knew that one cannot separate family life from that of business and remain happy. In fact, the more joy one brings out of the family, the more prosperous it would exert a profound impact on work. Apparently, a joyful family would add value to the business prospect and happiness of the individual.

"What do you intend to do now?" Joyce asked wishing to understand how that incidence had affected her and above all what her next action might be. They spent the whole night and early morning hours together dissecting the problem and trying to proffer an ideal solution to the most devastating problem.

Hours on end, Esitima wept out the guilt of infidelity. She could hardly open her mouth to give information as what happened in that one week when her kin and kith were lost in emotional turmoil concerning her safety, without tears rolling down her cheeks.

As a mark of respect for their friendship, Joyce decided to leave her alone. She felt that it was better Esitima cried out her pain, necessary she offloaded her mind of the guilt, frustration, pain and indignation that usually accompany marital unfaithfulness.

Nevertheless, Joyce was dumbstruck as Esitima recounted her colossal mural breakdown. In her mind, Joyce wondered why her friend would be so naive as to prevaricate regarding her lifetime vows of virtuousness and faithfulness in marriage.

"Ima, I know you as a woman adept at hitting men attempting such advances below the belt with precision. And without any iota of doubt, I always cherish and admired with enormous respect your doggedness, self-preservation and tenacity in this regard. However, if what you're telling me is true, then, the man who had succeeded in unlocking that aged-long iron door; that invincible gate of youthful pride, that put many a man in passion ride, is overtly lucky at stealing the show.

What an exceptionally charming gentleman he must be, infectiously greedy with a poisonous goad, that removes respect for age-long landmark creed, with a mere twit!"

Joyce regarded her with indifference in her heart, and as far as Joyce was concerned, Esitima was unimportant before her right now. Her action was disgusting because of bringing herself down to the level of contempt and disrespect to her connubial union. Joyce looked at Esitima unsympathetically with an aversion for her action or inaction before continuing.

"In any case, Ima, it was an adventure not worth making-a price too costly to pay at the age of forty five! The very timing itself was an infringement on the honour of your youthful pride that you jealously flaunted before our very eyes with conviction as a Christian"

Esitima became too embarrassed to look Joyce in the face; she buried her head between her knees sobbing uncontrollably. Joyce on her part regarded her with reservation.

"Joyce, it was like a dream when I woke up, it became too difficult to pick up the pieces of my deep sense of self betrayer" Esitima intoned with a cracked voice and a jittery mannerism.

Joyce looked at her feeling pity for the dislocation with which an impulsive act might bring to their marriage in a long term.

"Self-betrayal indeed Ima" Joyce replied "You could betray your family by not being present at the birthday party you arranged just because of a man? How did you expect your husband to know exactly what to do in that circumstance? Ima, your action has tarnished your image to a point that people don't trust you any longer in family matters.

"You also betray my trust and confidence in your abstinence amongst us your friends for that number of years. Shall I fail to talk about the loyalty and respect which marriage stands for to which you have trampled under your feet? Ima.

"Your treacherous action has seriously betrayed not only your husband, marriage, your business and reputation, above all your age of indulgence in such a demeaning affair. Your husband's astute faithfulness, devotion and commitment on realisation of your worth-the index of course, which drove his passion to lead you walked the aisles with him, have been seriously betrayed, Esitima"

Esitima burst into uncontrollable moan writhing in the pain of her own undoing-the emotional turmoil and wound grilled her to her disgrace. She expressed regrets feelings very remorseful for behaving in an unacceptable manner towards that birthday programme she arranged and invariably couldn't attend. Though Esitima had understood the enormity of her action but had still wished, as the human that she be shown a little bit of kindness.

"Joyce, I acknowledge my mistakes without being told. I know what I've done is the most grievous sin not only against my husband but my family and friends; and to you, my beloved. All I only wish I be shown mercy. The reason I decided to see you first as a friend"

"Mercy is not really mine to give in this circumstance but your husband's. We may talk about it as friends, the onus lies on him."

Esitima's emotion boiled up within, she was conscience-stricken for being a disappointment to everyone, especially her husband.

'It's bad to buck up one's ideas' Joyce reasoned. According to her, repressed energy might lead to the degree of mental illness in future. But it had been in her position to pluck up Esitima's courage, by creating enabling environment to ease her tormented mind through the expression of repressed emotion. It wouldn't be much better to just bottle up her problems in the inside. That, Joyce, had resolutely determined to do.

"Look at me, I hate myself. I am unworthy to be called a wife anymore. How could I ever commit such atrocious sin against my marriage? Can I live with this without a permanent scar? No, I wouldn't! Better to end it here and now without my care."

Joyce's assertiveness and robust self-confidence were going through serious evaluation as Esitima laid every trust and ability to solve the problem under her footsteps. She had to face the herculean task of not only consoling her despondent friend but properly providing a definitive solution to this threatening problem.

Esitima had reposed enormous trust and confidence on Joyce's ingenuity at finding a convincing solution to pacify her husband that no love lost had existed between them. She earnestly looked forward to Joyce in recapturing that romantic feeling, that passion and essence upon which her marriage had always rested. Indeed, Joyce was her last bus stop.

CHAPTER 20

IT HAD BEEN A DISTRESSING moment for Esitima, so distressful that she wouldn't know what exactly to do next. She considered this time of chat with her friend Joyce a defining moment of rescuing her marriage. And so, found it necessary, honestly telling her nothing but the whole truth. Esitima couldn't hide her that emotion as she continued recalling the days of her youth and what that really meant for her.

"Joyce you know me from youth, despite celebrity perception of people about me, I've always kept my sanctity intact. This was the promise I made to myself 'I shall never break my virginity outside of marriage' and I've been able to keep that promise to the later. But what has become of me at this old age when I should be consolidating and celebrating the gains of that virtuousness. Look at me, old tart, breaking the bond of an everlasting relationship with a pinch of distrust? And the most painful part of it is that Joyce, it happened with a stranger, and in a foreign land!"

Esitima sobbed with tears, her heart increasingly became heavy with emotional build-up. She brooded and groaned in the shame of her undoing.

"It might be better to die, stabbing my husband on the back than live walking with my back straight in agony. And I earnestly wish to end it all and be buried in an honourable way than live a miserable slut the rest of my life."

Esitima sprang up from where she sat running straight towards the kitchen door. She pushed on it, but the door resisted the move. It took Joyce sheer luck; because her kitchen door was jammed lock, to rescue her despondent friend from the wounds of deliberate self-harm, or outright suicide.

Joyce rushed down following her from behind in desperation that Esitima would leave a sinister trail of a mess behind in her house which could lead to trouble with the Police and difficult to explain even to their husbands. She imagined if Esitima wasn't losing her mind too.

"Not here, you can perform that chicken-hearted act in your own house where I'll not get involved," Joyce warned her sternly.

"Look" she stressed "to be weak-minded is a pain but gain in boldness. Esitima, so adultery has eaten deep into your mind that death becomes an inevitable weapon for you?"

Tears ran down Esitima's cheeks on both sides of the face trailing down into her cleavage, the front of her blouse was wet and was she absolutely devastated.

Changing from the appearance of a princess which her coiffures conferred to a snobbish character whose hairdo scattered on her head somberly presenting her with a pent-up image in crisis. Her personality and forbearance became subjects of evaluation now in Joyce's eyes. That enigma of class which identified her as a woman not given to mean choices was thrown overboard.

"Look if you would not comport yourself and show maturity, I shall wash my hands off this matter, Esitima. Someone once said 'fools die many times before their deaths'. I know you to have a very intrepid spirit. Where is that courage, where is that stubborn mental strength; have they dissolved into the thin air of disloyalty, or blown away by the tempestuous winds and guilt of infidelity? I demand that this suicide ideation stops here forthwith. Get going with mistakes of yesteryears and live today to amend their wrongs.

"Now, tell me, if you die today, the worse Bassey could do is mourn for you a few months, and then cleave to another lady for a wife. Come on girl" Joyce said "pull yourself together. Put on your thinking hat and fasten your seat belt. Life is full of inexplicable turbulence and, only those with fierce determination and strong resilience survive. Cheer up my baby; you're not alone in this mess" Joyce finished her fierce reprimand.

Esitima appeared sober running to hug his friend. And Joyce with a gentle pat on her back and a peck on her cheek drew Esitima close to herself consoling her. They took a cursory stare at each other on the face and revered the awesomeness of the situation, something which they have never done before.

That action really helped to console and soothed her flared nerves. It demonstrated the strength of their friendship and how seriously Joyce had really wanted to help her. They remained in thoughts for a while letting that awesome emotion linger on before Esitima spoke.

"It's not as easy as that Joyce when you recall the path you've worked and how far the journey has taken you. Then, at the very verge of success, you lose the prize." Esitima moaned "Do you think that wouldn't call for something the unthinkable, Joyce?"

Joyce had acknowledged her but wouldn't agree that ending her life would be the ultimate price for her to pay in that circumstance. She encouraged Esitima in finding a workable solution that would address her worries remained as the only remedy-an option they would have to explore.

"Yes, it's would, definitely not suicide! Death ends it all, but the desire to live dwells in every gallant heart that is not afraid"

Joyce looked at her with pity. "Please stop working up yourself, baby okay. It's a problem which demands a solution. And that solution is definitely found in your attitude toward the problem itself."

Joyce thought for a moment while still cuddling her. Esitima still very much depressed wasn't in the right frame of mind to articulate any point, but Joyce pressed her to express her own desire about the future which seemed quite uncertain.

"It's actually no-brainer, you can figure this out yourself. Now would you want to deny or confess? The ball is in your court"

And for a while, they remained silent. None spoke. Then Esitima raised her head slowly and began speaking with a preconceived perspective.

"Deny or confess, Joyce, how do you mean?" These adjectives hit her like ballistic missiles driven into her very soul. "Confess or deny" she turned them on again on her mind silently.

Invariable these were the exact words that Esitima had been battling with soon after the act.

She was deeply touched by the urge for denial any issue in connection with Las Vegas ordeal but felt that it would be an outrageous blitz-a barrage of defeats to her husband. Would denial save her from troubles of life with her husband or confession? If she denied though maybe that her husband wouldn't come to that knowledge, but her mood could be altered considerably before him or if she confessed, how would he react? She turned it repeatedly on her mind weighing the pros and cons and the consequences on both actions and inaction to evaluate where the scale tilted.

Honest people find it quite easier when confronted with a choice to tell a lie or be truthful, and in most certainty; they will go for the later no matter what the situation might be. Doing otherwise would put their integrity and goodwill at stake. So was with Esitima, she took a serious exemption denying this saga, therefore must find a way of telling her husband however she could. Otherwise, she might be hunted for the rest of her life. She could become the most miserable.

Her mood could alter for the rest of her life especially before her husband to the extent of depression. Therefore, it's better to find a way of confessing it now than later. That was exactly what brought her to Joyce-finding a practical way of confessing it without causing pains to Bassey.

Joyce made a mental examination of the whole saga and imagined the repercussion it might have on their marriage in a long term. She thought of pains of having to live with depression and guilt the rest of her life, remaining silent for a while trying to work out the most difficult of situations. Resolutely Joyce must find answers to these nagging questions but meanwhile, Esitima continued with her tears unabated.

"Well, I don't know what you really want. But if you ask me, as I know you really do, I will propose plan A and B. The final application of whichever Action Plan would be absolutely your decision to make." Joyce told her.

Then Esitima quickly dried her eyes and adjusted her position staring at Joyce intently for a moment. Joyce continued holding onto her hands with the caress of friendship while unfolding her celebrated action plans.

"Plan A:-Behave as if nothing had ever happened while you were out there. Perhaps the reason you couldn't come to the party was that your flight was cancelled at the dying minutes. And you couldn't have any connecting flight back to Idiaimah...

"How do you explain my failure to call home and report the inability to return? Remember this birthday party was meant to be a very special gift to Bassey. Therefore, I should have called to put it off without his knowledge".

"Well, in the midst of that disappointment you lost your cell phone where all numbers were stored, and couldn't remember any offhand, therefore unable to access home."

Esitima thought for a while, then said "Mmmh, that might sound right, okay." Looked at Joyce with the expectation of solving the problem threatening her at hand. She said, "And Plan B?"

Joyce was ready with what she thought to be an indisputable action plan that might address her problems and she quickly downloaded it to her mind.

"Plan B, resolve to be an honest faithful wife I always know you for, tell your husband the whole story!"

Without allowing Joyce to finish the last sentence, she rushed in... "Honestly, Joyce that has always been my thoughts, it's my wish to let Bassey know that someone else has tasted the forbidden fruit. However, doing so without causing any injury to his feeling is what needed to be worked out"

"Oh yes sit him down, cry your heart out, then, break the news of kidnapping and rape to him. Let Bassey see in you the guilt, post-assault depression, fear, anxiety and low self-esteem associated with rape.

"Not only that, let him touch in you that humiliating scene which made it hard to comport yourself and move out of that disgusting situation you were taken, hostage. Impress upon Bassey a case of mistaken identity which, unfortunately, got you into that trouble waters in the first place." Joyce finished fixing her eyes on her. "How do you see that?"

Esitima considered the option thoughtfully. She thought it to be the magic wand that would seal her evermore porous and leaking connubial roof. As Joyce went on to give more details to make the point of mistaken identity undeniable. She sat down and drafted a letter supposedly written by the rapist to indicate how the mystery lady must have disappointed him. In it, he was so angry and waiting desperately for the next move to set his eyes on her.

For Esitima then, it was by the grace of God that she was still alive. The initial intention of the rapist was to kill her, but a change of mind was only by a stroke of luck. Frightened, humiliated, insulted and bruised Esitima was left to wallow in the emptiness of that shame.

Her invincible pride had been punctured and it collapsed like a pack of card. Her ego diminished within a twinkle of an eye.

"How do you see that Ima?" Joyce sought for evaluation.

"I think plan B is a brilliant idea, Joyce" Esitima was emphatic.

"But let me sound a note of warning here. None of these action plans may be fool proof. If you go for plan A, the repercussion will be yours, but if you adopt B, you'll throw caution to the wind, exposing your darling husband, Bassey, to some irrepressible dangers"

"I don't understand, Joyce?" Esitima stared at him in wonder. Joyce explained that Plan A will eventually leave Esitima with the greatest guilt of betrayal which she rightly deserves. If she chooses that, from time to time, Esitima may experience some flashbacks into the real scene of her actual love nest situation in Las Vegas. That might hunt her for the rest of her life.

And Plan B is an intelligent way of making true confession; it's confessing a real-life situation to your husband without letting the cat out of the bag. In this way, you download your mind of any traumatic consequences which might follow you in life. However, it's a landmine, a catastrophe and an accident waiting to happen, and unfortunately, its victim is likely to be Bassey. Depending on how he will perceive the news, Bassey may be plunged into a deep sadness that may affect him and his job badly. "How do you see that?" Joyce finished fixing her eyes on her and expecting some answers from Esitima.

But Esitima remained thoughtful for a moment. Her mind wished there were many options to choose from.

"I wish there was a plan C that might stand on a neutral ground, capable of addressing the culpabilities that might be eminent in the course of time." Esitima thought aloud.

"Well, for me there's no neutrality in life. It's either you're for or against; positive and negative attributes define the very essence of our existence. Therefore, when we go out to do a thing; we weigh the pros and the cons to see where the scale tilts."

"Da, you can't be serious." Esitima expressed her objection "You mean one-night stand has turned the hand of the clock? Goodness me!" And she was scared.

"Absolutely, it has changed your family significantly. And things might never be the same again. Let me tell you Ima, adultery is the greatest dislocation of family life; it snags you before realising what has happened. It's like passing a flatus-you can't fail to perceive the odour, even though no one else would"

Esitima felt the pangs of her action. She imagined life without meaning. How would she cope without her husband in event of death; or would the impact be on her? These thoughts left her with much more pangs of sorrows.

"Joyce, I thought we're here to solve a problem rather than creating one?"

"' Experience is the best teacher' they say. And all I know is that the skill of solving any manner of life's problem develops through experience, the more intercourse we have with life, the more rational problem-solving skills we acquire."

"And perhaps the more problems we generate along the way too?" Esitima quipped.

"Esitima, we're here to find a practical solution to a disturbing problem. We are here to sort out delicate issues threatening your marriage to the verge of collapse." Joyce told her "Therefore, there mustn't be any pretence. No playing to the gallery. We need to face the fact, and we must be factual. In every stage, Esitima, honesty is the watchword."

Esitima sat down digesting answers to her problem. She thought if these indeed would alleviate and lighten the enormous burden and challenges which she is facing. All through the night, Esitima was not sleeping but ruminated on and on and on. Her mind was turned apart, she saw deeply saddened of the incident thinking this has affected her and her marriage.

The following morning, Joyce dropped Esitima at the arrival wing of the Airport from where she called home. Esitima decided to go early enough to have ample opportunity of aligning her plans with her feeling well ahead of her husband's arrival. She needed time to be alone for a while to think things through. As far as she was concerned, this marriage must never fail.

CHAPTER 21

I T'S A BEAUTIFUL TUESDAY MORNING; the sun smiled from the empyreal radiance blue sky, planting colourful rays of halos on the single-glazed bedroom windows where Professor Bassey Mbede had been sleeping. Usually, he doesn't stay in bed that late as his wont, but events of last week have taken a toll on his coping skill despairingly impacting on his thought process and behaviour.

Increased level of stress, tension and panic exposed him to vulnerability to his daily routine. And for five days, Professor Bassey Mbede lacked the adequate capacity to navigate or take control of events around him. Therefore, he was away from work spending much of those times in idle thoughts and increasing worries about the safety and security of his wife. While his wife on her side spent the same night placating on her deceitful game, she had hoped to play on him.

Professor Bassey Mbede had only gone to bed in the morning by 05:00 am. Prior to that, he spent the whole night ruminating on the circumstances surrounding the absence of his wife from home for a week. And he tried to put in place adequate strategies to solve this debacle.

Startled to wakefulness by the crowing of cock a few metres away from his window, and instantaneously a gentle knock on the door; Bassey sat up with daunting fear. His heart jumped to the roof of his mouth, but he held back remaining speechless staring at the door agape. And with both hands folded across his hairy chest like letter 'W' momentarily, he responded stretching out himself giving a loud yawn.

"Whoosh" noisily indicative of fatigue. "Come on in" was the next command, still holding his heart in hand and praying to be Esitima. But Patrick turned the handled slowly and opened the door. He moved in sounding proud like the world held no problems at all. Radiance of beaming smiles brightened his face.

"Good morning Daddy. Oh, I am so sorry you're still in bed?"

"Good morning my son, how are you this morning. Never mind..." Patrick was laughing at the same time. And his mood and manners got his father confused 'is this not the family that want to bet yesterday sad?' Bassey had taught 'what has come over his son, Patrick?'

"Patrick are you alright?" He said fixing his eyes on him squarely. "What's the matter"

"Daddy there's no problem, I am alright" he was laughing at the same time.

Daddy guess what?" Patrick said heartily with excitement! Waiting briefly for his father to say something.

"Patrick you know am not good at guesswork, what is it?" He was obviously still very depressed. His present problems were nagging and rumbling on his mind.

Before he received that call from his mother that morning, Patrick, like the rest of the family members, was very sad. His mental preoccupations with worries and anxieties about his mother's whereabouts got the whole of his being. He laid in bed ruminating on the possibility of her death and what they would do in event of his thought becoming a reality. Suddenly, a strange number called his phone. He felt reluctant in answering at first, but as it persisted Patrick picked up his phone,

"Hello," the person at the other end had said. "Patrick is Mommy. How're you"

He quickly recognised the voice as that of his mother and was very excited

"Ah! Mom, it's you, wow, oh my God! Is that you indeed?"

"Oh yes! The roaster has finally come home" Esitima tried to bring humour into a bad situation "What of your brother, Etimbuk?"

"Oh mommy, this is heart-warming, am so excited indeed to hear your voice" he ran out of his bedroom to Etimbuk's, unfortunately, he wasn't there. "Etimbuk finds but worried as everyone else of your safety"

"I know, I am alright, Patrick please tell dad that I'll be arriving at the airport by 12.30pm this afternoon"

"Mom, did you mean today?"

"Yes, today by 12.30pm. Don't worry again, okay, cheer up, I am coming home eventually"

"Oh mom, I am so happy, you are highly welcomed."

"Thank you"

So as Patrick relayed the news to is father immediately, he was still feeling the euphoria of that interaction, something that reeled excitement in his heart.

"Mom called a moment ago to say she'll be at the Airport by 12:30pm" Patrick held back to see how his father would react. He noticed a sudden radiance of brightness lighting up his face with interest at the mention of his wife. He adjusted his position on his bed looking at his son intently.

"What?" He asked, surprised!

"According to her, she thought your line would be switched off"

"You can't be serious Patrick" Like bolt from the blue the message caught him with frightening impulse. Bassey sat up in bed adjusting his bedclothes to cover his bare hairy chest properly.

"Your mother called; when, from where?" Bassey queried.

"Well daddy I have no idea, I never asked her those questions. I was too excited about hearing her voice and..."

His father cut in sharply "You're right my son. You're dammed right. We shall be there to take her home." Bassey said in a calmer tone.

It was customary of Bassey to switch off his mobile phone before going to bed to help him catch some sleep, and so was this night, which he spent sleepless in depressing thoughts about his wife's absence from home. Worried feverishly why Esitima couldn't call when she realised, she had overstayed her expected date of return, sleep refused to come.

Bassey still piqued by his wife's decision to keep the plans and programmes of her 45th Birthday Anniversary away from him. He saw this as a slap on his authority and influence as husband and public figure.

Inconclusively, Bassey had lined up plans to contacts few friends of his and hers as the perspective of solving the problem. And had contacted the commissioner of police to bare his mind on the matter. Though he was not unaware that there may be very little the law enforcement agencies in Idiaimah Nation would do to help in this case, but as a public figure, he thought it ideal to first explore all possibilities.

He was therefore waiting to see some actions on this direction. Although the commissioner came in to brief him on the progress of the investigation, he had not been optimistic of any positive outcome from Idiaimah police.

Now that there was breaking news that his wife is alive and expected home today, all his earlier thoughts regarding her search launch must be put on hold. This is a welcome relief for him. He can't wait, there's every reason to celebrate! Out of excitement, Bassey put a call through to the number given.

"Hello, Kpan Eka" was a voice from the other end, sounding very dull and quite unenthusiastic.

"Hello Ufan, are you okay?" Bassey greeted. He doesn't seek to verify the problem right now, but to ascertain that it was indeed his wife.

"Yeah, I am alright. So sorry I would have called but knew your phone may be offline. How are you? I spoke with Patrick to let you know I am arriving by 12:30pm this afternoon"

"Yes, he told me and the reason I call to confirm the breaking news. Are you alright?"

"Yeah, very much so," Esitima said.

"Expect to see you then" Bassey added.

"Kpan Eka, I am so sorry. I'll explain everything when am home."

"That's okay. Take good care of yourself. See you soon, bye"

"Bye Bye"

Both hung up the call.

Bassey breathed a sigh of relief thanking God for his mercies to his family. He can now go to sleep peacefully after a really distressing week with turbulent nights.

At least the thought of his wife's return gave him the consolation to look forward to the future with hope.

But Esitima felt the compunctions of her raunchy game deservedly, the emotion which eventually left her heartbroken.

CHAPTER
22

THE TAVERN, A RESORT BAR was situated two kilometers away from Mbede's residence. It had been a good Rendezvous for the couple since its opening date, five years earlier. At The Tavern they unlocked, refreshed and rekindled their love life whenever they needed to be spoiled a little. And Esitima's choice as a place to talk her husband into believing her cooked lies was indeed worrying. That wasn't right. With this she had given The Tavern a new imperative in their romantic relationship.

A well laid out property, and scintillating features dotting the whole landscape. Victorian buildings and impeccable features of golden nature in their respective locations in the vast landmass. Along with them were marbled footpaths, fish aquaria and other aquatic animals and plants. These took their strategic positions around the central lobby of property.

Beautiful sceneries captivate attention as one got into the property which covered an approximate area of a football field. And every customer passing into the property was digitally recorded from the mounted Close Circuit Television (CCTV) cameras surrounding the property.

At the entrance was a boldly written notice, "This Property Records Your Details for Your Security." and with a rider "*Management assures all her customers data protection, privacy and strict confidentiality*" Stating that such was for customers' protection.

This had been one of the many fundamental features which defined the uniqueness and selective positioning of The Tavern in Mkpasang and its environs. These too invariable, endeared this beautiful Resort to Professor Bassey and Mrs. Esitima Mbede with engaging passion.

The Tavern was a distinctive resort to be. Improvement and satisfaction of customers were in the heart of service of the amazing staff at the resort. As delicate ideals knitted in the heart of service, it brought out The Tavern as a beacon of culinary and cuisines excellence in and around Mkpasang.

And their unique principles built around value of their customers. They knew that once customers were satisfied, their business succeeded. Excellence was at the heart of their existence, they built business with these principles in mind as the only place who provided playing areas for children to enjoy balanced leisure and value-added time activities.

We found children playing around and having fun as one resort in Mkpasang with equality program contents. Truly, The Tavern gave people the option for relaxation.

The couple drove and stepped out holding each another hand on the palms as if nothing had happened. They moved to a choice corner marked 'PRIVATE' – often one of their reserved spot the past five years. It is here that they were far removed from inquisitive eyes of other customers, the pressure of academe and business to enjoy profoundly, the absolute natural beauty surrounding the vicinity.

At the 'private' the couple would be assured of freedom from any interference. They looked forward to invigorating the essence of their marriage and happy days ahead. It's was here that both celebrated the tenth anniversary of their wedlock. In that special occasion, Bassey in his magnanimity overshadowed his wife with his urbane praise. He presented a diamond ring to celebrate the memory of that epoch event.

They had that superlative memory entrenched in golden as a mark of deep sense of respect for one another. It was an evergreen memory not to be forgotten in a hurry, memory meant to last the rest of their lives. And they cuddled it with affection and gratitude.

Esitima placed an order for their usual drinks and traditional delicacy '*Iwod Ebot*'-specially prepared goat head dish in a spicy source. Settled down to feel the crux of the matter-real business of the day.

Usually, it had been the tradition that Bassey would serve his wife frequently, the tradition he imbibed in England. But on this special occasion, the reverse was the case, Esitima took the driver's seat.

"Kpan Eka" she said "let me play the man today. Please sit down and enjoy yourself"

Bassey remained silent without a word. Anxiously waiting to be told the reason for bringing him there. With heaviness of heart, he grudgingly gave his approval.

"It's okay."

She stepped into the centre stage doing it with extra dexterity and utmost sense of indulgence in her heart to her husband. It took a great deal of time for Bassey to rearrange his thoughts and come to accept the idea of eating or drinking with his present frame of mind. He remained silent without a word. Esitima on her part, was so concerned about the present mood of her husband.

"Kpan Eka," she looked at him silently. Then crossing over, she held him by the shoulder giving a kiss and hissing with utmost heaviness for his present mood.

"Cheer up, Kpan Eka, whatever happens I am here to tell the whole story. I know, after the whole truth is told you'll be convinced that I acted in good faith."

"Look, I just want urgent answers why it took you so long to return. Are you aware of the trauma you put all through? I, children and guests, it was horrendous. The party which I knew absolutely nothing about. Even after that, the pains and sadness and anxiety in the family. I can hardly think, and for the first time in my life I couldn't concentrate. What was the matter, that's what I want to know?"

"Sorry my love, I know you weren't in the position to know, and I had no choice than put up with the situation as it was. Yes, I do know, but please cheer up and let me explain everything"

"Then make it snappy, that is what I want for now."

"I am so sorry not informing you about the party. I thought to make it a special gift of my love to you, Kpan Eka. My lack of returning is obviously regrettable, and I hope to explain that too"

"That's what I am waiting eagerly to hear."

Esitima remained quiet for a while weighing the problem from different angles to see how her husband would react.

"Eat, please" She said pushing the plate towards him.

Then they summed up courage to enjoy the delicacy in silence. And for a while, they couldn't talk to each other. They were examining the situations silently.

After a while Esitima reached out for her golden-coloured handbag; zipped it open pulling up an envelope with no specific name or address on it. Esitima then tossed the envelope over to her husband, with a whoosh sound as though waves gusted through trees in the field.

"Kpan Eka, here is it"

"What?"

Bassey at this point was still managing to munch his mouthful delicacies. Washing down with a glass of chilled beer in front of him, he searched his breast pocket for his reading glasses.

Reaching out his hand, Esitima deposited the white envelope on it. He slipped opened wearing his reading glasses. Bassey scrutinised every word and sentence in the spectacle of a professor.

"Suits you aright, isn't it? Remember 5th May? Think you can eat your cake and still have it. Blessed your soul I change my mind, now heaven or hell will be you call. When You are back, then find way through. Goodbye"

"What is it; I don't understand" Shaking the paper instantly as he was talking. Before Bassey lifted his eyes from the letter, Esitima had collapsed on the floor, sobbing.

"What's the meaning of this?" Bassey became more confused.

"Ufan, are you alright; Oh my God, what's happening here?" He resisted the strong urge to shout for help, for the sake of being ignorant of the issues at stake. Bassey threw the piece of paper on the floor, holding his wife to stand up first.

"Ufan pleeeeease get up and tell me what the problem is?" It took another few minutes for Professor Bassey Asuquo Mbede to get attention of his wife to give him a clue of this nonplus situation.

After she got up from the floor, Esitima hissed and mussed with tears running down both sides of her face-her supposed sad and emotional tension, she thought to draw sympathy from her husband. This emotion, she conjectured as post-birthday gift to her husband!

And Bassey having been increasingly irritable of the whole drama, stayed there tapping his feet with so many thoughts running on his mind.

"What is the matter with you; can you let me into this puzzle; am I safe, Esitima?"

His wife suddenly stared at him surprised at hearing him call her by her first name! Since their marriage twenty-seven years earlier, Bassey had chosen to fondle his wife with the nickname, Ufan, and for the first time in almost three decades, Esitima could hear her husband calling her by her first name. This is an indication of danger, she reasoned rightly. And in no time, she bust once again into hysterical frenzy rolling on the floor groaning and moaning in disbelief.

"I am finished oh; my own is gone forever. Where do I stand this time oh? Oh my God save me. It's better to die now than later, where do I hide my face o o?"

Bassey became much more shocked and confused. Having lost the will power to restrain his wife or get her to express the myth surrounding her strange behaviour and the piece of paper, he sat down quietly praying for time. And in his mind Bassey was making analysis of the whole episode.

"Perhaps there's something-some secrets you're hiding away from me. Now, what do you take me for; unless I have full explanation of this mystery, consider all else closed, Esitima."

He got up on his feet angrily in readiness to move away, but Esitima held unto his overflowing Agbada restraining his movement. "No no" she shouted and stopped him "I'll tell you. The simple reason I brought you up here was to properly lay bare my secret to you, despite what has happened. It was to reassure you that I still love you as ever before. Kpan Eka, don't disgrace me, please. I still pledge my unwavering love and absolute loyalty to preserve the dignity, sanctity and integrity of this marriage, please."

"Esitima, for the third time I ask you again, what is the problem? What is the meaning of this letter? You mean you got me out here to insult and abuse my sensibility? I want to pretend you don't understand the gravity of this your action."

She regarded him cautiously while standing up and holding him close to herself. With whimpering cry Esitima wiped her tears and stood to her feet. She fidgeted with nervousness to gain his empathy. Bassey on his part had been absolutely disgusted of the situation but managed to play it down as usual with his lopsided feeling as the price he must pay for being husband to beloved Esitima.

She persuaded him to sit. Then wiped her eyes with a handkerchief she had earlier got from him. She then started unfolding her nefarious story.

"Kpan Eka, it all started a normal business discussion, but before I realised, I was already in the midst of a gang of kidnappers who demanded nothing but sexual intercourse from me."

Dumbstruck, Professor Mbede adjusted his position in his seat; he remained speechless with words evaporating from his mouth. His mind went completely blank temporarily.

"You mean you've been... raped? Jesus!" He found his voice at last. Esitima nodded her head in agreement like a woodpecker. She went again into another hysterical frenzy.

Rolling on the floor shouting and crying her eyes red. She succeeded drawing empathy from her husband who was ignorant of her gross. Bassey moved forward holding her by the shoulder and got her to stand to her feet.

"I'm very sorry indeed, so sorry." Holding and consoling her. He held her to himself and she dropped her head down his right shoulder with his right hand patting her back.

"So sorry indeed, Ufan" he emphasised. Holding her head up, he asked.

"Now tell me in detail, what happened?" She had successfully drawn his mind and will to her purpose, Esitima then wanted a better word to placate him of any doubts, subtle words that would be quite insinuating causing him to cool down his anger. And she found that in utter silence.

Esitima maintained a moment of silence that if a pin was dropped on the marbled floor, one would hear clearly from a distance. For sometimes there was absolute and perfect stillness that enveloped everywhere such that gave her time to think of what to say and how to say it. Then after a while she broke the silence, she began to unleash her folly.

"Taking a short domestic flight from New York to Las Vegas and unfortunately sharing a seat with a man who, during interaction, decided to offer assistance for me to get some goods from the shop where his cousin works. And being my first trip to Vegas, I was quite appreciative of meeting a lead to my need. And most importantly, I saw it as a divine arrangement in easing my load of problems.

"On arrival, the stranger, Jeremy introduced me to a lady whom he said was his girlfriend. That boosted my confidence to trust and do business with him without any iota of doubt or fear. We sat down and had a good chat. After a while, Jeremy's girlfriend; Chelsea offered me a cup of tea which I accepted without any suspicion that it had been drugged. And within minutes of consumption of that liquid, I was dazed, and mentally dumb."

"I don't remember how I got into the car, but I awoke later to find myself in a hotel room with a man pointing a shotgun on my head with the command, 'Hei, sit up and get those silly dress off quick, ok, you bitch'"

"Stupefied with pronounced fear for my dear life, I passed out temporarily. My cell phone, money and passport were snatched away from me leaving me to the mercy of God. And before I could say please, my skirt was writhe and pant ripped apart. The rapist was already pulling my pant aside while still pointing a rifle on my head with one hand."

"Kpan Eka, I had been bruised not only physically but emotionally too. My pride of womanhood was abused, dignity trampled upon, and ego assaulted. Well, I had no option than to relax and cooperate to see if my life would be spared after that horrible experience."

"I tell you" she continued "I had the most brutal and rough coitus ever in my entire life. Of course, you know that since I was born you happen to be my one and only sex partner. My virginity was broken by you"

Bassey looked at his wife feeling absolute sorry for her undergoing such gruesome ordeal.

"You mean you went through such anguish?" he found his voice to assert his indignation and disgust. Bassey expressed sympathy for such inhuman treatment meted out to his 'innocent' wife in a foreign land.

"Kpan Eka, when I got out of that frightful scene, I lost control of my life. I even forgot my name too! I was weeping my heart out. And sincerely, I never thought I would ever be a living person again. That I am still living today is a miracle, as far as life is concerned, I lost mine then."

"There was anger written all over me, I also experienced numbness of my hip coupled with fear of my dear life. I blamed myself for agreeing to go with him, he ceased my simplicity to launch such grievous assault on me"

"I tell you" she continued "I had the most brutal and rough coitus ever in my entire life. There was soreness and I was unable to walk properly, I thought I've fractured or dislocated my hip bone after that terrible ordeal. The mayor reason I was unable to return immediately"

"I am so sorry indeed" tears rolling down his eyes. He pulled his wife close to himself and consoled her for the misfortune which had befallen her in a foreign land. Bassey thought for a while about the consequences of such violent attack on his wife and the effect this would mean to his family.

He thought of urinary tract infections, Acquired Immune Deficiency Syndrome (AIDS) and many other sexually transmitted diseases. His plan would be for Esitima to see a Doctor immediately. The stigma of such ordeal and possible loss of self-esteem occupied his mind heavily.

Bassey then understood why his wife was unable to comport herself and come home from the effects of that ordeal. He imagined her suffering from psychological effects of daydreaming that impaired proper functioning and abilities to concentrate. He was completely devastated but still found voice to manage his anguish by asking for clarification.

"And this letter then?"

He asked. Esitima took a deep breath closing her eyes and tempting to soothe the pains rolling in her heart before responding.

"After that devastating experience, I passed out only to wake up and found it lying on bed beside me with whatever was taken from me, except money"

She held back in order to read her husband's countenance and since it didn't happen, she continued.

"First, I thought to disregard it, but then I realised it to be a veritable proof of evidence I might need-something to convince you of my story and innocence; I said this letter is it.

"And sincerely without this letter, I might not have told you this sad story. I would bury the tormenting experience within the dark confine of my mind" She concluded with tension in her heart.

She watched Bassey suddenly transfixed with light headedness, sweating, general malaise and disorientation. He was staring into empty space with fluctuating consciousness and temporarily shot out of reach. Within a split moment, he fell face flat on the floor foaming from his mouth.

Startled! Esitima switched sides from a deceitful actress at gaining sympathy, to an honest active First Aider, eager to restore life back to her dying husband.

"Kpan Eka, Kpan Eka. Someone pleeeese help me." She was shouting on top of her voice and rushing out to seek help as her husband had swooned by the verge of the eaves.

"Please help me, I am lost, my husband has suddenly collapsed. Help me, please." She shouted, pulling the arm of another customer nearby.

Without waiting for full details, Johnson Ndubak ran faster than Esitima to the scene of the incidence to see how he may be of help. Quickly, he ran back driving his V-Boot Mercedes Benz to the scene while beckoning on others for help. And within minutes, Professor Bassey Mbede was in the Cardiac Unit of the State Hospital where he was treated for heart attack. And from now onward, the 53 years old Professor of Agricultural Engineering was never the same again.

His life suddenly changed from that of an ebullient academia to a debilitated and bed-bound individual who had lost the use of his left arm from that accident. Life would never be the same again.

For several weeks, Professor Mbede was in the intensive care unit of the hospital where a total nursing care delivery was given him from personal hygiene, to continence care or eating and drinking.

"This is a very trying moment of my life" Esitima told her father In-law, Deacon Mbede who rushed in to see his son.

"My daughter, I lack the exact words to describe this paradox of life. My expectation had always been that life would lead me on and my son shall bid me final farewell in a grand style, but here I am looking at a different world entirely. It's more than trying moment; but a moment of great trial indeed"

Some from Mkpasang gathered in groups to discuss the event. A good number of citizens were putting bits and pieces of information together to form a plausible theory and reason for this sudden dreadful illness.

"No, it's ancestral deities associated with marital unfaithfulness. Any woman sleeping with another man must confess to her husband else, her man would die. And everyone would suspect Mrs. Mbede, an International lady might err in this regard. She needs to do something urgently to save the life of this man" Etim offered his conviction convincingly.

"My brother such a high-class lady, a celebrity, can't be free from adultery especially as she is so frequent in her trips abroad. Besides her kind of business brings her so close everyday with men" Mbuotidem chipped in.

"I pray that this good man does not die, he promised to help with my job vacancy. You know since I finished my National Youth Service last year, I have not yet secured any employment" Theophilus was praying with a shaken faith while carrying his heart in his hand.

"Boy, not only you but Prof has been quite supportive in ensuring Mkpasang indigenes have hope and a secure future. I am so scared, praying hard he survives this kind of illness"

"Would you talk of only that, what about ever-increasing infrastructures scattered about in Mkpasang, without Prof, we wouldn't come close to getting what we have now. May God help Mkpasang." Was the observation from Margaret.

Effiong who has been listening attentively demurring their utterances. "Ladies and gentlemen, I never knew that the future which we fight hard to secure is seriously beclouded in a mere imagination. Who would have thought that we of all people, educated minds could be so quick to rush into conclusion and be lost in such unsubstantiated superstition?

"I earnestly believe we begin speaking from facts and evidence. The reason we have so much trouble in the society today is that we are still living in the superstition of our fathers, speculating on everything we see without evidence.

"I am surprised you could rush into apportioning blame and insult on the integrity of that respected lady without verifying your claims. Please watch your words; they become your actions, okay?" Effiong said while walking away from the band of malicious scoffers.

"Go away; people like you allow what you've been taught in school distort your thinking and behaviour about the society. Are you the only educated youth in this community; didn't Prof a well learned man, also believed in our tradition and culture?"

Mbuotidem poured his anger on Effiong, and so did others. Men and women too gathered to wag their tongues on the issue. The community of Mkpasang was thrown into deep sadness. Everyone praying that the end to this saga would never be a sad one.

Professor Bassey Mbede although a very intelligent gentleman never knew he was a potential victim of heart attack. When last he visited his Doctor, three months earlier, was advised for frequent visits for cardiac investigations and assessment. But because of approach to medical treatment in Idiaimah nation generally, the last appointment rescheduled was missed because the only Specialist Cardiologist, Dr. Ndipmonguwem was on a Sabbatical leave.

His next appointment was due in a month and Bassey was expecting to keep it. Bassey underestimated the gravity of his ailment therefore never considered a priority to tackle it early enough outside of his regular General Practitioner's private clinic. He hoped that whenever the Specialist is back, everything shall be sorted.

Now as he lay in the Cardiac Intensive Care Unit (CICU) his mind roved from his family to work and the impact of his nonchalant attitude towards his health. He recalled the event at The Tavern which had brought him to where he was, Bassey felt sincerely sorry for himself and the future relationship with his wife.

'Had she listened and paid attention to my frequent concerns about her travels, maybe this wouldn't have happened to her, and I maybe he wouldn't have been where I am today' He thought.

Moreover, Bassey also faced the reality of shoddy health care delivery system in the country. He felt that if we had had enough Professionals and equipment to handle various departments in our health industry perhaps, his condition wouldn't have deteriorated into the present irreversible level.

And many more are dying daily of various treatable ailments in the country which are attributable to activities of witchcraft and sorcery. If the healthcare delivery system was good and the masses educated on the causes and prevention of diseases, many would still be alive today.

He therefore apportioned blame first on the political framework of the day for failure in delivery of excellence, efficiency and effectiveness in the healthcare industry, and indeed all spheres of life to the masses. For him too, this is just a window to view the level of negligence in almost all aspects of our national life.

Corruption has become a hydra-headed monster that continues to eat deeper destroying the very fabrics of this Nation, he reasoned. For him, this undermined delivery of excellence service by government of the day. Corruption has reduced accountability and eroded ability to providing the citizenry with infrastructures that could make life easy. Basic infrastructure like good road, pipe-borne water and good school buildings are lacking in Idiaimah.

In Hospitals and schools, as in every public office, there are very little or no continuous training of staff and basic equipment due to shortage of finances. Yet many stories abound where people embezzle millions-even billions daily from treasury with impunity. What type of country is this?"

As he continued to labour his mind with the impacts of kleptocracy in Idiaimah Nation, his health deteriorated gradually, though his intellect was intact. He could not communicate his feelings because of slurred speech. However, Bassey hid under this to learn some lessons. To help him assess the level of truth society holds in matters like this. What information his wife would share with whoever may care to ask whatever about his health and the genesis of the whole problem.

The Professor was conscious all the way through besides moment of the accident. To his pleasure, Esitima remained true to herself. She would never tell anyone beyond what they needed to know. The meeting at The Tavern was significantly a normal way to unwind as a family; nothing unusual about it.

Unfortunately, two weeks into the illness, Bassey slipped into deep unconsciousness. Hospital staffs were battling seriously in their effort to resuscitate him but failed. And he passed on.

CHAPTER 23

ONE YEAR HAD GONE BY since the death of Bassey and Esitima narrowly learned to live without him. She tried rebuilding herself and the family business silently with a lonesome spirit, attending and becoming interested in life generally as she could be. No matter what, life must continue, she had consoled herself. Esitima had focused her attention in nurturing her children, giving them the best, she could.

As far as she was concerned, they must have a superb lifestyle and a future. Even though Patrick wasn't prepared to listen to her, he was doing his own business. Esitima devoted all her attention on them wholeheartedly by giving them their due in life in the light of the present predicament.

However, the majority of the indigenes seemed to be quite envious of her continued presence in business. Murmuring and whispering had built up gradually in the village against her unabated.

The accusation of her being the cause of her husband's death increasingly torn her apart as quite a lot of people in the community had signed up to this negative bidding. Therefore Esitima, was uncomfortable with this development; she started looking into the direction of her friend, Joyce, as the possible instigator of such can of worms.

And, gradually, she lost a massive interest in her business as the day unfolded, staying away from her shop and leaving the business at the verge of collapse.

Esitima was so depressed incapable of attending to her regular daily activities anymore; she suffered immense anxiety and distressing thoughts as a result of the shock of losing her husband so young in life, coupled with Uyai's embarrassment in her office.

The display of symptoms of depressions like upsetting dreams, anxiety, intrusive thoughts and serious emotional upset got her mind entwined with other problems. Above all, frequent nightmares and flashbacks into Las Vegas ordeal-a thought which frightened her seriously and caused her loneliness with the wish to see her dead husband every passing day.

Esitima had no other choice than remained in the house crying for days on end. She would not attend to her daily activities or go to her boutique any longer. Her merchandise rusted away with customers dwindling rapidly; even the workers had decided to leave one by one.

Continued absence in her boutique made her finances to go down rapidly and creditors running down her neck in all directions adding up to her problems. Here began the unimaginable tragedy; the circle on inchoation, beginning of the woes of shame that savaged the beloved Esitima Mbede's fame.

She had lost massive trust in Joyce to the extent that Esitima wouldn't want to call her or pick her numerous calls and wouldn't relate with her on a regular basis anymore. Lack of interest in attendance of her normal engagements in life became pronounced as the day passed by.

She absolutely was not in tune with time. Frequent overseas trips came to a sudden sad end, unfortunately. And she had begun sourcing for goods locally in Idiaimah whenever she would, or Eduek became involved in filling the boutique with whatever local stock she could lay her hands on. This development was out of character with Ndiokko de Vogue, with tremendous negative consequences on the business.

Most of her clients, especially the A-list customers, turned away from Ndiokko de Vogue. Business dwindled, growing smaller and smaller each passing month. Esitima had changed drastically with the feeling of loneliness and pronounced desire to be with her husband each passing day.

Preoccupation with twilight state of dreaming and waking with compulsion toward necromancy became her bizarre behaviour. She spent a lot of time singing endless litanies to her dead husband at the graveyard. At times she would go there with burning candles in her hands uttering some words of incantations trying to communicate with his spirit.

Esitima was definitely out of her mind! She hardly had time for food, if she wished to eat or drink; alcohol had remained the possible alternative.

With this state of mind, Bassey's cousins, including some members of the community did not help matters; they added more pressure from all fronts to her already sinking mental state. They treated Esitima with contempt and outright insult, and Aritie decided to remain in the home so that she can perfect their mischievous plans.

Aritie became the real brewer of Esitima's trouble. Even with her present state of mind, Aritie became antagonistic. Often rollicking in front of her in frolicsome and peremptory manners whenever Esitima would be around. This was part of their heinous plan to foment more trouble for Esitima. To further pressurise her mind causing great amount of distress and sadness.

Aritie treated Esitima with contempt and absolute disrespect to her authority and orders despite living together in her house. But she wouldn't afford any open confrontation with her because of the fear of her children.

Obnoxious and vile behaviour had become something which Aritie used as her weapon to execute her insidious game plan, behaviour which exacerbated Esitima's symptoms remarkably. But in spite of that, Esitima lacked the desire and zeal to stop her.

Failure to open of her doors to any manners of friends and visitors became new normal, even Joyce. Greatness and fame that Esitima paraded with energy and enthusiasm waned with the passing time, this development had been a big blow to her children, especially Etimbuk, and Uduak who were the most affected…

"Mommy, it's so disheartening to see you and Joyce apart, I couldn't believe my eyes," Etimbuk said while arranging her room and keeping things in their proper order.

Esitima never commented, she sat mute observing her son and acknowledging how caring he was.

"Would you like me to invite her over, mummy?"

"No! Do you want me dead? Don't you dare!" Esitima was alarmed, she goggled and gawked at her son without blinking her eyes when suddenly she began to wink and squint in a bizarre way, murmuring some words to herself.

"Mum, you mean Joyce and you are enemies now and she wants you dead?" Etimbuk snapped at her. Then he realised what he had done and was full of apologies. "I am sorry," he said "so sorry indeed, mummy"

Esitima was silent, Etimbuk thought of what to do to manage the situation at hand; he must play down her emotion if indeed he wished to see her make recovery. He had thought he would need the assistance of someone like Joyce who should be the right person to know exactly what do to help her.

Esitima has rejected hospital admission on several occasions.

Despite the toxic relationship with her mother, Etimbuk still had hoped that persuading Joyce to take part in her treatment and rehabilitation was the ideal plan of action.

"I do not want to bring Enametti into this, no, it's good for friends to maintain a certain distance in domestic affairs. I am aware he knows the problem to some extent, that knowledge is what is needed now. Overt closeness and being aware of how bad the situation really had been, may not augur well after all" He had thought that if the situation worsened, perhaps he would involve his friend eventually.

"Well, mummy, pull yourself together and stop worrying, things will eventually resolve themselves at will"

Gradually, through his intervention, Esitima settled her grievances with Joyce her dear friend though it had not been without some regrets on the part of Joyce, for the inert love she had for Esitima and persuasive antics of Etimbuk.

She eventually realised the herculean task of rebuilding Esitima back to her normal life again. This had been her new challenge. And found out that she must, with all honesty, reverberate that enthusiasm, the spark which defined Esitima's personality during her hay-days.

Esitima had a definite need for proper medical treatment and rehabilitation if indeed she must be rebranded. She needed to be brought back to her normal state of mind as she had lost massive hope and interest in the future to a large extent.

As Joyce came to understand the extent to which Esitima had deteriorated mentally she proposed immediate visit to the psychiatric unit of the state hospital.

"I never kill him; I would never have done such a terrible thing to my beloved husband Joyce. My name is a song in the community. Tell me, where to hide my face" Esitima wept bitterly.

"Hold your peace and stop shading tears, things would settle at their proper time." Joyce re-echoed Etimbuk's earlier consolation to his mother, she looked at her and felt great pain in her heart. Joyce wondered why such a larruping good lady, her youthful friend, would become a subject of furphy news, a false report in town. For such an honest and straightforward lady where no false is ever found in her to be branded evil and contemptuous, is unbelievable.

"Tongues may wag in idle talks, Ima its remains for you to blink or gawp in an effort to be relevant. Yes, you need to be steadfast not allowing feeble-minded individuals intimidate you with things that do not concern you no matter the weight of the rumour flying around. No word or action should move you if the will in you does not wink.

"Ima, if you are convinced in your heart, then carry on with your business. Forge ahead don't give room for any intimidation. It's your own life we are talking about here; you either live it in honour or leave it to blemish. As for me, I have decided not to dwell in idle talks and old wife's stories which is the handiwork of people with small minds" Joyce was building a psychological ladder for Esitima to climb to a state of calm.

"I can't live with this shame anymore, it has gotten down to my throat and I can barely swallow it, Joyce" Esitima moaned. Joyce had pitied her while trying to provide a workable solution to her threatening fear.

"Ima, we live this life not by chance but by choice, ability to select what is relevant can assists us to make right decisions and live comfortably is what defines the progress of our happiness, or lack of it. Must you then continue to allow these petty talks carried by idle minds press you down, or should you think positively and continue exploring those heights that bring happiness to you? Be a woman that I know you to be, Ima, let's go for it.

"As you continue to dwell in this state of mind Ima, you may never fail to dance to its sinking tunes." Joyce was trying to cheer up Esitima with whatever she could.

"Cheer up baby there is more to life than sadness. How many years do we have to live in this world to spend even one in sadness? Ima, happiness is living and enjoying what we have and not allowing any sinister situation to destroy the rhythm of the moment. Better to be happy than sad for I take up the responsibility of doing so, not anyone else."

Joyce remained silent for a while thinking of Esitima's inability to make a meaningful decision due to her diminished mental capacity. In that situation, Joyce thought, someone had to decide for her by taking the responsibility of her hospitalisation even against her will. This is for the best interest of her health. And she discussed this important option with Etimbuk and his father-in-law.

Esitima regarded Joyce without a word. She examined her in silence while making note of Joyce's advice and encouragement which she saw as consoling to her. However, Esitima lacked resilience and strength to manage life and she saw Joyce's encouraging words totally a wasted effort as she had determined not to shift her ground.

"Ima, do you know if you're happy, you throw your enemies into confusion subsequently, they would be wondering if their intrigues really work? But being sad energies them with greater zeal for evils"

She had given Esitima time to digest what she had just told her, but Esitima seemed quite vacant saying nothing.

"Come out of it Ima." Joyce said with a note of concern for Esitima's welfare.

Esitima regarded Joyce from her head down.

"No amount of intimidation would work, no not even one from you!" She said eventually.

Joyce was surprised to see her react that way.

"I don't intimidate you; Ima I would suggest you see a doctor immediately. Probably a Psychiatrist"

"Joyce I am absolutely fine. All I need now is see Bassey. He was my pride, my joy and everything to me. It would be absolutely impossible to alienate myself from his side so gloriously knitted"

Joyce was aghast! She was afraid her friend mind had indeed gone soggy and spiritless so as to leave her with the thought of death!

"You can't talk like that and still be 'absolutely fine' Ima. Something is definitely wrong, and you need help to..."

"Joyce" Esitima interjected, "I say am alright! I don't need any hospital treatment, okay?"

Life had taken a new toll unfortunately for the worse for Esitima. As they say, all good things do come to an end, the euphoria that defined Esitima; that lustre of hope and imagination, unfortunately, faded away like the noontide. Joyce thought of days when Esitima was an enthusiastic lady, full of life and hope, then, she would twinkle with radiance like luminous light on her path drawing people along. But now, her mind is so daft lacking focus and rusted like an old door hinge incapable of flexibility with eminent signs of decay.

Occasional flashbacks and nightmares into that atrocious ordeal at Las Vegas intimidated the very essence of life in Esitima, leaving her with the bizarre appearance and with suicidal thoughts.

CHAPTER 24

ETIDO JOINED US AFTER HE learnt about the presence of Enametti in the village that morning. They had a very good time, laughing and joking and having fun together.

"Enametti, so you've grown so huge and tall just four years ago when we lost sight." I pointed out four of my fingers. "Boy, what's the secret; the magic formula?"

He hesitated for a while grinning and tapping his feet before we bust out together in unison:

"Hap-pi-ness!" Spreading out our hands.

With a long-drawn pronunciation of each syllable, we echoed the fun word carefully, remembering it as our usual catchword, something that meant everything to us. Together we went into tittering laughter like children discovering the magic wand of their new toys. As we did so, those nimieties of nostalgic feelings rejuvenated and the reminiscences that kept us noticed in the crowd of our peers yearned back to us.

"The evidence is so clear I apologise for asking."

I intoned while still being filled with affection that drew out the sense of extreme joy in me.

"There's no need for apology Etido. The joy of meeting with old friends rejuvenated old memories that light up the present." Enametti said.

"It good when those memories give us something to reflect on our relationship." Etimbuk intoned. "And as it seems, there's a lot to take home about, folks."

"This is it. The very essence of this meeting is that of bringing back those happy memories." I said with delight laughing out with them.

"And I can't stop filling the air with the euphoria of this meeting."

We had always believed that happiness is the bedrock of endeavours in life. People brimming with joyful thoughts and positive emotion will be absolutely absorbed in challenges at work and at play. We believed too such individuals would demonstrate evidence of healthy love life in abundance and freedom from all forms of diseases or infirmities.

"O yes happiness makes people be energetic and purpose-driven in their outlook to life. It creates new ideas that promote creativity and personal development as they interact easily with the environment demonstrating genuine kindness and passion for things that add value to life." Enametti was amused.

"And you're in control of your life". Etimbuk responded.

"Certainly! Your sense of taking charge of the situation increases so is pain and discomfort thresholds." I chipped in.

For us too, possession of overt joy, excitement, enthusiasm, and contentment put energy into peoples' lives exposing them to meaningful interaction and quality association with others.

"Ah ah" Enametti laughed as he rushed into the inner room to bring something for us to soothe appetite. He came out holding a bottle of Martini Vermouth.

"Oh, folks no day could be so fulfilling to be together again then today, after a really long time. The curiosity, joy and excitement that fill my thinking faculties are so great because I'm so very happy seeing you both. Hope nothing changes from those old days?"

As he said so, he was turning the bottle cap, opening it with delight.

He popped the bottle opened; the cap flew up the ceiling falling on the floor. We applauded with intent admiration as the fumes rose spiralling its way up the ceiling.

Enametti poured out the content into glasses carefully while we watched on. We picked our glasses and stood up holding the glass in front, a little above our waist level. And Etimbuk proposed a toast of unity and gratitude to our friendship.

"Nothing has changed except coming together once again after a really long time" Etimbuk said.

"Enametti, we drink to our health and wellbeing, to our friendship which has endured the hurdles of life. We drink to our future aspirations, hope, togetherness, and progress irrespective of life's challenges. To our God and our will. Hip hip hip!"

"Hooray!"

We chorused the response raising the glass, clanging together and sipping the juicy content with enormous satisfaction and gladness.

"This was a regular event in those days at school. When I would be the 'happening boy,' and the one who defined trends of social interactions around my peers.

See how events has turned the tide. For me, happiness, was available without asking and I would be brimming with strong positive emotion laughing and joking and making merriment among friends." Etimbuk submitted.

"That's in the past. The thoughts of it leave me with the feeling of emptiness" He laughed jokingly shaking his head.

"Don't worry, once a soldier is always a soldier. You're still resonating that euphoria, the emotion that portrays happiness in the present, Etimbuk." Said Enametti.

"Yeah, boy brace up. Bad time is not forever. We all do have one in different ways. What needs be done is understanding the way how to manage the present" I said to encourage him.

"And I know the reminiscences of the past energises the future interactions giving confidence we can do it again, Etimbuk." Enametti stated.

"That's true…" Etimbuk added.

Just then Enametti noticed a car pulled to a stop outside the compound. James highlighted and turned around to the passenger's side. Opened the door, and gently aiding a full pregnant lady out of the car with much care. They moved hand in glove smiling at ease with themselves towards the house.

Enametti who sat facing the door was the first to spot them. He jerked adjusting his position to get a better view and possible recognition of the lady. But hindered by the door blind dancing freely from the breeze coming from the fans that were blowing across in the room, he stared and gazed at them intently in confusion.

Etimbuk seeing his friend's movement turned to the door and looked. Just then, he noticed the couple approaching and Enametti who had recognised James his friend was still very confused about the pregnant woman with him.

"Look at them so lovely. That's James and his wife, James Etim."

Etimbuk said with a little risibility. He brought both hands around his mouth giving a chuckle and standing to his feet to welcome the guests to whom he was enamoured into the lounge.

"You don't mean it, Etimbuk. So, James got married. When?"

He stood in awe opening his eyes and widening his embrace in disbelief. Enametti expressed surprise for his friend to have gotten married without his knowledge.

"Precisely eleven months ago. See the wife is full." I said. Turning to James, Enametti said,

"You're a very good striker, James you play number 9, isn't it?"

They crackled in amusement as the pair walked into the lounge.

"Wow, that's goal number one, so good to know that you're Chelsea player,"

Enametti added with a chuckle. "No, I support Manchester United," James replied

Judith was wearing flowering maternity gown with facial appearance blown up considerably due to physiological changes in her body with pregnancy. She was barely able to walk, and the pregnancy was nearing its term. James supported her to sit on the cushion upholstery lying next to the door. And went ahead exchanging pleasantries and handshakes with his pals.

"I was passing by when I saw your sister Emedu, in Mkpasang Street. She said you came this morning, and I decided to breeze in."

James said with both hands on Enametti's right hand, his right hand on his palm, and left on the back of the hand. He held his friend for a couple of minutes with complete eyes contact.

"Boy" James said, "you look so fresh and full of life." Turning to his wife, "Treasure, meet my bosom friend, Enametti."

"Hi Enametti," with a smile "I've heard so many goodies about you. You're welcome home." She turned around and greeted Etimbuk and I. "What's up guys? You rushed in to see your friend, isn't it? You guys are just too much."

Judith said in her deep alto voice.

"Actually, madam I am a very bad guy, the reason I'm ignorant of your new status;" referring to her marriage.

James turned around in defence, first giving Enametti an apologetic look and waving his hands in objection of the statement.

"That's not true, Enametti, it was a miscommunication. How could I forget my right-hand man?"

"James, I didn't even hear the gist, the gossips or the rumours of your marriage. You decided to keep it a top-secret, didn't you? Anywhere, congratulations madam, he's still a man of the people and a worthy friend, his actions notwithstanding."

"I am so sorry, indeed."

"Treasure, that's not fair! You didn't inform your friend?" Judith asked, disappointedly.

"I must apologise once again, it wasn't deliberate, it's a case of forgetting to make the call again after I had tried and failed. I am sorry"

Enametti regarded him shrewdly with a discerning gesture before answering.

"Forgive him, I know the pressure on him was enormous, chances of remembering whom to call wasn't easy" I made excuses for James.

"It's true, Enametti. Forgive him" Said Etimbuk.

"James, Forgiven, apology accepted."

There was tumultuous laughter resonating in the house. And they settled down to enjoy a drink together and joked about a few things.

"James, I am so pleased you came around, especially so, with your beautiful and amazing wife."

Turning to Judith he said.

"Madam, you are highly welcome."

Enametti drawled, moving around to embrace Judith, laughing with a wild sense of amusement. As he did so he picked the bottle of Martinis, poured it into glasses he removed from a cabinet nearby. He then handed it over to Judith.

"I know it okay to drink, Madam. It's just wine, alcohol exclusive!" Enametti asseverated.

"No thanks," she said. "I am already full, no space to add more."

They all laughed it out aloud.

"Exactly, give strong drink to an empty stomach for it shall be filled." Etimbuk intoned. And all enjoyed the joke.

James accepted the drink on behalf of his wife. He sipped the glass and continued in his defence of the failure to inform his friends about his marriage.

"Enametti rushed into the inner room and brought something a wrapped small box, he handed it over to Judith.

"Madam don't allow him to see" referring to James. "Take, it's harmless, not a Trojan gift."

"Uh! Thanks so much, I appreciate it." Judith said.

Enametti was presenting a well-packaged baby toy to Judith for the expected baby. This had been the gift he brought home from Ubannde for any lucky mother whom he would meet. Judith, his friend's wife, happened to be the lucky one.

"Thanks very much, Enametti" She appreciated once more.

James gave him thump up the sign of approval.

"Thanks," he said "You know it's a milestone in life. The pressure, like Etido said, was much on me and I rarely had time for all my good friends… But I did try your number once without success."

"With all pleasure sir, I know," Enametti replied. "…but you'd feel hurt to be excluded, isn't it?

"That I know, my apologies"

"That's alright"

"Stress and anxiety are emotional problems that can make a person forgetful. Both can interfere with an attention span that block formation of new information or the retrieval of old ones." Etimbuk stressed. "That's exactly what happened to James. He was overtly stressed up, so needs your pardon, Enametti."

"I've said I've forgiven you, Jimmy boy," Enametti responded.

"Thanks, Etimbuk for that observation" James said laughing.

"James is a distinguished personality now. See, he has added some weight already." Turning to James he said; "O boy you look good!" Etimbuk laughed with so much pleasure in his heart. "And his wife is so beautiful and special"

"Etido, what of Aritie, we haven't met for sometimes. How's work?" James asked.

"Oh, she's fine, she started work at The Tavern about a month ago"

"No wonder I haven't seen her recently. That's good. My regards to her"

"Thanks"

"What of mummy and daddy, Enametti, are they around?"

James asked while making passing glances at the inner room.

"No, daddy has just gone out to pick mummy who went out for shopping."

"Oh, Obong Ebosom, the Iroko of Mkpasang. They're people holding the moral compass of this emerging city with firm grips."

They settled down enjoying the drink together and joking about many things. James was delighted his friend looked healthy.

"Boy, you're handsomely healthy, not looking like a student at all.".

"In fact, that's what we all said. Really living like a king out there" I said.

"Thanks, for the compliment. You're all not different; looking good, aren't you? Strong, tall, handsome funny, dependable, and above all-very good friends. Looks like this gathering shouldn't disperse. I love it."

All broke into a burst of long laughter.

Judith twisted several times on her seat. Etimbuk watched her and was very hilarious. James quickly noticed his wife's discomfort on the seat. He dropped the glass of drink he was holding on the table and moved quickly in to attend to her.

"When you are married you lose your freedom and everything else is tied up to the apron string of your wife." James asseverated moving near to Judith to soothe and lessen her discomfort. His pals looked on.

After a while, "Gentlemen, I'll see you again soon. Everything that has the beginning, must have an end, but Enametti, I wish it goes on and on and on" James said

"Oh, is anything the matter?" Enametti said.

"Not really," James replied. "It's the usual women's trouble, I'll handle this."

"Be careful" Etido opined.

"I do," James said with a sense of haste hurrying his wife out of the room.

"Madam, sorry oh" We empathised with her.

"So sorry you have to leave so soon," Enametti said.

"Gentleman, we'll see you again soon," Judith uttered in a low tone.

"So sorry Madam." We chorused again.

"Oh boy, we hadn't enough time to chat. Expect to see us again this evening, cheers." Enametti finished waving them goodbye and they sped off.

Immediately they departed, Etimbuk told Enametti the story behind their union. He said James and Judith were serious members of a pious organisation in the Church, very devout Christians. James thought of committing himself to Judith in marriage if indeed they must continue in their Christian journey faithfully.

"But he had no money to pursue this dream and that was a huge problem. James and Judith were fresh graduates with Bachelors' Degrees in Management and Education respectively. This stood as strong assets to their commitment. Hopefully, they'll make a good union, the future looked brighter"

"Approaching the family of his wife-to-be for their consent, without money, was James' biggest problem. Especially her Pastor brother, it was difficult. He stiffly rejected the wish right away. He refused because there were many suitors, men with lots of money who had already made proposals to Judith. Judith was thought to be a reserved bride for one of such important suitors that the family had in mind. They were unwilling to accept what they considered 'a mean choice.'" Etido added. Enametti listens attentively.

"Nevertheless, Enametti, negotiations began, especially with her pastor brother. The pastor rejected the proposal instantly, but James and Judith didn't give up the fight knowing that nothing good comes easy. They persevered and believed it to be a good choice.

"After six months of strong resistance, the family gave in on their opposition to the marriage. They allowed Judith Nda and James Etim to embrace their union in very happy wedlock.

"Do you know their wedding was one of the most celebrated and an epoch-making event in the annals of Mkpasang Enametti. Planning and arrangement were superb. Dignitaries thronged Saint Valentine's Church in the most parochial astonishing gathering of the century. Indeed, it was unique of all matrimonies ever in Mkpasang. The whole city fell in love with the couple as it seemed!

"It must have been very remarkable" Enametti replied.

"Enametti, remarkable is an understatement. The whole of Mkpasang was agog for the couple. And we friends were excited for him"

"Enametti, for such a young man to pull a crowd like that left everyone amazed at the splendour of the moment James was spectacular," I said with excitement.

"Do you mean James could create such a momentous effect in Mkpasang?" Enametti remarked rhetorically. Laughter continued

"Oh Yes, o o! The remarkable moments were captured in a video that would feed your eyes and stir your mind with love." Etimbuk asserted. That will be a memory you take along from modern Mkpasang."

"I wouldn't have expected James to get married soon after leaving school. I am surprised. He is too young" Enametti said.

"For your information, mine is coming very soon," I added.

"Wow! Congratulation in advance. Maybe, I'll consider it also…"

"Etimbuk?"

"Not for me yet"

Like I said after the wedding James was employed in the Oil and Gas industry. Cash started rolling in. Today, James Etim's house in Idoro has become a rendezvous for many of his in-laws, including the pastor brother.

"We'll go to their family house in the evening. I am so glad to see them."

That was the response from Enametti who was full of mirth of gladness in his heart.

"That's life folks! Those you place so much hope and confidence could disappoint you regrettably, while people with very little hope can spring surprises."

Enametti finished as he turned attention to other issues of concern.

Coming to see Enametti was an adventure James really wished to make, but his wife had resisted the move vehemently, insisting she'd rather wait in the car if she would go with him. But James reiterated that it would be an honour for them and his friend to meet for the first time after their wedding.

Reluctantly, Judith gave in to the request even though she had had a premonition she might not be able to spend long hours outside due to her proximate due date. Nevertheless, their inability to stay and enjoy the visit and the company of Enametti was regrettable; so, they went straight away to Maternity Hospital, Idoro where she gave birth to a bouncing baby boy.

The news of the birth of James' first son was spectacularly thrilling not only for them as parents, but also to their wider family members. Judith was overly grateful and happy, and James showed his happiness by calling for a big celebration that lasted for days. Enametti, Etimbuk and I were part and parcel of the epoch-making celebrations

And Enametti particularly relished in the pleasure of that visit from his friend. He felt true that he had come home to enjoy the presence and company of good people.

CHAPTER
25

"**M**ADAM, I CAN UNDERSTAND HOW you feel, how traumatic the loss of your husband had been" the Psychologist told her. "Of course, there are some basic things you need to do to manage the problem, and prevent it from getting worse"

Esitima sat staring at him. She was not in the right frame of mind to articulate anything with the Psychologist.

"I don't think you do, Edet" Esitima squirmed bizarrely bringing her hands to her eyes and rolling the eyeball weirdly "my mind is overflowed with extreme images of catastrophic nature, no one would understand, not even you!"

She pointed her finger aggressively at Edet as she finished the last word. "Madam, take it easy, calm down. We aren't fighting, are we?" Edet said fixing his eyes on her squarely without necessarily staring at her. This he did in case she would attack in a violent way he would however know how to de-escalate the situation.

This had been the first time Esitima was ever seen with evidence of any form of aggression. Throughout the illness, she didn't show any aggressive behaviour or violence not until this episode of verbal rage.

No doubt, this was triggered by her dislike for Psychiatric hospital admission and seeing a Psychologist presence in her house, she thought he is coming to force her against her will into hospital. She had always denied being sick.

Esitima had distanced herself from her sickness anytime she had an opportunity to talk with anyone. Distraction with agitation had permeated the course of the interview and assessment. Also, she demonstrated evidence of auditory hallucinations and delusional ideation but on the whole, the Psychologist was able to elicit his assessment on her with the help of Joyce and Etimbuk and another medical staff present who accompanied him on the visit.

"The Russians are out with their warheads to destroy the aliens" she lifted her eyes unto the ceiling as if she was seeing arsenal of 'warheads' flying. "And water in the fridge is polluted with alien stuff, I can't drink it anymore" she stated.

"Madam, in as much as Russia is a world power, but they can't bring their arsenal of warheads this way. There isn't any war going on in Idiaimah, besides there are no aliens present here. Everyone, of us, is a real human, we're here to help you, madam. Comport yourself, I know this can be traumatically painful" Edet stated. He acknowledged her delusional ideas without necessarily agreeing with her.

Her statement left Joyce with great sorrow. She was devastated as to why her friend could deteriorate into an awful state of mindlessness. Teardrops rolled down her face as she snivelled and groaned with extreme sadness in her heart.

For Etimbuk, he was taken back with such outrageous statements expressed by his mother. He realised, indeed that his mother was obviously not in the best of her mind. He had been so saddened that he went outside carrying his hands on his head crying and feeling the weight of the problem.

"Madam I do understand the problem to some extent; your subconscious mind keeps bringing back the memories of your husband to you, is that right? He must have been a very caring man" Edet told her, waited for answer briefly, since she never answered, he continued.

"People do experience this emotion in one way or another, you are not alone, the only difference is that of managing it so that it doesn't escalate into a bigger problem. Am aware, it can be most traumatic and painful"

Verbal poverty like staying for a couple of minutes without saying a word dominated most part of the conversation.

Joyce and Etimbuk were struggling to get her to the State Psychiatric Hospital after the visit but she was unwilling to stay. Esitima was disgusted with the stigma of being a psychiatric patient and would not stay in. According to her, she preferred dying at home rather than be exposed to ridicule and prejudice of being a patient in the mental health facility.

"I don't want anyone to see me as disabled, evil and unable to live a normal life. No, I rather die here than be a patient there"

Esitima had been emphatic. She eventually left home with some medications.

The Psychologist repeated his visit two days after. He was able to have a very rewarding interaction with her. The bizarre displays had reduced remarkably.

Edet had let bare some psychological remedies which he thought could make landmark inroads towards the management of flashbacks and nightmares. These could bring Esitima back to the real world. He told her that she needed to constantly remind herself that she was safe.

And if possible, could carry some valuable items like a piece of jewellery she loves most, and cuddle to distract her attention whenever she had a premonition of a trigger. When threatened, it would be better to say her name repeatedly.

"Madam, it would be wise to stay calm; never to be anxious at all. Anxiety is the enemy with the state of health that you are in. If you can, write down the contents of the flashback or nightmares and talk with a trusted friend, like Joyce. Talking could make you feel confident you are in control of the situation it could boost your confidence remarkably" Edet asserted.

"How is your sleep pattern, you may not be sleeping at night, or do you?" Edet waited a while for an answer, but Esitima lifted her eyes regarding him cautiously and displaying strange arrays of bizarre movements of hands and body. Lachrymal tears ran down the sides of her face. This was her constant problem in those grieving days.

"A little bit"

Edet expounded those therapeutic remedies he thought would encourage Esitima to sleep. He told her to establish the routine of things well ahead of bedtime. For instance; listening to soft music, wearing pajamas she likes and making necessary preparations well ahead before she actually go to bed. Taking of hot beverages would be very relaxing for her, he said. And focusing on relaxation technique like breathing, stretching and if possible, yoga can help.

"Otofiakwa!!!" She exclaimed! Was alarmed, shocked and astonished! "You can't be serious Edet, yoga you mean?" Staring at him…

"Yes, of course, yoga Madam. This is one of the exercises to help you get some sleep if you can do it. It will bring back your mental clarity and calmness. Relaxes your mind and increases body awareness so that your mind can concentrate on things that matter to you."

Esitima rolled her hand many times over her head bizarrely and ended up throwing it in front and murmuring some words to herself.

She regarded Edet carefully with a note of rejection, feeling that the Psychologist was insulting her beliefs and customs. She, at this point, had seriously wished that he would go away.

"Go away; I don't need any Psychologist, please. I rather die than do yoga. I am a Christian for crying aloud and yoga is contrary to my belief. I say go away." Esitima was quite upset, she became very irritable.

Edet got up stepping back with intention of leaving.

"I am so sorry to hear that Madam please calm down. I never intended to annoy you. I am a Christian too"

"Your type of Christianity is a figment of the imagination. For you to sit here and tell me to practice Joga is unthinkable. Please go away, I don't need you, okay? Christian my foot"

"Mummy, I don't like the way you go about this, shouting at him is not good, he's here to help you. Can you give him time to finish his work, mummy?"

"Ima, enough! Enough is enough, don't you dare." Joyce was so firm with her. "Do you understand the implication of your action; must you send away him that is here to help you?"

She remained calm looking at them with apologetic gestures.

Meanwhile, Edet who went outside for a while giving her time to relax come back in and continued with his therapeutic proposals.

"Madam so sorry about that," he said, "We can do this in another way."

He diverted attention to the management of anxiety which he highlighted as something which had prevented her to deal with everyday living, like getting out of the house to her shop.

"Madam, anxiety is a psychological response to fear as the body gets to a fight or flight situation, this does not in any way mean necessarily that one is going crazy". Edet told her. "But continuous anxiety can prevent your functioning capacity. Life, in general, could become exhausting, as the worry and fear associated with different situations take so much energy to overcome. You might find it difficult to relax, sleep and eat or avoid certain situations.

People with anxiety find it difficult to access any social situations such as work or new and unfamiliar experiences. Try to see why a particular situation makes you feel nervous which could result in mental pressure like going out to your shop or doing any particular chores, like cooking or even watching television could be stressful.

"You can of course overcome this by staying calm. You can prevent it from becoming chronic which might, of cause expose you to some degree of difficulties in everyday life.

"Learn how to challenge your unhelpful thoughts and control your anxiety. If you are faithful to this anxiety therapy, it will help in the alleviation of most, if not all of your distress.

"The disability associated with anxiety disorders will be relieved without recourse to antidepressant drug management"

He knew he had gained her confidence, so he introduced his earlier aborted topic on sleep as the last lap of his psychological treatment.

"Madam, you can see on this list" Edet handed a list to her with numerous exercises "You select from the list whichever agrees with your belief. They are very vital and potent in the management of your type of situation"

Esitima collected the list and examined it, she threw it on the floor staring at it without any interest. The psychologist observed her action with rasp attention noting her behaviour.

"What is that mummy? That's not necessary" Etimbuk said sadly.

"No, he's given me the most sinister object I have ever see and I can see his intent is to harm me, right?" Esitima cried out.

"Oh no, I think you're wrong. The list is presenting arrays of excises that could help tune you to sleep and not in anywhere intended to be a weapon of harm, madam" Edet stated

"You can keep it to yourself, I don't need it" Etimbuk picked up the list from the floor and held it in his hands thinking what the end of this sad saga of her crisis might be.

"Madam, try and make good use of the remedies, you'll like it eventually, I promise you"

Quite reluctantly, Esitima accepted the list with the encouragement of Etimbuk and Joyce.

"Keep it there"

"That's right" Edet responded and left her before she could become more stressful with his presence.

With the encouragement of Joyce and Etimbuk, she was able to try out these therapies and they helped her benefit from their efficacies.

CHAPTER 26

I
T WAS FULL OF FUN as Etimbuk and Enametti came together and continued after coming back from the hospital. They got back home enjoying the bliss, frills and thrills of their friendship. Exploring one other's feelings in a way to establish the true meaning of their friendship after four long years apart. Really, this was a thing they mustn't forget to engage with. Just to be sure they were still those old pals they were four years earlier.

It was quite uncomfortable to remain within the soaring temperature in the room even with both the table and ceiling fans blowing across the room. Getting downstairs to sit under the mango tree was a choice. This allowed fresh air to cool their bodies launching them into atmosphere which allowed for easy and friendly interactions.

Etimbuk sat watching the field as the wind blew across pushing the grass towards one direction. The leaves and flowers swerved winding beautifully following the direction of the wind as it frizzled noisily across the long alley! He admired the beautiful scene with attention and optimism.

"This is absolutely amazing Enametti, and the scene captivating, telling the beauty of nature"
He sounded quite thrilled and enthralled both in his voice and body language.

"That's God's creation giving Him praise" Enametti responded in a similar way.

Etimbuk stooped down picking the stalk of the blossom flower that felt on the field; he smelled the gardenias and ambrosial fragrance and then thought for a moment about the present Idiaimah political atmosphere. He thought of how the repugnant smell had scared people away from the system because of its continuous unpleasant and volatile odour emanating from its political scene and responded.

"It's concerning how we're forced to live in this unfriendly situation for so long. Should we allow fairness and scent of God's glory move and permeate the political atmosphere like these grasses, we would have achieved the desires of our hearts without much constraint and people would embrace political freedom burning in their hearts"

He looked at his friend with the thought of expectation as he continued.

"Whereas we continue to labour and struggle amidst fumes and petulance corruption and attended negative impacts threatening the society."

With mirth of joy Enametti practically roared with pride as he spread his arms on the rail of the cone-shape sofa. He asserted after placing the glass of wine on the table.

"Oh Boy, politics has nothing to do with religion and indeed Christianity; politicians may go to church, they are not integrated into the Word, they don't allow the Word of God sink deep and move in their circumstances, conducts and practices. The reasons you'll continue to witness chaos and anarchy swelling the corridors of power"

"In other word politicians are hypocrites." He said leaning his back on the tree "Jesus graphically described them in Gospel of Matthew as whitewashed tombs. Those with very little or no regards to the true love of God and others"

Etimbuk tried to place his drinking glass on a little table but missed it just by a fraction of an inch. The glass with its content felt and hit a piece of stone on the field, then broke.

"Oh my God!" he screamed bitterly stepping backwards.

"Be careful, mate" his friend cautioned.

Etimbuk looked at the pieces of the glass on the field with deep sadness in his heart.

"I'm sorry I broke the glass, so sorry," He said.

"No no, it's an accident, no worries, nothing to be sorry about"

Enametti rushed back into the house and brought another drinking glass and placed it on the table. But his friend was still feeling the heat of that loss. He felt guilty in his heart for what had just happened. So, Etimbuk stayed silent regarding the pieces of glass on the floor for a minute and see it as something that told of him as irresponsible. After a while, he started picking them carefully into the bin.

Etimbuk is known to have great compassion for any loss, be it material, financial or otherwise. So, with what had just happened he felt he should have been more responsible. His action, he felt, indicated a lack of seriousness in dealing with issues of life. How can he break that glass; was he that careless? Murmuring with discontentment and bearing the great burden of loss in his heart, Etimbuk remained very worried.

His friend sat down assessing him and thinking why he should be so remorseful because of accidentally breaking a mere drinking glass. Why would he gloat over a thing like that, showing much concern? But Etimbuk is someone with a positive outlook to life; he is known to be circumspective in his behaviour. And very cautious, prudent, and astute in dealing with anything, especially as he had become the sole home administrator, planner and thinker for the family.

"Boy, I told you there's no problem; it's just a glass for God's sake!"

"I know, Enametti, I know. But you but don't understand...it's not your property, is it?... It belongs to your parents!"

"Oh! Is that why you look so scared? ...come on boy, cheer up, it's not your fault; it's an accident"

"I know" He squirmed under the presence of his friend with remorse.

"I should have acted responsibly"

"But you are my friend. Honestly, the way you bear the responsibility for this accident is completely out of limit, Etimbuk. Calm down, okay?"

With the mournful expression of sadness, Etimbuk reluctantly dropped the problem behind him adjusting his mood to suit the moment. He mustn't spoil the fun; he should do away with sadness and enjoy the company of his friend for time being.

"I am so sorry" He repeated.

"That's all right. Anyway, I am surprised about your behaviour, mate. It doesn't warrant this.

It's just an accident! Mum or Dad wouldn't raise an eyebrow even if they were here. Cheer up my friend, there's more to it than merely broken glass."

"I know, but I should have been a little careful, that's all."

"Forget about it, we need to explore Mkpasang and possibly, be at the stadium for the match in the evening. I want to watch the terrifying Mkpasang City in action. If I can recall those good old days!"

They all engaged in a peal of good-natured laughter.

That action was quite telling. It indicated the extent of their friendship how it had endured long years of absence yet remains resolute. Though they were miles apart, shrewdness among them as true friends had been what drove them along during those years of absence. They remained with humane compassion, understanding and trust.

More so it demonstrated dependence, loyalty, empathy, and good listening ears in the face of difficulties as qualities expected from any sustainable relationship. Both appreciated the situation which was a booster to their continued intimacy. It was really a thought-provoking reflection of the whole incidence with some degree of self-assessments for them.

Enametti felt Etimbuk was indeed an indispensable person that he has ever associated with. His response to that incident, at least, had clearly presented him as thoughtful and calculative in dealing with things that matter in life.

Etimbuk in own judgement saw Enametti as a warm hearted individual capable of holding genuine role in fostering an enduring friendship. In their hearts, both resolved to contribute to building the relationship to its greatest heights.

"Boy, we were talking about those who go to church but do not allow the Gospel to go through them" Enametti reminded him "this is the end-time mind you; one can even see Mr Lucifer himself parading like Angel of light. Jesus said this."

But Etimbuk responded by acknowledging his warm-heartedness which helped him to manage the situation that just took place with the right frame of mind.

"Thank you," he said "it's really good to have you around, your forbearance saw me through, I really appreciate this, thanks"

Enametti gave him a gentle look of appreciation, a feeling that transcended a mere word of mouth or routine. He then offered a double handshake, a social norm they had acquired previously.

First, he made a fist extending it towards Etimbuk who responded with the same gesture; meeting Enametti knuckles to knuckles. And then, opening the fist both grabbed each other in their palms with a little squeeze of the hand, maintaining complete eye contact. Then they brought the gesture to a bosomy embrace.

That gesture communicated sincerity, warmth, and friendliness. It also conferred the message that honesty, trust, and camaraderie were the defining principles to cement their friendship. And both identified this warm hand from warm hearts message to mean resolving to move along with oneness of the heart and oneness of the hands in dealing with their many challenging issues in life.

That feeling lingered on far beyond that meeting point. On his part, Etimbuk allowed the deep-seated feeling to settle down completely, before roaring with hilarious laughter.

"We're heading for the State stadium to watch the match between Idoro United and Mkpasang City which is slated for 15.30 for this afternoon. Hope you're still playing football?"

"Yes, sparingly"

"Come on, you're not serious with the round rubber game again, Etimbuk what happened?"

"It's a long story"

"Tell me a bit, please"

Etimbuk hesitated.

"After the demise of my father, I wasn't able to attend the practice session of the team for a long time. The coach/teacher was also on his way for further studies abroad, meaning there was a dearth of the team for a while. For months, I lost interest completely. Though in my first year at the University I got back into the game"

"Oh boy, it's a pity… But you shouldn't lose that fire. You were so good at football to leave it behind. Whatever happened, sharpen your enthusiasm and get back to play, who knows, that may be the way you'll make it in life. Through football you can live a life of passion and determination, you know.

"As for me, sports hold a distinguished place in my agenda as you know, most importantly athletics. I can't stay without running or throwing. I represented the University of Ubandde in the just concluded Idiaimah Universities Games"

"That's good, I always knew you'll make into the national league in sports. It's not a surprise" Etimbuk said, "Any prizes won?" He added.

Enametti left him and went inside briefly then resurfaced with hauls of medals he had won during the four-year period as a student. His friend wasn't surprised to witness the achievements he had made, he praised Enametti for the job well done.

However, Etimbuk felt that given his talent in football had he pursued it to the depth of commitment required, maybe, he would have been in Idiaimah National Team by now. Nevertheless, he praised himself for the courage to participate still in the game given all the happenings he had been through the past two years.

"Etimbuk, no matter the situation, you shouldn't lose that innate talent, that fire which caused you popularity with everyone. You've mourned your dad long enough, it's time to get on your feet and move on with your life. He won't come back again, you know. Get along and be yourself. Activate that 'Windy' skills, a name that caused a sensation among everyone that knew your worth. That talent mustn't be waisted"

With that comment, Etimbuk realised that the needed to face the world squarely with his life. He should relearn those skills howbeit with the commitment demanded even in the face of his problems-by taking his training seriously.

He was so challenged by the progress made by Enametti and then resolved that he too, should do something towards winning laurels, like his friend by getting back to his sporting life and rebranding himself.

"Thanks, I am aware football has grown to become the world most decorated sport with massive potential for young people with enabling skills. The role it's playing in society and culture is huge. I'll try my very best to make it a part of me"

"Please do. I can't wait to see you in Chelsea or Barcelona" Ememetti chuckled with delight.

"Thanks" Etimbuk concluded.

CHAPTER 27

WE'RE JOINED BY ANOTHER IMPORTANT friend, Animah; an indigene of Mkpasang community and youthful friend. Although he couldn't have the opportunity to progress further educationally due to financial constraints of his parents, Animah still maintained strong bond of friendship with us, nevertheless.

His probity and uprightness in manner and attitude to issues of life generally endeared him to a good number of people. Animah's sagacious and jovial character earned him many accolades among his friends and acquaintances. In Mkpasang, by and large, Animah's peers including, Etimbuk, I and Enametti held him in very high esteem. His intelligence and unparalleled sense of humour was second to none by all standards.

He was on his way to an important errand for his mother and in a haste to catch up with time before meeting the three of us clustered together in a relaxed atmosphere under floriferous tree.

Economic incapacitation of his parents put him at the risk of not going beyond secondary school level and he had never been particularly happy for this. His parents were very industrious people who were struggling under the weight of economic depression to fend for them. His father was a palm-wine tapper while mother engaged in various legitimate ventures that could put food on their table. From petti trading to peasant farming and hired labour for any job in the community.

Animah's thoughts wandered as he walked briskly along with cloak of misery written all over him. 'When shall I get liberated from the fetters of poverty and inequality? My contemporaries have all gone to the university while I am the only one left to roam the village streets.' He thought as he moved along looking dejected and bewildered, Animah was lost in thoughts as he drew nearer us. He had no iota of knowledge that we, his mates were sitting under the mango tree.

He neither had the idea that Enametti had come home nor did he expect to see him with us clustered together at that hour of the day. Nothing was said about Enametti's presence in the village when he met Etimbuk returning from school the previous evening. Although such meetings often brought sad memories of his inability to achieve his academic dreams and ambition.

The pain and frustration that such encounters always brought to him were tellingly depressing. He wished with all his heart that he would be like us.

Animah was going to a nearby compound to purchase some food stuff for his parent on credit, a thing that was almost a routine in their household. The idea of always buying on credit bogged down his mind immensely each time he went on such errands. Although his skills and ingenuity had brought him fame and recognition within the village community, ultimately, he couldn't settle for that level of popularity.

Animah always thought of life goals, fame and respect. His mindset was on achievements that would add value to his life and others. He had been hoping and wishing he could be counted amongst those that define values and trends of direction of that society. Therefore, he was not happy that he couldn't meet his dream of a higher academic pursuit four years after secondary school education.

When he thought of the educational attainment of his friends and other youths in the village, he always felt like a sharp knife was being passed through his heart. Animah was very passionate and had a strong penchant to be a thoroughly educated young man.

That he had the freak and fervid desire of getting his mind illuminated by the beauty education can bring was evident in his constant involvement in reading anything challenging to his mind. Animah wouldn't pass a newspaper stand or see it lying on the road without peeping through it headlines or major stories inside the cover. Indeed, he had the hunger and passion for knowledge.

He suddenly stopped when he realised us, smiles radiated on his gloomy face and he surged into the compound with confidence.

"Wow!" he shouted laughing aloud "Who is this tall, handsome, and amazing dude hidden away from Mkpasang for so long? Enametti! What a surprise!" Turning to Etido, he said. "The chair, I greet you my man." And to Etimbuk he chuckled amusingly, "Etimbuk, union of three owls, is it vultures?" He looked at them with open mouth. "Oh, when did you come in Enametti?"

"Ani Baba, you're highly welcome as the fourth owl or vulture, whatever. Continue your hooting spree: coo-coo-coo-coo-coo-coo-ooh-hoo." Enametti responded with a hearty laugh. "Or make the raspy, drawn-out hissing and grunting piggy sounds like vultures do."

Enametti brought his two palms to his eyes making them into circle with holes in the middle, he was also taking small steps backwards. A demonstration of large eyes of owls with excellent vision and hearing during nighttime hunting. And of vultures feeding on carcases. Enametti stood on his feet offering handshakes and welcoming Animah in.

"No, I don't ever want to play that nocturnal game with you." Animah responded while still giggling. "That will be too costly or dancing backward in the style and rhythm of vulture. Jek, jek, jek" He was laughing his heart out.

"Oh yes, you can." Etimbuk said with air of congeniality. "The presence of these creatures signifies ill luck and bad omen. They never ever portend anything good for humanity, except occupation of spaces for nothing. And their presence announces nothing but death."

Animah looked at him with open mouth. "No no no, you've misunderstood the economic importance of these beautiful birds completely. Owl presence signifies good luck, wisdom and even fertility for women. They maintain the balance of food chain by killing smaller insects preventing them from overpopulating our environment. It's a very prideful birds that hoots to deter men like you from entering their territories." Said Animah in a gruff voice, laughing and pointing his hands at his friends.

They were all filled with good natured laugh that lasted a couple of minutes.

"And even committee of vultures that roost together to scavenge a piece of shit, plays important role in cleansing the ecosystem of the carrion that would have piled up to become breeding grounds for diseases. They cleanse our environment of decaying corpses of dead animals"

"Ah Animah, the lecturer. Your thoughts have shifted our believe system. It has given us the new perspective of viewing the world." Enametti quipped.

"For me!" Etimbuk was surprised, "I can't see anything good about them except some negative psychic power of control. My friend, owls and vultures are bad omens to association with man, period." Turning his back on him.

"Yeah! You may identify them with evil intentions Etimbuk, may see them as symbol of mischief, but they remain what there're: birds with distinct economic values and ever surpassing knowledge of things and events." Animah said emphatically.

"I am yet to find that out, folks. Oh! Don't mind them Animah the divine! Full of jibes and vibes capable of setting new standards for our cultural heritage forever." Etido laughed with glee and Enametti joined in the laughter.

"Anyway! Animah, you're grown so tall how does that make you feel?" Enametti said.

"Just take a good look at yourself, Enametti, you've changed in four years." Pointing four of his fingers "Surprise? Academic knowledge, skills and general outlook to life. Do you think I do? In fact, am jealous of what I see here"

"So are you AniBaba."

But Animah's countenance changed instantly, fueled with his recent frustrations and challenges.

"Hmmm...!" He gave a low mournful sound of sadness, weighing them from feet up.

"Is this not you folks? Look at me! Do you think it's well with me?" He waited briefly and then added. "No, not at all. Life is too short to waste away one's youth in the village doing nothing. Allowing a lifetime opportunity to slip away really hurts. Well, I'll keep on trying, perhaps there will be a chance for me to seal this golden moment that seemed to elude me." He made full eyes contact with Enametti eventually.

"Well, you sound defeated Animah. I know you're still young, miracle do still happen, you know" Etido asseverated, and Animah groaned under his breath.

"Well, the chair, time waits for no one, they say. Every passing day brings with it the aging process. In fact, we're growing older every day. So, the need to make hast while is still day for the night shall come upon us"

"We need to pray for good opportunity, man" Enametti said.

"Anyway, when did you come around? Boy, you look handsome and I know Matilda will be head over the moon when she sets her eyes on you?"

He finished the sentence with a funny laugh beckoning on him to take his seat.

"Sit down Ani Baba before you break the curd or spill the milk. That will be a disaster, mate"

Animah with inquisitive eyes assessed him carefully, shaking hands again with both I and Etimbuk, he cackled with satisfaction before replying.

"Curd and milk, what's that all about? How did that come in here?" He asked.

"Have you seen her recently, I heard she is hooked-up with another man and soon to say, 'I do'?" Enametti ventilated.

"Hooked-up or not, you circumcised her!" Animah responded. Meaning he was her first boyfriend.

"That was hilarious, Animah. I never did that. Mathilda was my good friend, not what you think"

"Good friend indeed, and a good bedmaker too, I know." Giggling. "For me, I have a new address now, I live outside my comfort zone. No messing around with them" Meaning Animah does not engaged in any social activities currently.

"Animah, you always know the way around a subject. But she never did that. In fact, our relationship transcended arousal intimacy. She was like a sister to me" Enametti argued. "And besides, I don't ever want to put any sand in another man's plate of food"

Mathilda was Enametti's former girlfriend whom he never thought about for a long time, therefore mentioning her at that point brought back happy memories. Feelings of affection and heartthrobs associated with such experience. However, Enametti left the relationship with his former girlfriend in limbo and although she was still in the village, he feigned complete ignorance of her where about.

"Well, let's leave it at that. Wither she aroused you or not, it was widely known that Enametti Ebosom and Mathilda Ibaha were intimate friends. Isn't it, Etimbuk, or am I lying, Etido?"

Etimbuk acknowledged by expression on his face and holding his thumb up, but for Etido, he wasn't obvious in his reply because he wasn't around by then. Etido was in school in another city far away from Mkpasang.

"The beauty of an elephant is known in its dwelling place, but when he makes an inroad into the dwelling of men, it becomes a destroyer and threat to humans, and all deny that beauty. Enametti, you deny your heartthrob of many years?" Enametti can answer his question as I finished assessing Emanetti.

Animah continued "I don't mind you, according to the fowl, when the wind blows, we shall see whose butt will be blown open to the public."

He screeched with a hearty laughter and then added, "then the gourd and milk shall be weighed on a scale of romance." More laughter continued. "We aren't ostrich, are we, Enametti?" Animah finished his critiques.

"Of course, none of us is. I do recognise Matilda as a reference point, but there's time for everything. I shall neither curd nor milk with her any longer."

"I know there are many Matildas over there, aren't they?

He sipped his wine from the glass. Enametti continued laughing all the same.

"Etimbuk, how're you, Etido how is Aritie? I hope her new work gives her the needed ease of comfort"

"She's okay, thanks" Etido responded.

"I am fine, thanks." Etimbuk asseverated

"So boy, when did you land?" He assessed the environment. "I know if it was in those days when tortoise was still in communion with the lion, I would have been among the first to kiss your presence."

"But you're Animah. It just happened this morning and I haven't had any time yet to see anybody, fortunately we're here"

"So, what about these two, they knew it via internet, isn't it?"

"O yes, social media like Facebook, Instagram and Twitter define communication these days. They make it easier to relate in the global stage as we're moving into global village of today. Do you have an account?

"Hush! Who dash monkey banana; do you even see me with a cell phone?"

"That's the trouble, if you had one, the world will be in your pocket, and we would communicate easily" Enametti intoned.

"Never mind, I'll get there sometimes" was Aniamh's wishful consolation. "Etimbuk, you didn't even mention when I saw you last night?"

"By then he never came around yet. I woke up this morning to be greeted with the news of his presence in the village" Etimbuk replied. Enametti laughed elegantly putting up stiff defense.

"Ani, be internet literate and connect with the world, would you? He roared with laughter to diffuse the tension in Animah, but Animah dropped his head low thinking how he felt like a dwarf amongst giants.

Although he was not exceptionally intelligent in school, but he was good enough to make good grades that were adequate for pursuance of his dream carrier in Journalism. He was comparing his academic records with those of his compatriots and felt sad that life had really cheated on him.

Those who are educated do so not really because they have the intelligence to absorb academic pressure, but because their parents had enabling financial buoyancy and muscles to wrestle them through school. While those languishing and vanquishing their God given intelligence, like him, were doing so because they were poor.

Inability to adorn themselves with the beauty that academic knowledge confers came down to their social standing in the society. Indeed opportunity, he reasoned, was what had eluded him; what had seriously let him down!

"Enametti!" Animah ventilated, "poverty is indeed an orphan while wealth begets many descendants. My predicaments are many and varied. I will be quick to add that I hate my current situation and...."

Etimbuk cuts in sharply.

"I know you'll be very proud to wear the emblem of distinction as an educated person in the future. Won't you Animah?"

"Oh yeah o, certainly!" He affirmed with confidence. "Who wouldn't? Yes, that shall give me enormous respect and honour. In this world, you know, money begets beauty and honour while poverty brings perpetual repugnance and ugliness", They all went into another round of loud tethering laughter.

"Animah, so you never stopped being funny?" Enametti added.

"Funny is an understatement, he is a Rockstar, a comedian extraordinaire and commentator of happenings in Mkpasang and Idiaimah in general" Etido said.

Animah was proud that his folks recognised the potentials he has.

"Thank you for the complement, Etido. Enametti if you have any occasion, as I know you'll soon do, I'll be pleased to play your guest."

They all drank, laughing, and enjoying the jokes and wittiness of Animah.

"Ani Baba, I've heard your remarks. You're my man, nothing spoils mate and at least no party for me to host soon, but in case I do, you'll play a centre stage, mate" Enametti responded.

"You look good, anywhere. How is that side?" Animah asked about Enametti's city life.

"Not bad!" Enametti said with worry and pain of seeing an intelligent and promising folk wasting away in the village.

"I'll leave now before I forget my mission; lest I break the curd and I don't ever want to spill any milk. But before I leave, I remind you all not to forget Ani Baba. Remember that he has creative imagination and could reach greater heights if he gets any opportunity!"

"Ani, whether you break the curd and spill the milk doesn't really matter. What matters is the reason behind your action" Etimbuk intoned.

"And how it happened" Etido said.

"Okay, before I run out of steam and break the curd, let me first hurry for the cause of my mission so that I don't leave bad omen, the omen of vulture and owl that'll hunt and seduce my compatriots. Maybe we'll rekindle the flame of this conversation by next meeting when I shall have done with the milking mission to my mother. Meanwhile folks, keep on hooting, bye"

"Ani Baba, the omen you'll leave shall never distraught but wrought us to accomplish greater heights for Mkpasang community. This is our aim. For you my friend, take heart, things shall sort out themselves at will" Etido said.

"I so much cherish this union, it has lifted my enthusiasm and hopes. The sooner we met again to milk the future, the dearer the opportunity to curd again, bye"

He walked away thinking when he would measure up with his peers.

"Ani Baba, I'll like to see you again. Come back here in the evening let have a heart-to-heart talk, okay?"

"With all pleasure, sir be reassured of my presence unfailingly. See you then!" Animah responded hurrying away.

"Bye!" his friends chorused as Animah walked away and disappeared in the corner of the street. They look at each other in silence pondering with empathic gestures toward their poor, but intelligent friend.

"Wow Animah, such an intelligent boy couldn't go to the university. It's terribly absurd." Enametti empathised with him.

"That's what poverty can breed. Nothing but waste and frustration as he rightly said. I feel something be done for him. What or how? I don't know. I am just thinking aloud." Etido concluded with so much compassion.

Etimbuk shrugged his shoulders in astonishment; his body language suggested the ambivalence he felt for Animah's ordeal. He was quite unsure of what to do to alleviate Animah's frustrations just as he was uncertain of how he could handle his personal challenges. And Enametti remained absorbed in uneasy thought for Animah.

CHAPTER 28

"ETIMBUK, 'TIME CHANGES EVERYTHING' AND I can see a great change in you."
Enametti is not talking about any positive changes but a marked depreciation in the appearance of Etimbuk regrettably.

"Looks like you've been burning the midnight oil seriously. Boy, slow down, take it easy please for the sake of your health."

Etimbuk groaned heavily sipping his glass.

"Well, in me if there is any noticeable change, its emotional pain, sorrow, and disappointment amongst other repulsive happenstance I've come to live within recent years. And the synthesis is that Enametti; they have almost corrupted my sense of reasoning."

Enametti assessed him with a nod of regrade. His current appearance was his concern.

"Well, corruption has bearing on the physical ability of a person to think and act sensibly. When our leaders divert what belongs to the people into their private wallets, when people cannot be assured of the security of lives and properties or one square meal a day; these result in hunger and starvation as evidenced in physical and psychological debility of the masses to think and act properly."

"That's true Enametti; it has worn me down considerably to the extent that I can hardly think and act with the correct frame of mind"

Enametti was only trying to impress Etimbuk, all along, and immediately he arrived in the compound his lean appearance was very apparent, but Enametti was playing it down until now.

Etimbuk obviously was not the same energetic, laughing and outgoing boy he knew four years earlier. He has become gloomy with the lethargic appearance and decreased energy level of the body.

Etimbuk had lost significant body weight making Enametti wonder if his friend was still having any more interest in pleasurable activities and hobbies. So sad, he wouldn't be the happiest, laughing and outgoing lad he had always known him.

Enametti went into the room emerging with another bottle of drink. "Boy! Drink and be merry, it's long since we met. After lunch, we're heading for James' end to cuddle the euphoria of the new baby"

"Drink responsibly Enametti. Alcohol isn't good for your health." He looked at his friend with a sense of pride concerning James' newborn baby.

"She almost delivered under your watch. Looks like the baby was waiting for your arrival" He said.

"Oh yes. God does everything at His own time."

Enametti filled the glasses on the table with drink; he picked his and fell back on his chair. Etimbuk picked up the bottle examining the name and alcohol content carefully.

"Pinot noir, the name sounds French, isn't it?" Etimbuk asserted while still examining the bottle

"Oh, Yes, you're right. It's one of these common wines from viniferous-yielding grapes grown in France"

Etimbuk took a sip of the liquid; he left it to linger in his mouth briefly as he rolled along exposing his taste buds to the sparkling sweet sensation of the wine. He held it briefly trying to see if he could acknowledge its taste.

"I think the taste is awesomely satisfying." Etimbuk intoned sipping the glass again "Eh! And its scent really tastes like sweet wine from the grape. It has that sommelier satisfying flavour! This is one of those noblest red wines I've tasted for so long."

"Boy, let's enjoy the rich Raspberry flavour, the savoury fruitiness of a tart that dispels the negative political spectrum hovering around us"

"It's an absolutely amazing, rare blend. Superb alcohol content, only 10%, this is lovely"

"Boy, that's what makes this life go around, the uniqueness and its sommelier content. Its satisfaction rolls away chaotic memories of this political deception forced on innocent citizens" Enametti finally said.

"Honestly Etimbuk, it shall take long years to write off your father's indelible footprints from the annals of Mkpasang history, he was an epitome of uprightness," Enametti said as they left the luncheon table moving with the bliss of new vigour over into the lounge.

"But one consolation I do have is that you have such a dear loving and caring mother to fill that huge vacuum."

Etimbuk had just sat on the upholstery in the lounge when Enametti made the statement, he listened attentively to his friend.

And at the mention of his mother, he put the glass of wine on the side table, dropping his head down low sadly. His countenance changed instantly, and he had remained speechless for a moment beating his feet on the floor and shaking his head incredulously. Enametti observed this sudden shift of composure and hesitated a moment before asking.

"Boy, what's up, is anything the matter?" Enametti looked at him in silence… "You're not talking!" He queried.

Slowly, Etimbuk became emotionally tensed, he lifted his eyes to Enametti regarding him calmly with the look of innocence and with the incorrigible tone, he muttered.

"Enametti, you can't imagine how unlucky life has treated me of late. Life has really delved despairing blows on my destiny, and I come to fear what exactly tomorrow might hold for me."

"How do you mean? I know it would have been even worse if mummy was not such a brave and courageous lady with international connections, she has really tried, isn't her?" Enametti responded.

Standing on his feet with a sudden shift in his personality, from that of a calmer individual becoming verbally aggressive, he poured out his anger and bitterness. Etimbuk spoke with such force that most of what he said were hardly understood by his friend. In effect, his words intimidated and scared Enametti. Enametti looked at him in awe.

"Enametti, better if both of them were dead and buried together, that would serve me the trouble of living with the painful knowledge and shame of homicide." mumbled and he could hardly be understood clearly.

Enametti was taken aback, he looked at him with disbelief, and wondered if he really understood all that he was saying, or does his words made any meaning at all? He stayed silent trying to work out the meaning. Eventually, Enametti responded.

"Homicide! Did you say homicide?" He responded with a surprised stare, waited for a couple of minutes before adding. "Come on boy…eh are you serious?"

Without any hesitation Etimbuk groaned with the emotion of regret, "I am sorry for raising my voice" he apologised "You cannot imagine what I've been through these few months"

"So?" Enametti questioned his outburst of anger going ahead to address the issue at stake

"Are you suspecting your mum of your dad's death or something eh? Quite unthinkable"

"It may not be, Enametti"

He became sober groaning with shame for allowing his emotions to run wild out of control before his friend. Etimbuk regretted his erratic behaviour then spoke in a much calmer tone.

"I speak to you as a friend that we have been all our lives" he maintained unmatched eye contact with Enametti without necessarily staring at him. "There's a threatening rumour making the rounds in Mkpasang that my own mum, my very dear mother may perhaps be the reason for my dad's brief ill health which eventually ended him in the grave, leaving my future in jeopardy."

Enametti looked him over for a while with dismay and felt surprised for such devastating and derogatory remarks towards his mother.

"What are the rumours? The usual old wife's story, perhaps a new way of defaming someone's character was born in town these few years I had been away?"

He screamed with laughter to ease the tension that had built up in the room.

"It's not funny" Etimbuk objected "it has really worn me down more than death itself."

And Enametti was full of apologies and wishing that he had not laughed.

"Etimbuk, I am so sorry, please pardon me." They stayed silent for a while and Enametti thought of the right way forward.

"This is unfortunate" he addressed the situation eventually "Unfounded allegation against the integrity and personality of your dear mum can't be taken seriously. Honestly, this kind of rumour is capable of inflicting a considerable degree of damage to the reputation and integrity of your dear mother."

For a moment, Enametti looked him over, with strong admonishment he objected the spat of error in his views. He reiterated the possibility of a strained relationship with his mother as far as his advancement in education was concerned.

"Enametti, it might appear unfounded though, but there may be some good reasons to investigate this. And in fact, I am determined to conduct a full-scale investigation into this allegation."

"Wow! This is getting interesting Investigation!" Enametti responded with a composure which appeared more of a sad person.

"Oh, how do you intend to do that?" he sought to know.

Without hesitation, Etimbuk dropped his blueprint.

"Asking people that matter, the opinion holders. Perhaps they could give me the headway" with a sombre look on his face.

"They smacked you, and you complain to them?" Enametti quipped.

"How do you mean?" Etimbuk was curious.

Enametti had pulled himself to the nearby seat and then began emphasising the need for caution.

"Well, what you and I see today are the standards that the so-called 'opinion leaders' set for us yesterday. The ills of society were midwife by them. The corruption and infightings you see around us today are the brainchildren of our beloved opinion holders, including the rumours going around now.

"They are those who hold their faces as if they love you when you're around but tear you into pieces at your back. There are hypocrites, tricksters, betrayers of trust and lip servers. You should be quite wary in relating to those kinds of people Etimbuk, won't you?"

He thought carefully about their conversation since his friend came in. "Etimbuk, we were talking about leadership a moment ago, then prove that you could be one. Show understanding and integrity expected of leaders here. Remember, you may lose a friend and have another.

"May lose one opportunity and take up yet another, but it's difficult, if not impossible, to mend a mother-child relationship strained with such unfounded rumours as deadly as suspected murder of a husband! Be very careful Etimbuk, it may be just a rumour."

Enametti reminded Etimbuk of our culture of accusations of a living spouse on the event of the death of a partner. This social battering has been going on for ages and of recently taken a new toll, the impact has risen significantly. He even cited life examples to dissuade his friend from forming a wrong judgment on his mother.

"...the rumour in town is not new, but an ongoing age-long society demented prejudice on its subjects. I remember Okon Asuquo was accused of killing his wife so was Affiong Edet of her husband. Men and women have equally been indicted on the death of a spouse."

But Etimbuk remained adamant. He informed Enametti that he knew and shall move with caution at all times.

"It's not in me to appear captious or accusatory towards my mum. I was only sharing my deep concern with a good friend. Nevertheless, anything worth doing must be done well. I think my investigation is set to achieve several goals, one of which is the exoneration of my dear mother from this malicious society demented prejudice.

"Also, this shall give me the courage in future to challenge such blatant infringement and absolute disrespect and disregard for fundamental human rights. Of course, the result of my investigation is set to impart resounding confidence in me to move with caution in the midst of a spiteful people."

But with lucid wisdom, Enametti warned "Your agenda is audacious though, maybe too ambitious Etimbuk; all the same I wish you good luck. But in whatever outcome, remember 'blood is thicker than water' the adage goes. In all cases, move with caution. Don't ever appear to be on a collision course or accusatory before that lovely lady.

"Continue giving her due respect, honour and trust expected of you as a son."

Etimbuk was left in the loneliness of himself to reflect on the word of Enametti. Ultimately, he came to the realisation that in life, the opinions of other people matter in making a personal decision.

CHAPTER 29

Etimbuk and Patrick lived a life of comfort and affluence right from their formative years; getting virtually everything they needed without much ado. Any of their requests were just for the asking. And Professor Bassey and Mrs Esitima Mbede graciously filled their presence with pronounced opulence both at home and in school. However, they almost corrupted their young minds with the negative meaning of parental love.

Fortunately, it wasn't without verification of the impact of their benevolence on the young boys. One day their father had called them. "Etimbuk and Patrick, I wish to speak with you both today on a very personal topic. You may be tempted to believe that wealth of the family would be handed on a platter of gold just like that to you. No, it's not so. Both of us your parents have struggled to acquire what you see us with today."

Bassey went ahead to admonish his sons on the essence of hard work. He led them into his struggle in England to build his carrier in the academic world, and hassles of his wife in business. As a student in England, he never minded the evermore availability of his community scholarship; he did odd jobs to push his educational pursuit upfront beyond the first degree which was the limit of that support.

"Daddy, I understand what you mean" Etimbuk was the first to speak "and am here to assure you that you'll not be disappointed in me. I am determined to be a child you both shall be very proud of."

For Patrick, he was either not listening to his father, or as usual, preoccupied with his idiosyncrasy. Professor Bassey Mbede was happy that Etimbuk was not just enjoying a wealth of the family, but also determined making his. It was gratifying for him to learn that Etimbuk shall carry the good name of Mbede with respect and honour expected of him into another generation.

His father thanked Etimbuk with a hug rubbing off his hand on his head.

"I am very proud of you, you're my son indeed. Keep up the spirit for your honour and for Mbede, the future looks very bright indeed." When Etimbuk left that meeting with his father, he looked more determined, focused and committed to his educational pursuit.

However, Bassey was worried Patrick may not be the son he would be proud of. He reprimanded him for his negative outlook on life. Bassey was worried about Patrick's truancy that he may be experimenting with drugs because being prone to violence and aggression; erratic discipline, coupled with lack of heeding advice of parents amongst other repulsive manners and behaviour he exhibited lately which were quite disappointing.

He warned Patrick seriously against playing pranks but facing his studies with the seriousness required for in it laid honour and respect. "If there's anything I mustn't let go of, it's the love and friendship of my parents. As I continue to demonstrate to them that I appreciate their largess on me, they shall be very happy filling my cup always." Etimbuk told himself.

And he was committed to that pledge.

Etimbuk determination to seek information on the possibility of his mother's link with the rumour was non-negotiable. Whatever it might cause him to break the ice with the meagre resources at his hand, he must forge ahead. He headed first to meet with his granddad, Deacon Jonathan Asuquo Mbede.

CHAPTER 30

Late Obonguforo Bassey Mbede, was one of 'Mkpasang Five,'-pioneer indigenes of Mkpasang community sent abroad to study through community support in the late 1980s. They all studied at various locations in the world, including the prestigious Cardiff University, Bassey earned is scholarship.

He was decorated with a Doctorate degree in Agricultural Engineering as a well-deserved honour, the world was in his pocket. Bassey had worked hard to overcome all sort of contending obstacles on the way to his studies. That he attended this prestigious position of honour in life was no mean feat for Bassey Mbede, he did this for all the Mkpasang people. Deacon Jonathan Mbede told his grandson.

His homecoming in December 1988 was the greatest epoch-making event in the annals of Mkpasang history. All were overwhelmed with exceeding joy for producing a pioneer "Doctor" to heal the community of many ailments arising from long years of pronounced economic and social ills, years of neglect by various administrations of Idiaimah.

Deacon Jonathan Mbede recalled with nostalgia, events that marked the reception ceremony almost two decades past. Many of those who attended still treasure with profound enthusiasm those incredible memories that had defined the height of that gathering.

"Yes! This is our own. What we have been hearing in other communities has reached us today, May God be praised?" Madam Nkoyo Umanah had told her friend Ikwo Okon, as they hurried towards the Community Primary School, venue for the reception ceremony.

"Ah! This community shall never be the same again. We're people united in words and in works. That's what it takes to produce a Doctor." Ikwo responded.

They recalled with immense fondness, the incredible contributions the community-made to send Bassey abroad. Individual use of palm fruits in the community was banned for three months. It was agreed that only the communal harvest would be made after that period. This was so as to generate enough funds into the common purse for that purpose.

The two expressed profound happiness and gratitude that they were alive to witness the magnificent fruit of that sweat. Indeed, it had been a huge sacrifice of love that everyone in the community made. Both danced exorbitantly to the joy of the moment expressing profound happiness and thanking God for bringing such unparalleled progress to the community. They relished in the pleasure of such epoch-making days.

"Have you forgotten, Mma Ikwo, that they were five of them; where are the other four?" Nkoyo asked rhetorically.

"Well, maybe as they left one by one, shall also return that way too; for now, nothing to worry about". Mma Ikwo retorted.

Both women continued displaying various dance steps as long-standing inner caucus members of the famous *Ebre* cult-a socio-cultural group which had held its rein firmly in inculcating moral principles in the community.

Ebre society had groomed, nurtured and moulded the characters of the maidens preparing them for marriage and family leadership. It also promoted oneness and progress amongst the people through the encouragement of individual development, self-discipline and financial contributory scheme of members.

The society had also trained women of Mkpasang to good moral uprightness, maintenance of values that had made Mkpasang a delight to many communities surrounding Mkpasang.

They organised themselves into worthwhile economic ventures. Membership in *Ebre* society had been the pride, their heart and mind of everything for women in Mkpasang.

To this society belonged seasoned women of reputation, those who defined territorial integrity and behaviour components of the village, Mma Ikwo and Nkoyo were forerunners. Among other things, they prided themselves as skillful and famous rain doctors! Causing and stopping rainfall at will were the incredible powers these two witches possessed.

Anyone who had wished to do anything in the village at any time-dry or rainy season, must consult with them if he or she wishes to expect good weather, other than that, the rain may be imminent. And on a day like this, it had been very cautious to heed such warnings.

Their mission, therefore, was for these two witches to perform their incantations in a way of managing the skies to avert possible rainfall! So, they intoned a song and danced thrilling themselves with the beat of the wooden gongs and traditional rhythm and rhymes specifically composed for that occasion

> Bassey Mbede oh oh Mbede our own (2times)
> Tall and handsome
> oh oh Mbede our own
> Treasure for Mkpasang
> oh oh Mbede our own
> He's tall; he's English,
> the only cure for Mkpasang ailment.
> Light for Mkpasang,
> healing and comfort
> In him no arthritis
> Sickness run afar,
> We have the medicine we wanted.

"Nkoyo, don't kill the rhythm of the dance, this happiness must go on forever" intoned Ikwo.

"...and the rains shouldn't become close to sight"

Nkoyo responded with a stylish rhythmic jerky movement of her waistline.

They laughed gleefully and continued their dance steps making way towards the venue of the reception.

His granddad reminded Etimbuk of Mkpasang Community Primary School as serving six other villages surrounding Mkpasang. The only educational institution most of the contemporary leaders in Mkpasang, and the surrounding communities had passed through, including Bassey, his late father.

Established in the late thirties as a bribe by the colonial imperialists dangled out to entice our elders in exchange for the enslavement of the area. It's the only memorial to immortalise our painful history for near hundred years!

Years of servitude, waiting and hoping to see and feel liberation from captivity and embrace freedom march to occupy our destinies and common intents. This we have been hoping and waiting for so long.

"The Queen's Land exploited rich material and human resources in Mkpasang, impoverishing the area through egoistic pride. They took away the most vibrant of men of this community in exchange for Mkpasang Community School.

"And apart from annual Parents Teachers' Association... celebrations which usually brought the community together, the School had never hosted any other major event right from inception. Therefore, its use as a venue for the celebrated reception of such an important personality in the village was iconic with lasting memories."

Deacon Mbede had been very emotional close to the verge of shedding tears but managed to hold back his emotion had remained silent without words. However, from time to time, tears streamed down both sides of the face as he had continued in his narration. He was groaning and moaning at intervals for the loss so great to bear.

Etimbuk waited watched and consoled him.

Suddenly he got into the conversation again after drying his eyes.

"We watch our future ebb away mercilessly for so long, years of economic deprivation and marginalisation. We see a community of vigorous and responsible men and women with so much energy and enthusiasm languishing and vanquishing away in poverty because the government of the day do not care about them.

"My son, we have been betrayed and marginalised for being good people, our future becomes perilously endangered for lack of development.

"Bassey was the only light that illuminated this community. He was our hero, our hopes and inspiration. He was someone whom we all looked up to. And in fact, what we see today as a glimmer of development come from his singular effort.

"The numerous road projects, the advent of tremendous youth empowerment and development programmes in a level unheard of in Idiaimah. Bassey had transformed Mkpasang to the level the community cannot be ignored further. Unprecedented housing projects scattered about in the community were his treasured legacies. We can go on and on, the list is endless.

"But lo, death snatched him away suddenly and we are left with yet another long year of sorrow and pain. The anguish that awaits us could only be better imagined than felt"

"Someone else may perhaps step into his shoes, who knows, but that person will not be Bassey. Bassey was unique, Bassey was an outstanding figure that radiated love and togetherness, and above all, Bassey was my son."

Deacon Mbede again gave a long pause only to continue in his narration of events of the reception ceremony something that gave him a little radiant of joy and consolation.

"So, drumming, dancing and merriment were in the air. The whole of Mkpasang was agog with joy radiating from the faces of attendees in a remarkable way. They were solidly united at the mention of the name, Dr Bassey Asukwo Mbede.

"Ah, doctor!" Etukudoh, a 73-year old man exclaims with the radiance of unquestionable joy on his face, "and I am so happy that the cure for my arthritis has finally arrived"

"Ah ah ah ah Etukudo," laughing uncontrollably, "I tell you something. I am told your "Doctor" only knows the cure for maize and cassava, not man," retorted his friend, Ubokudom.

"Whatever that means, Ubokudom, give me your snuff-box please, I have forgotten mine at home. I suppose you bought it from Ekaette Ekott and not Anwaan Okon. Hers is usually overdone with excess limestone."

Ubokudom took a good pinch of the tobacco stuff himself pushing it hurriedly into his nostrils before attempting to give to Etukudo.

"Ah!" flaring his nares, "Ooowashiee!"

He sneezed out the stuff, tears ran down his cheeks with chocolate-coloured nasal discharge that accompanied it.

Ubokudom stood one place gesticulating in rejection of the offer to Etukudoh who was in desperate need of the tobacco stuff himself. Etukudoh asked with disappointment as he forgot his own snuffbox at home. So, Ubokudom then brought out a squalid piece of cloth from the pocket of his shorts-a cloth he wore underneath his three-piece wrapper wound around his waist. He wiped off his nasal discharge and eyes meticulously before, in reluctance, handing over to Etukudoh.

"An old man would hardly have a life without it." He said before handing the box out to Etokudoh. He collected it then intoned.

"A doctor is a doctor, Ubokudom" he pushed the stuff hurriedly into his nostril and breathed a sigh of relief. "Ah! I can't wait for him to find a lasting remedy for my persistent pains after all that is what we sent him out to bring to us" Etukudoh concludes in an incoherent voice.

"Maybe he will, maybe not, but all I can tell you now, let's hurry on fast so that we don't miss item number six." Ubokudom suggested.

"What's that?" Etukudoh queried.

"Ah ah, of course, the overnight palm wine. That may be served first"

"Oh yes o, you're damn right Ubokudom; overnight has the yeast which is the real condiment of up wine!"

"Exactly".

Hastily, both men increased their labouring steps towards the Community Primary School, venue of reception for Dr Mbede.

"Attendance at the reception although not compulsory, but together everyone had a burning desire to attend. The young, the old even the weak and vulnerable came together relishing in the pleasure of history being made in Mkpasang. They all converged at the Community Primary School to receive the most distinguished son of the soil, Dr Bassey Jonathan Asuquo Mbede.

Their faces were radiant beaming smiles. And a charged environment ensued with urgent and profound eagerness for everyone present to feel and appreciate the pioneering personality of the community. The one who had made Mkpasang exceedingly proud, Dr Bassey Jonathan Asuquo Mbede.

"Groups of traditional displays gathered outside in the field. Each group brought his own set of the display which added zests to the occasion. The most prominent and famous was *Ekpo Nyoho* masquerades which thrilled the crowd. *Ekpo Nyoyo* appeared very scary with their regalia and voices like someone speaking through the nose or water in the mouth.

It was a secret society which had had a long traditional history in the community with only male members. It was a seasonal display usually out to maintain discipline and single out deviant individuals in the community for mockery and disgrace. Anyone who had misbehaved while they were off-season became subjects of such derision. It was usually said that no secret can be hidden away from *ekpo nyoho*.

Their horrible voices and fast-moving dance steps brought a sense of fear to women and children in the village and even men who were not inducted into the cult. *Ekpo Nyoho* was the traditional government of the day.

Maintenance of discipline and order in the village was their duty. Besides, *Ekpo Nyoho* cult was designated to enforce the norms and will of the ancestors whom the villagers believed, their spirits were still alive and active amongst them.

They were weird-looking creatures groomed in seclusion with their faces like monsters and body smeared with black stuff too scary to behold. Some even carried pots with smokes on their heads. They moved in their numbers and perambulated the whole arena overshadowing other groups. They traversed causing panic, fear and excitement in the crowd.

Ordinarily, women, children and non-inducted men into the cult were forbidden from catching even glimpses of these daredevil creatures. Such people would usually remain indoors peeping through keyholes during the season of displays as the masquerades prowl the community. But on this very special occasion, there were no such restrictions.

Everyone who can withstand their intimidating appearance and manners of the 'mother ghost'-that's what they otherwise called, had to feel and see what they really look like. Invariably those who can withstand their horrific voices and threatening manner were permitted, although they still stood in awe.

Ekpo Nyoko masquerade had a long history of association with villages in the environs. They were some myths surrounding it of the dead coming from beyond the grave to visit the living. Such ghosts usually sent greeting to their loved ones whom they left behind and received messages of consolation from the living back to the dead.

And indeed, it was an unforgettable day in Mkpasang.

A man dressed in full traditional regalia walked into the crowd with a piece of paper in his hand. He eulogised with a sense of pride and respect to all present before placing a piece of paper on the lectern specially placed in the podium for it. He read eloquently from his well-scripted verses over the microphone.

MBEDE

Mbede, the name is like music to our ears,
A name full of respect by all and for him,
Particularly for Mkpasang, and all its surrounding.
A name so wonderfully encrypted in our hearts,
By our elders who painfully sourced our future,
that we may live our lives devoid of worries.
With Bassey Mbede, the doctor to heal our land!

Like music, the name strikes a chord of praise,
the rhythm of melody fills the air with dance.
Young and old, gyrate without restrain.
Dancing to the sequence and harmony and praise
Our hearts swell with the chorus of unending praise.
With Bassey Mbede, the doctor to heal our land!

Our community once excluded from the comity of nations,
And cast down for lack of direction and leadership.
Now, the light of hope breaks in all directions,
Glowing radiance; with combustible flame,
envelopes Mkpasang, its embers burn
With Bassey Mbede, the doctor to heal our land!

Many ailments berserk our community for ages,
Our hearts sank and bled with pains and sorrows.
But today repose of healing and cure have arrived.
For everyone with pains and headaches to be healed
Mbede, we drink and wallow in health and joy!
Bassey Mbede, the doctor to heal our land!

Loud standing ovations of applause rented the air. The persistent and consistent echoing of cheers reeled on intermittently as he read his well-scripted poem.

And going further he changed the rhythm.

Never shall we forget
The city of Mkpasang agog in adoring splendour fleet
Cars, cyclists, and human traffic converged

Amidst shouts of joy and unity of mind on feet
Heralds of songs and human voices echoing
In ecstatic oneness consumed.
All for Mbebe our benefactor and umbrella

Never Shall we forget
From Ibattai to Ubenefa down to Mkpasang agog
Trailing in splendour of majesty for Mbedes
With songs of love and integration of mind.
Poured out for Bassey Mbede our son.

Never Shall we forget
Those years of marginalisation and lack of care for us
When Idiaimah government forced its creeping corruption on us
With impunity, they stole, lied, killed and divided the common purse of the people.
Now in Mkpasang, their monstrous embers will cease.
For our beloved Bassey Mbede has taken control of the land.

Never shall we forget
Hunger and starvation in the midst of plenty
Abundance of corruption in government that squeeze the masses.
Punishing us with Kidnapping, killing and robbery so sad to quantify.
Leaving many us to groan in the weight of despair and fear.
We shall never ever forget the forlorn of our comfort.

It was a great stem winder line resonated within the crowd and spilling into the community. Some of the lines became expression that was used eloquently by many in Mkpasang in their daily conversations. Making Emediong the poet, a sort of celebrity in the community.

Bassey moved up with grandeur of majesty offering handshake with Emediong. There was an uproar-thunderous eruption of the shout of joy by everyone present. Every indigene present and residents of Mkpasang community and the environs were delighted to be part of this epoch-making day in Mkpasang.

Many were anxious to shake hands with the distinguished guest of honour as the privilege of attending. The skies too joined in radiant gleaming smiles, indicating divine approval.

For Bassey, since he left home, more than eight years earlier, was profoundly surprised as many villagers, some of whom may not have known him well, so excited about his success in life. This was the turning point in his life-an aspect of the reception ceremony which really drew his heart for Mkpasang. And that he saw as an honour.

CHAPTER 31

DEACON MBEDE WAS VERY EMOTIONAL recalling the captivating event that happened over three decades in the community. He was particularly thrilled with the event which had remain evergreen in his memory.

"Amongst the dignitaries present at that gathering, I, Deacon Jonathan Asuquo Mbede was the proudest of them all. And I found it very resistive to hide such a boundless joy that radiated on my face for a day like that.

"The memorable speech I gave on this red-letter day still remains evergreen, and indelible in my mind. I started with traditional greetings:

"Mkpasang isongo!-(the crowd responded) iyah
Isongo!-iyah
Oh oh oh!-Oh ooh.

"My dearest people of Mkpasang, I greet you. Let me use this auspicious occasion to express my deepest appreciation to you all for the magnanimous and incredible love you have demonstrated to your beloved son, Bassey".

A shout of joy greeted the crowd, clapping and music from the band hired for this very special occasion responded with special rhythm and melody that churned the whole arena over and over again. The trumpet sounded, echoing of cymbals reverberated in the hall with everyone shouting for joy.

I began as I offered to make this closing remark on behalf of Bassey. Invariably, he was too distracted, seeing such a crowd of people that came on his behalf, to organise his thoughts to say something.

"Today, as never before, Mkpasang has made a futuristic statement. The people of this deprived community have come together with one accord and passion to build a United Mkpasang, one nation community, which no one can destroy.

We have come to announce to the whole world that a ray of light is breaking through the generational darkness of this deprived community. And on behalf of my family, we are so proud to be the beacon of that luminous light.

"Thank you for your insurmountable contributions to the realisation of this dream-the dream of deliverance from economic marginalisation of Mkpasang.

"Yes, the dream of recognition of Mkpasang in the comity of States in Idiaimah nation. The dream of liberation from the long years of political doldrums, where those we spent our lives and hard-earned money to elect into National Assemblies would turn their backs against us without any feasible dividend of democracy.

"So sad that we are soon forgotten once our votes were counted-the proverbial goose that lay the golden egg. Therefore, from now henceforth, we have hopes in a voice to speak unequivocally in defence of justice which has eluded us for ages. We have one who will represent us in this community. So, continue to hold the fort and be the people of love you have ever been.

"However, let me be quick to add that we need more of these than one. A tree cannot form a forest, we all know. I am aware there are those still left to return. However, we still need a forest of educated people, young men and women in this community.

The more forest around us the healthier we will be. And truly, forests are reservoirs of food and fuel, and today there are enough resources reserved in Bassey to fuel and feed the wheels of progress of United Mkpasang Nation"

There was clapping of hands in appreciation in acknowledgement.

"Every parent in Mkpasang should resolve to task his ability with joy at sending their children to school. Bassey has made us all proud today because of attainment of academic independence without which we would not have been here today. Yes, education for the liberation of the entire minds of the people.

"Please my beloved youths from Mkpasang; we need many more educated indigenes of this deprived community. Invest your lives; time and talent in education for yourself development and for Mkpasang.

"This is what shall liberate us from long years of neglect by successive administrations in Idiaimah. Moreover, we shall have freedom from youth unemployment, idleness, crime, boredom, and destitution; with their attended negative impacts on our community that have been living with us for ages.

"As many more young people in this community are educated the more lights, we shall see. Remember, development starts with the acquisition of knowledge. And I want to be confident, before long; we shall come back here to celebrate yet another distinguished indigene of the One Nation People-Great Mkpasang community.

Once again, thank you so very much for your unflinching support which is the reason for this epoch-making day. Thank you for your time. And may God bless Mkpasang"

After the remarks, there was an upstanding ovation as he took his seat.

"Proud father" echoing of voices lingered on with unceasing applause in acknowledgement of this landmark speech of appreciation.

Thereafter after this heroic reception, Bassey went around exchanging pleasantries and thanking the old and the young for the mark of the honour done him and his family. He presented two live cows to thank the community, including some undisclosed amount of cash.

CHAPTER 32

BASSEY WAS EMPLOYED BY THE Federal Government of Idiaimah in the newly established Federal University of Agriculture Mkpasang (FUAM) as a Lecturer. He made rapid progress on his job. Academic brilliance and inventiveness stood him out as an outstanding scholar in the University community. This too earned him appointment into the prestigious Academic Board of FUAM, and other such fellowships in the University community.

Four years into his career as a seasoned lecturer in the University, Dr Bassey Asuquo Mbede, a brilliant boffin, served as the first indigenous Deputy Vice-Chancellor of the University.

Bassey had a penchant for excellence, a knack for being the very best in his chosen career and above all, he was a man on a mission, mission to make things happen, and effectively he had used his charm and ingenuity well in this direction.

His engineering skills contributed to the inauguration of two new Faculties in the University, his most coveted caps earned him many acolytes. It had not been surprising then that at the expiration of the tenor of office of the expatriate pioneer Vice-Chancellor, Professor Jones, the young Professor Bassey Jonathan Asuquo Mbede assumed the mantle of leadership in the administration of the University through a keenly contested election.

As first indigenous Vice Chancellor of FUAM, Bassey was keenly loved by the majority. He brought his wealth of experience to bear in the necessary challenges within and around the University campus. He harnessed and reshaped available human and material resources maintaining sustainable development in academic and infrastructural development in the University.

Everything was done in line with the policy thrust of the State administration and, in consonance with the regulating body's benchmarks policy and best practice.

Successful implementations of these by the Management had culminated into the approval of some additional faculties and programmes for the University. This made FUAM one of the few in Idiaimah to be so decorated.

This position of authority had also launched Professor Bassey Asuquo Mbede into Idiaimah hall of fame.

"It was during this time of his Academic fame that you were born, Etimbuk. And your brother followed two years later. Professor & Mrs Bassey Mbede had been married for years without any children; your birth then was a double blessing to the fortunes of Mbede dynasty. Etimbuk, you instantly became the most loved, sought after, wanted and of course, a near spoilt child.

"Your parents had overindulged you with everything that money could buy, except their presence. While your father had been completely embedded in his Academic work at FUAM, your mother, a seasoned Economist, had chosen life of an International fashion guru, she had no time for domestic affairs.

And found faith and pleasure trotting the globe leaving you without parental care."

Deacon Mbede took a pinch of his tobacco snuff remaining silent for a while. He appeared quite moody and utterly downcast; he was gnashing his teeth and guessing into the empty space in the wonder of how cruel this life had been.

Deacon Mbede unwittingly dropped his chin on his palm supported by the right thigh which he shook repeatedly, groaning and moaning for a loss so great to bear.

"My son" he reiterated "I am so worried about your junior brother, Patrick. He doesn't listen to any legitimate piece of advice. His absolute negative behaviour, quite unlike those of Mbedes, is so worrisome"

The swipe on Patrick further exacerbated Etimbuk's dislike for his brother's attitude and behaviour. His granddad informed him that he had seen Patrick the other day with Edet Okon, a notorious boy who had mortgaged and sold off all his father's properties while the old man was still alive. This had been the type of friends that Patrick kept company with, those who dragged him into waywardness and defiance with authorities.

Deacon Mbede took Etimbuk along memory lane of history he stated that they were lucky because right from birth, their education had been insured and guaranteed. Quite unlike other children their age, they attended the best of schools right from birth, were thought by the best teachers and treated exceptionally well as children of the rich.

According to him, when he started school, there were problems with the educational system in Idiaimah. Government schools were in total chaos and shut down for months because of perennial strikes by teachers due to lack of payment of salaries and other entitlements.

Children remained at home stranded and some even lost interest totally in academic pursuit swerving back to illiteracy.

"In the midst of these tales of woes, your parents had to send you both to a privately-owned school. According to your father, it would be a shame to see his children not attending school and not living their full potential in the future. Therefore, he considered your academic pursuit far more important above anything else. So, you and your sibling Patrick received foundation education in privately owned Nursery School up to secondary school level.

It was in Secondary Class four that Patrick started showing some strange behaviour. He showed no regard for rules and regulations and felt that he was in charge of everything. Things that seemed important not only to him but those with a communal interest he became antagonistic to them.

Patrick's truancy was quite concerning; therefore, efforts were made to address this deviation, but he wouldn't just listen, wouldn't take any pieces of advice. But he managed to come back home with Senior Secondary School Certificate result which is still very doubtful as to his own.

Soon after the death of your father, your mother registered him into the University of Harcourt, a school located about 200 kilometres away from home, on his request. According to

Patrick, that would help him escape bad friends and accomplices around here. But little did we know it was a ploy to get him into increasing freedom with the phalanx of bad companies.

"Where is he now after squandering away his future and all that money? He is back to square one, nothing to show for it. He pressurised your mother to open a similar business of hers for him. That beautiful shop your mother opened for him, where is it now, all gone with the wind. He sold it to satisfy his yearning for cannabis and other drugs."

As his grandfather continued recounting prodigal escapades of Patrick, Etimbuk listened with so much pain in his heart. His mind had been too scared to continue hearing wastefulness on that scale by a boy of his age!

"Have you seen him recently?" Deacon Mbede asked with regret and disappointment.

Etimbuk being too ashamed to answer that question hid his face in shame. He was absolutely embarrassed to open his mouth and speak about Patrick, therefore had stared at the floor for a moment shaking his head in disapproval. Sighing he replied.

"That boy is a complete waste of space." He found his voice at last. "Even with the present predicaments, the way things are now, he still appears as if nothing does concern him at all. I am so sorry for his waywardness-it's so disappointing."

After this, Deacon Mbede filled with a heavy sense of grief and despair in his heart, remained silent allowing his feeling not to generate into an outburst of tears. Nonetheless, his emotion was soaked up by nostalgic memories of his son's immense contribution to the advancement of Mkpasang community.

He managed to push his emotion back rubbing his moistened eyes with the back of his hands, groaning, moaning and grinding his teeth, revealing his vulnerability and helplessness. Deacon Mbede was obviously still very much depressed. Ultimately, he managed to accept the situation as a real and inevitable end that all mortals will embrace eventually.

Etimbuk, full of sympathy commiserated with his grandfather, he looked at him with pity for the loss so great to bear. On his part, he tried as much as possible to play his emotion down which burned inside him with pronounced intensity.

"Etimbuk, for me to be the person left to mourn Bassey and not the other way around is the greatest loss which had broken my bones. Bassey was my hope, my joy, the pride of my life and I was confident on the day of my exit, the whole world would gather to bid me final farewell in a grand style. But where is that hope? I am lost" More tears rolled down his wrinkled face.

Etimbuk held unto his grandpa consoling and reassuring him that by God's grace, he himself shall fill the vacuum left by the demise of his father. It was this tears that would have brought the meeting to a fruitless end without gathering much-needed information he searched for.

Quite unable to ask further questions, Etimbuk bid his grandpa goodbye after consoling him for a while and letting him understand that he really appreciated him.

But as soon as he got up to go, Deacon Mbede held up his righthand sleeve reassuring.

"My son, your parents were a courageously happy and loving couple"

He stopped suddenly, his head went down between his two thighs and with a heavy sigh, he then continued. "Not one day in their over two decades did me or anyone else I know of, wedded into their privacy to settle any dispute"

Deacon Mbede took a pinch of his tobacco snuff inhaling the powder into his nostrils slowly, in small quantities one nostril at a time. His reddened eyes were fixed on unimaginable distance as he felt light-headedness usually on taking snuff.

This habit he developed two years ago following the death of his son, he recalled those glorious days when his son made a significant impact in the community and the country at large.

Recalling the outpouring of love and gratitude he received from all and sundry people in Idiaimah, he maintained unimaginable stillness, guessing at his grandson and thinking how he resembled his father not only in physical appearance but in manners and attitudes. Profound sadness rolled along in his heart. He allowed himself to feel the flood of loss and emptiness rolling and glowing in his heart.

Etimbuk too, remained silent praying for times and opportunities to be a person he had always wanted and most importantly, Etimbuk wished that his educational pursuit could become a thing he would carry as a token of appreciation and tribute to the evergreen memory of his beloved father.

"That may not necessarily mean that your parents hadn't any disagreement" Deacon Mbede struggled to complete his sentence "as marriage people, but love conquered all in whatever happened"

His grandpa went on to imply that but for frequent travels of Esitima abroad, Etimbuk could have had either another brother or sister in line beside Uduak and things may not have been the same.

"Nevertheless, my son, I am satisfied that you shall step into this inheritance successfully if you look down and stay focused. And if you need anything, don't fail to ask me"

Etimbuk considered this an opportunity to explore. He gesticulated reaching for his handkerchief which he had left on the small side table. Clearing his throat and responded with a note of reservation, quite unsure of how to present the problem, but he did manage to say something.

"Grandpa…em" Clearing his throat again "what about the rumour in town concerning my mother's involvement in the death of my father, do you share in this"

He held back to see the reaction of the old man. Deacon Mbede shocked unable to show this apparent uncomfortableness immediately and Etimbuk continued,

"… honestly, grandpa, it makes me quite uncomfortable?"

And for a while Deacon, Mbede couldn't find the exact word to express his feeling. He remained with blank stares and suspected his grandson may be hiding something from him. He assessed Etimbuk cautiously with worrying gestures that his good intentions may have been misunderstood. And clearing his throat he said in a hoarse voice.

"My son, the evening sun casts its shadows a long distance away, while that of the afternoon is planted right under your feet."

Etimbuk waited for a while to see if his grandpa would explain the proverb, but since that didn't happen, with a grin he said,

"Grandpa," appearing blank and lost "I am sorry I don't understand I am not good with proverbs."

Waited again for answers to his puzzle. Etimbuk was not in the best frame of mind, therefore, became a bit hesitant though not expecting straight forward answers from his grandparent.

"Sit down" he beckoned, tapping the chair with his left hand and then waited. Etimbuk slowly lowered his buttocks on the chair before his grandpa continued.

"...my son, when an adult over eighties dies, little or no questions are asked. But as soon as a young and promising person departs this world, significant others are suspected of being the reasons for the untimely death. No one would be happy to lose such a treasure in the community"

Deacon Mbede explained to his grandson the culture and traditions of the society putting blames on a living spouse once the other dies. And in this case, he excused the genesis of the rumour because Bassey's death was a grave loss to Mkpasang as a whole not necessarily the Mbede family alone.

"It was a dearth of progress, growth and development for numerous projects that he started for Mkpasang. In fact, his death brought the whole of Mkpasang and indeed Idiaimah, on their knees.

"People won't fail to blame close relatives for missing such an indefatigable icon in the society. Of course, accusing the wife and I satisfies that tradition."

Etimbuk was taken aback by this news. So, it means that his efforts have begun to pay off, he saw a gleam of light in the tunnel. At least some mysteries which do weigh him down for sometimes have begun to unravel.

"...grandpa honestly I only heard the accusation concerning my mother, and not an inkling in the least of you"

"My son, you aren't heard anything yet. Keep your ears and eyes to the ground and don't allow what you've heard, seen or shall hear later in this case weigh you down. Keep on keeping on my son, you have your future to tend. When an animal is like a bunch of palm fruit, the butcher finds it very difficult from where exactly to start separating its parts."

He finished the proverb with eyes fixed on the grandson.

"Oh grandpa, you've come again with a proverb. What's the meaning please"

His grandfather explained to him that anything that is beyond imagination is not worth wasting so much energy on. That one shouldn't try seeking for answers to those things he knows are too far deep beyond his grasp.

Although the latest information got him by surprise, he, however, welcomed the grace to have found it. In his mind, he was very confused. What is happening here, he thought. I'll have to seek more information on this; more inquiry is needed if he must crack the code of this puzzle.

"Could it be mummy and grandpa joining hands to perfect this atrocious evil? No, I don't see this as a possibility."

Certainly, this was worrying times for Etimbuk. But what he failed to understand was that death by what appeared ordinary means is very difficult to investigate the cause. It would be quite impossible to dig into the evidence of the cause of his father's death. Idiaimah had no capacity to exploring into the concept of forensic science. Except he wanted to learn the language of esoteric and speculate.

What he set out to do with this recondite act which is far beyond ordinary understanding, a mystery only known by the initiates of witchcraft or sorcery is unthinkable and unimaginable.

Must he let go the rumours at this point; does it really worthwhile expending his energy and time in this direction?

However, Etimbuk needed time to go over this. He must keep an open mind not dismissing anything on any possible lead that could potentially solve the mystery.

"Everything must be on the table; nothing taken off for now" He was very worried.

Well, he would resolve to consider it a project of a lifetime exploring into the unknown. After all, at the end, he might learn some more lessons about life itself as he had started to learn already. There is nothing to lose but greater gain. He concluded in his mind.

CHAPTER 33

ETIMBUK WAS CHALLENGED WITH THE awesome badass of situations ever. He got inside his late father's bedroom and stood there for a couple of minutes without necessarily wishing to do anything. His mindset was on something desirable and wished he overcome this toughest challenge and create something better for himself and his future.

Etimbuk wished to be alone in solitude where he could think properly. In that state of mind, suddenly a poignant curiosity came upon him, a feeling that triggered the urge to search for something —something which he hadn't any glue about-just anything! And the intensity of the curiosity had been so strong and flooded his mind as he stood in the room guessing into the emptiness of his own mind.

Since the demise of his father, Etimbuk had been inside the room several times, but never had he been pressed on like this evening, by what appeared as an invisible hand, urging him on to do something. And reluctantly, he obeyed that urge.

He sat down on the cushion in the room opening two huge filing cabinets, one after another as he had done several times. He had been in the room many times and had searched into the cabinets a number of times over. But on this particular encounter, he was a bit meticulous about the process. Searching the whole pages of each document carefully.

Eventually, he came to the thin file embedded inside another file earmarked, *Important.* He spent almost the whole night meticulously rummaging over every piece of information inside the document that staggered his imagination. He sorted the file in great details noting information off the shelf on this notepad.

Information gathered was timeless capable of resetting time and circumstances in his life forever. It was a dividing line between success and failure, between his continued sadness and enjoying the bliss of happiness like never before. And between remaining uneducated and coming out of the university a graduate.

The details contained in the file earmarked boldly "debtors/creditors" embedded in *important* file still sitting in the filing cabinet in the room was mind-boggling. And yet, he wandered long distances miserably in search of succour.

It was there that he realised, to his astonishment, that answers to his most pressing needs were not farfetched, it was right inside the house waiting patiently for him.

'Sometimes, the most important question, the question that could change circumstances of lives and situations is not farfetched. These could be answered within the immediate grasp of reach' He reflected days after.

In the file were dozens of names, those who were indebted to his father and whom his father was indebted to, were carefully documented. There were also names of those his father did a kindness to which were not valued in monetary terms. These were carefully documented and stacked away in *important*.

Lost for words, Etimbuk was exceedingly excited, it was like winning an American lottery! The dossier contained exact dates of the transaction, amount clearly spelt out in great details including legal documents attached to each transaction.

"Could such a stunning discovery be the answer to my numerous pressing problems; or is it a dream?"

Etimbuk had been extremely excited. It was absolutely electrifying for him to see relief from his challenging situations. And that feeling denied him adequate sleep the rest of the night as he laid in bed thinking of so many possibilities for his future. His long search for liberty could have a glorious and happy ending at last.

Perhaps indeed! He could not believe his eyes that this was indeed happening. There was a sense of relief in his heart as he leapt for great joy for discovery a fortune! Etimbuk allowed the euphoria to sink down how to be it, throughout the night.

> *O Mbedes, your stock will never run dry even in austerity*
> *The spirit of love endured for posterity*
> *Procured forlorn imagination and dexterity*
> *I'll ever remain grateful for eternity*
>
> *How could I roam the streets with uncertainty?*
> *While wealth is stocked up at home in abundance*
> *My soul would dance eternally*
> *For the joy which abounds without measure.*
>
> *My feeling expressed without taciturnity*
> *But full of mirth of the confraternity*
> *What would have been impossible*
> *Has resulted in joy eternity*

Etimbuk got up in the morning filled with the freshness of hope. He was however dumbstruck and overwhelmed with shock and amazement, why the matter had remained hidden for so long he thought. And imagined from where exactly he would start celebrating his sudden haul of wealth.

Although it had been like winning an American lottery, a state of ambivalence came upon him suddenly with a bittersweet feeling as he lay down in bed reflecting. His thoughts centred on the possibility of recovery of the funds two years after the death of his father.

He thought of man as being wicked in nature otherwise how can such debts be still standing two years after the death of his father!

The debtors, some have been seeing him regularly. Why shouldn't they take steps indicating their indebtedness and commitment for repayment? Or would they wish that these be written off just like that? Many unanswered questions had crossed his mind.

"To take pleasure in the misfortune of this family is very sad, unfortunately. It shouldn't be those my dad did kindness to that have paid him back in bad coins, no. And sadly, most of them are in business. It's unfortunate that those in business should engage in this schadenfreude, such an idea shouldn't be heard of with those who run the economy."

Feeling happy when something go wrong for us by our detractors is an outrageous lack of integrity and honesty. Otherwise, how can it be that his father had done kindness to them, and in return, they repay him back in bad coins?

His death supposed to trigger some emotion of sympathy as ones who have benefited massively from his largess, but here they are, turning their backs on the fountain that quenched their tastes.

Humanity indeed should be feared. Even with his present predicament, these sadists wouldn't mind, they still enjoy seeing him roam the street like a pauper. Etimbuk continued identifying reasons why such behaviour shouldn't be possible in the first place.

"But I'll not be destitute, I shall rise to reclaim the lost grounds and be the person history shall talk about with a glowing sense of respect and pride," He thought aloud.

He considered it expedient to keep the information away from the rest of his family members whilst still working out adequate plans and strategies for recovery.

Out of respect to the memory of his father, Etimbuk decided to mark that night a very special one, very significant in his journey for educational freedom and attainment in life. That night shouldn't be forgotten in his life.

The joy of such discovery made Etimbuk have insomnia, he had stayed in bed awake, sleep refused to come the rest of the night. So, he stirred in motion plans for an aggressive debt recovery programme. And he had planned seeking information pertaining to debt repayment from some legal experts and searching advice on the internet.

Through these avenues, letters were issued to all the debtors by reminding them of their indebtedness and the need for repayment. In the letter were included a warning for repossession of identified securities in event of them failing to make a repayment which were overdue.

He also reminded all creditors that he was aware of the outstanding debts and will do all within his reach to make payments as soon as it was practicable and affordable. Etimbuk also wished speaking with them personally and appealing for their understanding.

Messers Odoroma & co was the only legal consortium willing to negotiate terms without any upfront payments. They agreed to pursue those involved with the necessary legal backing until all the debts were recovered. However, the problem with that was, Etimbuk was told he will pay twenty per cent of the recovered sum as the attorney's fees.

That arrangement was something he needed to consider. If he agreed to that term and condition, it would mean loss of a substantial chunk of money; therefore, he had to give it a second thought. Fought on perhaps there could be better alternatives to solving the debacle.

"I will have to think very hard about this," he thought "there are many outlets there that can equally handle this effectively and charge far less. Twenty per cent is an exorbitant price to pay. No, that isn't feasible"

CHAPTER 34

ETIMBUK SAT DOWN THINKING HOW he'll get to the bottom of recovery of his father's debts. He sat on the dinner table with the thought of life being quite cruel and unfair to him. His consolation had been in his discovery so huge beyond his imagination, something that can change his situation profoundly and that of the family forever.

He thought of how, as a young boy, he missed the company and friendship of his father through death. He thought about his present trouble with his mother's poor mental health along with his brother's carefree attitude toward enormous challenges around the family and care of his sister, Uduak.

At present, he had been faced with enormous challenges at home and most importantly for him, his eminent drop out of school as it had seemed. These problems had put enormous pressure on his coping skill despairingly.

"Yes," he asseverated quite audibly as he got up to drop the plates in the dishwasher "it's these troubles that make us grow up into a man. The more we overcome certainties of life, the more we acquire the skill to manage life with certainty. I'll push on and not give up, especially now that the road appears smoother."

In the midst of these thoughts, even with the discovery of what had appeared a fortune, he reasoned that the debtors might decline payment or could deny it altogether. If not so, why would they not own up to their indebtedness for near two years, or would they wish that the debts be written off?

"I wonder why life would be so cruel, so unkind to me. Had I foreseen the future in this way, I would have preferred a life of an orphan right from birth. But no one chooses his parents or place not even circumstances of their birth. And no one had consciousness before birth for such choices. Therefore, none should be blamed or seen as making wrong choices. My birth into Mbede family was not accidental but providential.

"The dogged determination to overcome insurmountable problems became quite sickening at every step on the way. And if l must indeed conquer this threatening fear, I have to develop a strong mental character. Mind adamant to happenings within and around my immediate environment; to finish what I have set before myself-getting this money to pay for my education above any other thing."

And he had absolute determination, by all means, to ensure that his plan was successful.

"Change!" he groaned within. "Haha, so I've changed indeed? Would this change be due to backlog of pains or sudden grab with a fortune-money not tangible at the moment?" he laughed sarcastically.

"Yes, things don't stay stagnant, they change over time, and this is precisely what I've come to be the last two years or so. But in spite of intangibility of my haul with fortune, it still remains a change!"

"Change brings about the beginning or an end to any course of action. Flowers do change, so do non-living things. Houses aged with time so are vehicles and dogs and hens and goats and human, and a man changes in appearance for good or for bad. My current change is of course, very challenging.

"Gone are the days when I was the happening boy, where everything changed under my beck and call, changes for me then were full of life and expectation. But here, I struggle with lots of cares and wants.

"The journey of life is all about money. The rich is challenged on how to make more and safeguard it from running out, while the poor struggle to eke out living and get it running in. The upheavals and hassles of everyday life we see in our world today are all effects of the acquisition of money. And this is what brings in the changes we see

"Would this change lead me to boom or doom? No, I earnestly seek life, not catastrophe! For in it I will stand better chances of ground-breaking changes in my circumstance as I prepare for greater positive changes ahead."

"Yes, I will not be a weakling to the toast of the mean so simple. Instead, I must forge ahead and write my name in the sand of time. In spite of losses so great and difficult to bear yet, life must continue assuredly; that future changes will bring joy, happiness full of hope and love."

He concluded his soliloquy putting a call to Joyce, his mother's bosom friend.

"Hello, Auntie Joyce is there a way I might see you today, please. I have very important information to share with you"

"Hi, Etimbuk am not in town right now but might be back in the evening. When am home I'll call to let you know? Is that okay?"

"Okay ma, thank you"

"Bye"

"Bye-bye"

He had locked his cell phone and put into his pocket, then sat down quietly in contemplation.

Joyce was terribly shocked and afraid concerning a recent problem with Esitima which, as Joyce assessed was getting out of hand. She was shaken as her friend continued to lock herself up in her room for months, she has barely eaten well or gone to her shop. But carefully, Joyce had avoided meeting with Esitima as she had refused to pick her numerous calls. Joyce, therefore, had to take ample time to think out a better strategy on how to approach this issue now to avoid annoying Etimbuk. She was sure the young man had wanted a discussion on events surrounding his mother's ill health.

"Oh my God, where do I go from here; I need to be careful lest I too slip into the bottom of the quagmires. Everyone would say I am her best friend and personal adviser. Hence knows basically everything about Esitima. Now that Esitima is down; I better give her time for things to fall their normal course"

Etimbuk had wanted to draw Joyce's attention to her mother's poor mental health and how best to go about solving the problem for her. As far as Etimbuk was concern, her mother needed help after concerted efforts to let her into hospital failed. And he was sure Joyce would know the best way to provide that help.

She had not eaten food except for some bottles of alcohol which had now become her regular companion in those tormented times of her grief. The great Esitima, a woman whose self-care could never be compromised can now afford to stay for days without a bath! This is outrageous behaviour, quite unspeakable of her!

She appeared quite bizarre with poverty of speech and mutism most of the times. Esitima could stay for several minutes without saying a word. She had gained a considerable amount of weight by massive kilograms due to her inactivity.

Since overcoming the shock of her husband's death two years ago, Esitima had determined to move ahead with her life. She had certainly resolved not to deny but ensure a good life for her children in the face of the present situation. For her, the bloodline of Mbede must continue assuredly. She must do everything, at all cost, to preserve that name, Mbede, through giving her children a glorious future.

CHAPTER 35

Engrossed by the rumours tearing his mother apart, and his inability of ensuring his continued educational pursuit despite his father's wealth left in the hands of some ungrateful folks, Etimbuk had a battlefield with extreme anxiety. He thought of feeble-minded people who paraded themselves like businessmen but lack the virtues of honesty and discipline.

Such outrageous behaviour shouldn't be heard of in the business, the agreement which they entered into. How can someone in business deny a contract he entered with a very reputable individual like his father, is it because he's dead? He can't believe his ears. Etimbuk spent the whole morning in distressing thoughts and plans for recovery of the money.

Lying, for business executives shouldn't be something that makes them feel important or some kind of image booster. Rather, lying is deception, full of contempt and dishonour, it robs the lair of integrity. He thought seriously of the implications of such an elusive attitude on him and his family in a long term.

He was worrisome of lack of completion of his degree programme in the University on one hand, and his family being perpetually left in the last prong of life on the other. Proffering plausible answers to these nagging and threatening questions around him became the subject of his unknown fear. Etimbuk continued analysing and reflecting on his misery.

Obong Edem, Chief Odotama and Obong Ndifrekke, had been the highest debtors who refused blatantly several appeals to repay their debts. At a point, Etimbuk even threatened them with court actions though Obong Ndifrekke agreed to some forms of negotiation, that still seemed distance miles away. But Chief Odotama and Obong Edem just couldn't budge.

They felt that Etimbuk had no right to ask. All that he had collected so far from sundry sources were meagre as compared to the total recorded debts owed. Therefore, Etimbuk decided to seek alternative ways of solving the problem.

After much consideration, he decided to inform his grandfather, Deacon Mbede of the development to enable him help to mitigating for plausible means towards a solution to the problem for the sake of his educational pursuit.

Deacon Mbede was exceedingly overjoyed to hear that such large sums of money had been eventually found. He was grateful to God but thought perhaps there would be still some undiscovered amounts of money as his son was a very generous man.

"My son, this is great news indeed, something to cheer us up at last" radiance of beaming smiles on his face "but I fear you may have only scratched the surface, I do believe you don't see it all. Many more may still be hidden away somewhere"

"Well grandpa, what we have seen we shall pursue with utmost energy and vigour, even if it means sacrificing twenty per cent for it, we shall gladly track down that course of action"

"Don't worry my son, we are set to discover all Mbede's money come what may in the hands of saboteurs, those who have undermined the cause of this family for so long"

"Can you imagine grandpa, fortune lost in the hands of an ungrateful bunch of idiots, those who want this family to perpetually be an object of mockery and derision?"

Deacon Mbede remained thoughtful how he can fast-track repayment deal for his grandson to further his education especially now that a new school year is about to begin. That thought had been so worrisome, so grave that his attention focused squarely on ways proffering immediate debts recovery.

"Give me today; I'll see you tomorrow morning after reflecting on it this night. My son, we shall see how tinny the masquerade is that the rooster wouldn't growl at the sight of the intruder invading its territory? If you can, sleep tonight we won't rest on our oars until every amount is returned to the Mbede, that I promise you."

"This is indeed a welcome relief, a piece of ground-breaking news that stirs excitement and optimism in us. It's like a piece of diamond hung around your neck; it gives out the radiance of fluorescence light without blemishes. A day of great delight and glory for us, the beginning of an end to your sorrow and wants, my son".

CHAPTER 36

THE FOLLOWING MORNING DEACON MBEDE met with his grandson and presented him with his thought.

"My son, when preparing to eat with a tempter, it's good you have a very long spoon because you don't need to get too close to him else, he gets grip of your hand and harm you. This is a combat; as such we need careful planning in order to overturn their tactics to our advantage.

"It was good you brought the matter to my attention so that we put our heads together and find answers to a threatening problem. We want to make a good decision which entails seeking the right information, and that too demands meeting the right people to share the information with. And until these are thoroughly exhausted, most certainly, no good decision is made.

Moreover, now we are facing economic depression my son. So, with scarcity of money prevalent now in the country, we don't have to waste the little that we have. Is good to find a way of avoiding The Court altogether. I believe there is a way we can do this.

"We are her to make a decision on Mbedes fortune. Getting repayments of all indebtedness, and God willing, none shall be lost."

"I think the Usonnyin would be helpful here. His son is a legal luminary that owns Usoro and Solicitors, a firm of Lawyers that successfully prosecuted the dreaded Nkembas and strip them of that ego and influence with which they enforced on the society in the late 1990s. The firm is trustworthy and capable of handling vicissitudes of life" His grandfather suggested.

Deacon Mbede told his grandson the story of how the community and the environment were subjected to incessant robbery attacks from a group of idle young men who robbed with arms in the late1990s.

They stole with violence resulting in insecurity of lives and properties, permanent disability on the victims, reduction in a state of development, poverty, death and wastage of resources to fight them. This social phenomenon prevailed exerting a profound negative influence on the community. The emotional trauma, financial loss and physical injuries or even death of victims were things most feared in the whole area.

"My son, people were absolutely petrified sleeping in their houses at nights, and if you may, you do so with one eye open. The government used all within its powers including intelligence, technical know-how, sophisticated surveillance equipment and other paraphernalia and gamut of intricacies without success.

Finally, the dreaded Nkembas were nipped at gunpoint and brought to justice. Usoro and

Solicitors successfully handled their prosecution which finally the almighty Nkembas were sent to jail for life due to the level of atrocities they committed.

And since then, the community had been at peace. Usoro and Solicitors became a household name, most respected legal consortium in this part of the world. I do believe this is very reputable company to handle this matter effectively"

"Usoro and Solicitors, that sounds like a good alternative anyway" Etimbuk asseverated. "The son of Usonnyin? How do we get to meet with them?"

"This is exactly what is in my mind right now-getting all debtors to pay off their indebtedness, grandpa.

"This has to be decisive, the reason I get you involved. We can't wait, we have to see Usonnyin and discuss this alternative with him to see how he might be of assistance"

"He is available, we'll see him"

"When can that be possible?"

"Even now"

And with a sense of urgency and great expectations, they left to Usonnyin's palace.

On arrival, they met with Obong Usoro, the son of Usonnyin whom they had hoped his father would talk into their problem. They also met his business partner, Mkpisong Idara. Both were having a good time in the palace with The Usonnyin.

These two were eminent legal luminaries and Fellows-at-Law, who had been in legal practice for many years. Both gentlemen were having fun and a good time over a bottle of wine and some snacks with The Usonnyin.

It was like a prearranged meeting with those expected in attendance. The Usonnyin was sitting comfortably on his royal throne on arrival chatting with his two guests. After the initial pleasantries, Deacon Mbede introduced the subject matter of their mission.

"His majesty, I greet you" as he stood on his feet clearing his throat "I have come to the palace on something very dear that had broken my heart bringing back the memories of the dead to arouse like streams of water in my soul." He stopped to read the faces of his hosts.

The Usonnyin turned around glancing with a degree of sadness at his son and his other guest.

"I am here all for you Deacon Mbede, state whatever your problem is, it may not be too difficult for me to handle. I hope you wouldn't mind my son and his friend listening in as you lay your case"

"Thanks, your Excellency, not at all, in fact, the case may rather be of interest to them".

The duo regarded him with interest as was set to give a rundown of the problem.

"Then go on," The Usonnyin said. Placing his hands on both sides of his throne.

"My lord, you are aware that my son passed aware about two years ago, his death was painful not only to me as a father but the whole of Mkpasang generally. The most grievous part of his death is that two years after, his son here." turned around and looked at his grandson Etimbuk. "Is unable to complete his education beyond secondary school level. That is a shame on my part, isn't it! You may ask.

"I am incapable of supporting him so is his mother who is very ill as we speak. Her health has deteriorated for about a year now, she isn't been out on business and as such, money is difficult to come by. Right now, we're down though not yet out.

"Besides, I met with great difficulties in my grandson's quest to recover his Dad's assets from those still owing him. Thousands of cash his father lent to people out of compassion are languishing in the hands of those who are happy about his death. Efforts to recover these have proved abortive.

"My mission here, therefore, is to plead with you to use your good office, in helping me get Chief Odotama, Obong Ndifrekke amongst others to please help me repay their debts to enable the continual progression of his education."

There was a pause as The Usonnyin turned and looked at his son for a moment, he then beheld his friend giving a sigh and acknowledged the situation as appalling.

"Deacon Mbede, I sympathise with you indeed" Mkpisong Idara responded "It was a huge blow to Mkpasang to lose such a rare gem; a man that stood tall amongst his contemporaries. It was a blow indeed to our pride and goodwill"

"It was indeed" Obong Usoro agreed to nod his head "His son, therefore, cannot be left uneducated. We'll do all that we can to ameliorate the situation"

"Please do, God shall abundantly reward you" Deacon Mbede pleaded.

"It was a sad day in Mkpasang and Idiaimah even the sun in the sky felt the loss and the stars prostrate in their galaxies. A day we shall never forget in a hurry. And as such, we shall continue to remember his good works. One way to keep the memories alive is to ensure that his offspring are properly educated" Mkpisong Idara asserted.

The village head, The Usonnyin, after listening to him expressed deep sympathy, concern and the situation of the problems with the education of his grandson. He urged Etimbuk not to give up or rest on his oars but continue in his struggle and resolve to pursue his dreams vigorously with renewed energy and enthusiasm.

"You've met with them, what did they say?" Obong Usoro demanded to know.

"I have written letters to them on the need for repayment, also met with face-to-face contact. All I get are promises, none is willing to pay. Some of them don't even want to see me, although a few appeared sympathetic. In all, what I have collected so far cannot be said to be substantial compared with the amount owed. Etimbuk gave a report of his effort so far.

"We shall do everything humanly possible to recover the debts, Deacon Mbede by meeting with the debtors and reaching possible resolutions on the issue"

Meanwhile, he felt it ideal that his son, Obong Usoro and his business partner, Mkpisong Idara had a discussion further with the debtors.

"This will provide them with the opportunity to defend themselves and give the reasons why they wouldn't repay"

"I trust you to use your good office in resolving this debacle for me, Your Royal Highness" Etimbuk said.

"We will, my son we will" Reaching out his hand the chief picked his hand fan and started fanning himself then looked at his son who was very interested in the case, the son cleared his throat before speaking.

"Deacon Mbede, the first thing we will do is have a discussion with the debtors to see the best possible option available to you"

"Chief, these are men with high profile companies, their finances are churned in millions every month capable of rebuilding Mkpasang bridge. Their schemes are to frustrate this family, they are unwilling to pay"

Mkpisong Idara opined "I know Chief Odoroma very well though I may not know the rest. Whatever happens my son, we shall have a discussion with them and analyse their financial situation, giving priority to the running cost of their companies.

This shall allow us to determine what exactly is the lower monthly payment to you might be. We will also make sure that payment made to your grandson is affordable for them and fair for Etimbuk"

"I trust you both for efficient negotiation. The son of Dr Mbede cannot just stay without meeting his desire for proper education. Therefore, I urge you both to do all you can to ensure an efficient and robust debt management plan in place enough for continuous servicing of his academic ambition." The Usonnyin charged them.

"We're committed to the recovery of the debt, Papa" Mkpisong Idara opined.

"Your monthly payment" Obong Okon said "from your creditors will be based on what they owe you, this debt management plan continues until they have paid off their debts in full. And if any of them wants to make a onetime payment, then he will be free to do so.

"If they still remain unflinching, should legal actions be taken against them?" Etimbuk asked in fear of debtor's refusal to pay

"My son," Mkpisong Idara said "the problem we have in this country is the inability of the government to formulate acceptable National Debt Management Programme. This is a formular to solving the countless number of problems with debts. Therefore, we are determined to see this becomes law by the National Assembly sooner rather than later. A way of providing countless people with the problem of debt management programme in this country.

"Yes, legal action is not ruled out in event of their failure to comply with our proposals, however, let's have a chat with them first"

The conversation was very robust as they stayed and dissected the issue thoroughly with the professionals themselves. Each party was very satisfied. Deacon Mbede promised to provide the necessary paperwork that would enable the legal team to start work immediately. The legal fee was quite affordable.

"I cannot thank you well enough for your immense help, looking forward to fulfilling days ahead" Etimbuk expressed his appreciation.

"The Usonnyin, this meeting has been a remarkable step forward toward a utopian accomplishment, that dreamland we so much yearn to cuddle with a passion and warmth. Thanks, gentlemen, your encouragement has raised our sense of optimism that was down before we came in, it's much appreciated. Deacon Mbede summarised.

"Do well to send the copies of the names of those including the legal document to the office soonest" The Usonnyin concluded.

"We will," said Deacon Mbede with gladness in his heart.

CHAPTER 37

Ebosom Restaurant was located in Ebosom Street. it stood out as an architectural masterpiece, elegantly adorning the landscape of the southern part of Mkpasang environment. The Taverns was situated on the north eastern side of the community.

Ebosom Restaurant provided an alternative centre of beehive activities for Mkpasang people and within the surroundings. Most of the University staffers cherished this cosy Cafeteria for launch and relaxation.

It belonged to Chief Asanting Ebosom, the father of Enametti, and The Mkpasang of Mkpasang who wielded much power and influence within the rank and file of the community. As the highest traditional title holder in the land, Chief Ebosom earned honour and respect of many. It was here that Enobong, Uyai and Aritie, the threesome, had chosen as the venue to talk about the final phase of their diabolical plots.

I was visiting my friend Enametti, son of Ebosom the evening. We had barely settled down to have a chat when I spotted Enobong's car outside the pavement. I called Enametti's attention to her presence in Ebosom and the need for us to be discreet because if they ever had an inkling that I was there, they'll turn away. Luckily, my car had been parked at Enametti's end away from the public parking space.

Enametti and I were among those who had bought into the vision of 'Mkpasang five' of the community. And we were very sensitive to Esitima's predicament and the negative impacts the rumours had created in the community. The appalling rumours of her involvement with the death of her husband we both were sincerely looking for ways of taming the increasing tides.

Our interest in dousing the flames of the inferno burning off the reputation, not only of Esitima, but Mkpasang at large was incensed by the plight the family was facing. The news of Bassey's demise had been a serious blow to Mkpasang in view of the teaming project that he started in the community.

We had been heartbroken on the news of Bassey's sudden demise then, and Enametti was looking forward with eagerness to step into the huge vacuum created in the community by his death. We carefully shielded ourselves behind the curtain, just by the entrance close to table number 9.

The three friends walked in sounding excited and choosing table 9 to sit. This part of the Restaurant had been less busy at this part of the evening and we were surprised that they had chosen it to sit and enjoy themselves after placing an order for their special meals and drinks. I watched carefully the threesome settled down to digest their nefarious plans at stake properly.

"Enobong, we should be thinking of the right way forward in this case as I am bemused by its outcome of lately." Aritie filled her glass and then continued. "This case has bucked up my mind right from the day of the discovery of that information at The Taverns, Uyai's fracas with her in the boutique; and I am absolutely confused right now what to do"

Enobong had barely settled on the table when the remarks came, and she looked excited that Aritie had finally come to her sense by realising the dangers of what delays on the case would mean.

"Yes, I know, I am happy you finally think out of the box" Enobong replied. "This game we started must be rushed to a conclusion. Delay could mean disaster, so let's crack on to the end today here and now and, do that hastily."

"Esitima, em...that bastard will have to pay for this sooner rather than later."

Aritie's response giving clear evidence from where the malicious propaganda tearing Esitima apart came from. Her answers had awoken our interest from where we sat observing the trio. All along, we were listening to them, although I did suspect they could be the brewer of the rumours, but this was the moment of establishing the real evidence.

We regarded them at first without much concern. But with that comment from Aritie, we were thunderstruck, our hearts hastened to listen attentively with so much interest. Meanwhile, the trio continued in their evil intrigues escalating their conversation and making it much more horrific plot full of evil machinations.

Aritie told Enobong after Esitima stopped going abroad for her wares the boutique became a complete shadow of itself. A-list customers hardly remembered Ndiokkos de Vogue anymore, her workers started leaving gradually because of irregular payment of salaries and entitlements at the end of the month. And her creditors were running down her neck from all directions.

"Can you imagine?" Enobong roared with delight.

"You know what?" She brought down her voice almost to the whisper "She's left almost with nothing, literary Esitima is broke. And the good news above these tales of woes for beloved Esitima is that Enobong, she's not in her best of health right now."

"I never could believe Esitima would be so affected after that encounter. I thought she is a strong lady. It's amazing how she's affected and went down into the abyss of nothingness. I never knew too that that fall she had then was symbolic of the fall coming to her company" Uyai commented.

"Certainly! She has fallen beyond repair. Good for her" Enobong said.

And she stared at her friends with the look of intent; her mind engrossed in thought of Esitima being her rival, prominent competitor in business. She was secretly excited that Ndiokkos de Vogue was closing down after all paving way for her brand, Asurua Galore outfit, to flourish.

Enobong's business had struggled remarkably due to her lack of adequate knowledge and the presence of credible competitors like Ndiokko de Vogue in Mkpasang, and many others fashion houses within and around Mkpasang.

Enobong may have been a Home movie geek, but when it came to business, the slyboots was a complete novice and a flop. The reason she found it hard to build a reputable brand for her failing fashion hub. So, with her involvement in Aritie's atrocious schemes, Enobong saw this as a welcome development to put a whammy on Esitima.

She had always suspected Esitima as her rival whose presence impeded the growth and expansion of Asurua Galore. And now that she had ample opportunity to stifle her domination, she mustn't throw away that chance.

They laughed and mocked Esitima to scorn; expressing such contempt, malediction and ridicule that could only be possible from a stranger's standpoint and not one with whom Aritie shared common values and family affinity.

"Pray that she suffers mental illness with all it takes" was the view of Enobong. "Look" she dropped her voice to near-whisper "if it is possible" turning to check to ensure no one was eavesdropping "she may be eliminated!"

Aritie was startled by such a callous and murderous remark, she knocked on the table which almost tumbled. And she wondered if she had heard Enobong well. Dumbfounded, she guessed at Enobong intently with her heart pounding fast.

"Eliminated ...how do you mean? It's doesn't come to that"

Uyai was also in wonder with such murderous remark by her friend. She brought her palms to cover her mouth looking at Enobong without a word.

"Of course, it does. It's a desperate situation the demands desperate action. Aritie, you live in the same house with her, isn't it?" Enobong asked rhetorically.

"Come on, Enobong, I do not wish her dead" Aritie stooped down in awe. She was flabbergasted to her skin and became quite uncomfortable staring Enobong on the face.

"I..." stammering "can't dabble into shedding blood; I can't stand to see anybody die in pains and besides, I can't just kill anyone, it would be distressing for me to take that route Enobong" She was scared.

"I will rather kill than be killed, murder and live the rest of my life counting gains" continued Enobong "with the pains she has inflicted on the family already, don't you think death would be her deserved destiny after all?"

"Enobong…" Uyai called and had wanted to say something.

"No" Aritie protested "that is not possible; killing her will not solve the problem, instead, plunges us into desperation and utter sense of panic"

She comported herself but was really confused observing Enobong with suspicion look. All remained silence for a while.

"Suppose we are found out and charged with murder, what do we do, Enobong? I think that would be an outrageous route to take; there must be an alternative way to deal with this than wishing her death.

Getting deeper and deeper into murderous schemes is not part of this agenda Enobong"

Aritie looked scared; it took quite sometimes for her to get herself together again. Nevertheless, she continued casting aspersions on Esitima.

"I know she thinks she's a superfluous lady, the only cock to growl in Mkpasang. I know she carries herself high, and not giving regards to anyone else as if she's so important in this part of the world. But that does not warrant killing her, in spite of that, she can be good sometimes" Uyai observed.

Aritie agreed with Uyai on Esitima's wonderful gesture nevertheless but still felt that she didn't deserve to die.

"I know she pays no attention to her family's daily needs. All that matters to her is travelling around the world and changing men at will" Aritie growl. "But that doesn't qualify to kill her.

"I think she should! She's a disgrace to womanhood and marriage. She has caused untold pains to the community of Mkpasang through her concupiscence by killing that nice young man. Nothing could be worse than that. Suppose she's eliminated through poisoning her food. Is that okay?"

Enobong held back to see how Aritie would react to the plan "do you think that is a good idea? I am not asking for any physical attack on her, that will be horrendous, but a subtle, an ethereal scheming that produces the desired result keeping everyone in wanders" she screamed with delight.

"You can't be serious" Uyai responded "So, you mean it, and bent on accomplishing it? How do you guarantee your plans are with hundred per cent success?"

Meanwhile, Aritie at this point was considering the option and weighing it to see if she can convince herself of carrying out the plan.

"I need time to properly digest this strategy. I need to convince myself that I can actually carry a weapon that might harm or kill someone else, Enobong"

"Aritie, there's urgency in this matter, I must repeat myself, a sense of haste is the only option available for us. So, the plan shouldn't wait another day any longer. We've got to put our hands on decks together and finish it immediately, okay"

"Finishing it is one thing, but to finish it well another. I haven't convinced myself that I can actually carry such a dreadful weapon that can kill someone else"

"Alright girls, shall we reconsider the option and be a little bit human?" Uyai counselled "After all, we all have a life to live, we know judgement awaits any ungodly action"

"Uyai, who made you a pastor over this matter. I'll demand you remain silent if you have nothing to say, okay?" Enobong cautioned.

Enobong turned and assessed Aritie carefully with reservation in her heart. She thought Aritie brought her to Ebosom to finish the plan they started months before. However, she still needed to push once more if she must accomplish her aim.

"Aritie, don't mind her, she wants to be a traitor. Certainly, we have a duty to protect ourselves from such deceptive people as Esitima who sees herself as an invincible individual. We have to put a stopgap to her voyage anyhow"

Aritie's mind was not too difficult to will in this case. In fact, she had decided just before Enobong finished her last comment and was about to say so just before she was interrupted by Uyai.

"I'll see what I can do" she responded with a sense of satisfaction.

Joy overwhelmed Enobong and she got up to click her glass with Aritie in appreciation for acceptance to be the hitman for their project.

"Esitima here we come to finish the work started in your boutique, this time not to leave you panicking, but quench that breath which makes you feel important." She turned around addressing Uyai without a word but with the feeling of disgust in her heart for her.

"That's a good one; we need to finish the project without a trace that might cause any suspicion. Do it we must if we are to be free from Esitima's continuous influence and domination over the family and community at large" Enobong pressed her case

"Perhaps we are caught" Uyai pressed on.

"But we're just alone here, no one will call us to account. However, we may need to plan B in place. Robust action to stand whosoever may insinuate into this. A watertight option that will give leeway in case of any insinuation into any mistakes made along the way, you know what I mean?"

"While this is between us Enobong, 'walls do have ears', as they say. You don't know who may be suspecting, are you?" Aritie's mind was pretty unsettled she imagined why her friend should be planning such murderous schemes. She never knew Enobong was so jealous of Esitima and wanted to get her off the scene so that her clothing business can flourish. Had she known this; she wouldn't have involved her in this business in the first place.

Meanwhile, we were eavesdropping attentively to all their evil conversations. Using our mobile phones, we secretly recorded not only the audio but the video evidence of their plots.

As their conversation progressed Enobong unwittingly turned around and beheld Enametti at the corner of the room few meters away from them. She knew he was with someone else but couldn't wait to identify who he was. Their eyes nearly met together as she regarded him with great suspicion maintaining uneasy silence. She remained dumb and mute with apprehension.

Her eyes roved from her friends to the strangers and back, but no clue could be drawn, then Enobong became quite unsettled thinking what information they have already given out, and what the stranger might have heard or not hear. Her mind filled with the thought of the unknown and, worried feverishly that they have been in the wrong place at the wrong time and obviously, for a wrong reason.

Enobong was distraught and stunned with fear running through her spine. She squealed and shivered feverishly then called for a bill making way outside in desperation. And for a moment, she remained in complete silence thinking of the repercussion of their nefarious actions. She was scared should Enametti heard their conversation, how would he react and what would they do? They left the restaurant hurriedly in a state of panic and confusion.

Through the long aisle into the twilight darkness approaching the car park, they hastened down. Enobong with sealed lips and worrying gestures in her eyes pulled Aritie aside.

"Oh my God," Enobong hissed disapprovingly.

"What's the hell you mean that you flew out so suddenly as if you've been chased by an advancing tsunami, l only hope you're not acting another movie scene?"

Aritie snarled staring at her with questionable gestures and aggressive looks in her eyes. Fear ran through Enobong spine, heart bounded heavily.

"Aritie, really like a scene in a thriller, but sadly this is a real-life tragedy. We are in soup, utterly finished Uyai!" she groaned, moaning her heart which pounded rapidly.

"Has any of you seen the blokes sitting on a chair by the corner of the Restaurant pretending to be engaged in conversation?"

Aritie and Uyai thought for a brief moment

"No" they chorused "what about them?"

She turned around checking her back to ensure no other person was listening, while doing so, shook her long curly wig backwards bringing her hands to keep the strands away from her face.

"That's Enametti, the son of Chief Ebosom, I will be surprised if we don't find ourselves in a big kettle of fish this evening."

"You mean Enametti; but I haven't seen him"

"Oh my God, what are you saying, Enametti?" Uyai expressed dismay.

"Exactly, he is sitting by the corner of the room now with another bloke, right behind us."

"And I can't understand the sense of urgency in you about him" Aritie stated without particularly being concerned.

"If that's what it is, we're finished. Do you know he is a friend with Etido?" Uyai observed.

"Never" Aritie was alarmed.

"Well, he may have eavesdropped into our conversation, that's the problem"

"And what makes you think so?"

"I think he might have taken notes of our discussion"

"I don't think so, Enobong it's your mere imagination. Come out of it. I can't imagine Etido sitting with him and giving him encouragement to ensure we're indicted"

"You can bet me for it, I pray he doesn't do anything funny," Enobong said sadly. A rush of uneasiness, nervousness and worry came upon her same was written on her face.

"I am so disturbed, honestly Aritie I am"

"This is what I said earlier on, keep the issue of wishing her dead out of the picture, you said it's okay. Now, what do we do?"

Enobong refused to answer, she was thinking of her role should Enametti decide to put a hook into their mouths with what he may have heard if any of their evidence might affect her in a negative way. She thought seriously about the legal implications of their stupid actions.

"But no one was there when we first entered the restaurant. When did he come in?" Uyai reasoned.

"I don't know" Aritie responded.

"Should this be blown open it will affect me badly."

"Don't ever think of that again, that will be a disaster for me. Where would I hide my face?"

They thought of the possibility of their names being dragged through the mud and therefore lost their acting job, the profession they loved so dearly. Aritie on her part couldn't imagine herself being involved in such a detestable and abominable thing. The very thought was enough to drive her insane.

"There must be a way out of this turmoil, Enobong" Aritie said. "Take it easy things done can never be undone, all we need to do is formulate adequate plan B to allay or mitigate our fear and anxiety, okay?" Aritie consoled her.

Enobong was still ruminating about the situation and blaming herself for their thoughtless action in the first place.

"That's true Aritie, and the reason for that meeting; we better leave this place of shame now"

And quietly they walked into Enobong's car; she drove away without a word. Their minds were polarised deeply by their undoing.

CHAPTER 38

As the three women left the Restaurant, my friend, Enametti began to imagine them being engaged in such horrendous and atrocious discussions. But I wasn't surprised, rather I thanked God for delivering me from the lion's den. I knew Aritie will manifest her true colour after all as she continued relating with Enobong.

"Etido, I am in shock. Is that not the girl you wanted to marry?"

"Marriage is an important institution, no one should ever rush into it blindly hoping for the best. The would-be couple should understand themselves thoroughly before the wedding takes place"

"Boy, you're a lucky chap, otherwise you would have been a victim one day"

"Immediately Aritie turned down my good intentions for her, I knew she wasn't a good woman. Esitima's problems is cooked and served in her own home; and in fact, I suspect, Aritie may have played a part in her uncle's murder."

"Look at three young women who ordinarily would appear innocent of harm. Why were they planning to murder such a high-ranking lady in the community, don't they fear God? I can now see where this bitter jealousy tearing Mkpasang apart came from, I can't believe my eyes. No wonder one's enemy is always a member of his household" Enametti was in total shock.

"We must do something urgently to deter others from walking this same route possibly, kill the rumour spreading in the community."

Both of us had a duty of care to intimate Esitima of the impending doom. And definitely, we had a very tedious task at hand which must be completed urgently if our aim of restoring confidence to Mkpasang must be accomplished.

CHAPTER 39

THE FLUTTER OF JOY WHICH hitherto defined the very personality of Esitima ebbed within a twinkle of an eye. She was left with pronounced hopelessness, emptiness, and despair. The great Esitima, bruised with guilt, had a rethink of herself. She recalled life and times past when she would refuse to heed repeated calls to slow down on her frequent foreign trips. She made a mental twist with a strong wish that she could turn the hand of the clock backwards, now everything was in shambles; the wall had stubbornly refused to move.

Yes, Esitima had definitely bitten more than what she could chew of life's bitter pills; now her mind was gripped with disgust and wanton drip. As things were working seriously against her now, she must rethink her way through before losing self-worth and respect the more.

She must either float graciously or sink woefully even shamefully, into the oblivion-bottomless pit of this precipice-the infamous tempest raging across, about to disintegrate her empire.

Esitima could recall her frequent exciting flying trips abroad, from Europe to America, Asia and Australia on business. The five continents of the world were her marketplaces, particularly Europe which she saw as a second home. Not to mention Africa whose astute knowledge was impeccable, incomparable with those of the World Affairs Correspondent of the British Broadcasting Corporation or Voice of America.

Indeed, her passion for travel was breath taking. Esitima could have her breakfast in Europe, book for lunch in Africa while preparing to take a nap on her flight en-route America, Asia or Australia the next day for dinner. She was fascinatingly an adroit traveller.

She had dined and wined in most of the world's renowned 5-star hotels that she treasured their memories at heart with engaging passion. Is it in Dubai, London, China, America or France? Just mention and Esitima would delightfully give a graphic description of captivating features of such places to the delight of many.

And each place was a different exciting experience altogether for her. Yet, she remained loyal and faithful to the bond of their marital vows.

It was this obsession with travel that almost led to the existence of a huge crack on the wall of their marriage relationship a couple of years earlier. First, it sounded like a mere remark, but as time ticked past, became uncomfortable, and then serious concerns were raised by her husband needing urgent attention.

"Ufan, I am worried about these frequent travels. We need to bring our children up in a way that ensures all-round development" Bassey had expressed his concerns.

"Yeah, I know, but are they complaining of neglect in anywhere. I've always made sure I leave them with enough cash at all times."

She portrayed her complete ignorance in skills of childcare.

"You can't be serious. I know you know that parenting is a huge responsibility that goes beyond what money can buy." Bassey was very worried.

Esitima ignored worrying signs on his face and ranted with unguarded utterance.

"But you know as well as I do that without money there is no comfortable home. If we must meet the challenges of bringing up children in the modern world, and running a meaningful home, then, we have to make enough money to pay for things that matter for us and the children. And we can't possibly do that on a lecturer's take-home pay. Can we, Kpan Eka?"

Bassey had appeared quite calm; he overlooked her for a second and tried to play the tension down in his heart as much as he could.

"While I do seriously appreciate your enormous contributions towards the upkeep of this family," response that he gave with much pain in his heart, "that mustn't be sacrificed on the altar of my children' all-round growth and development. Giving them proper parental care is not just about money, spending quality time with them is what counts the most. And for me, that shouldn't be compromised"

"Kpan Eka" Esitima's arrogance grew profoundly "hope you'll not expect me to still dangle them on my knees to sing them to sleep. They are 11 years and 8 years old and even the 6-year-old is comfortable with Aritie. I've tried my very best possible to give them all I've got, and I am sure Aritie is always taking very good care of them while being away." Esitima retorted.

Bassey took a mental examination of his wife's lack of adequate motherhood affection and felt sympathy for her regrettably.

"There's one thing you must know, Ufan, you do not have to monetise everything in life. Although money may give you enormous joy, comfort and exceeding happiness, that cannot, however, be compared with the amount of parental love and affection"

Bassey sat on the kitchen stool nearer while trying to work out her extreme ignorance in home keeping principles. And Esitima regarded him cautiously while still continuing with what she was busy with at hand.

"Tell me." Bassey was aggrieved "where is emotional resilience, hugs, kisses and expressive declarations of love you should give to these kids on a regular basis. Would those be purchased at Dubai stores, or must you pay monetary value for this delicate motherly warmth and affections? Could those mandatory values be bought at London high street stores? That to me is priceless, and I sincerely insist you reconsider your stance in nurturance of these precious little kids"

Esitima was sober; she dropped everything she had to do and regarded him with seductive gesture in her eyes. She obviously thought that her husband may perhaps misconstrue her frequent travel engagement for unfaithfulness. Hence, she was worried despite her promises to him; Bassey wouldn't take her seriously. And with reassuring gestures in her eyes, she dropped everything and pulled him towards herself for a passionate embrace.

Bassey slowly stood to his feet drawing her to himself. Once again Esitima reiterated her unwavering loyalty to the bond of their marital union.

"Don't worry, Kpan Eka," she said "I am still that Ufan you can always count on me. Come rain or shine, Esitima remains unshakeable, unassailably fortified, untouchable bonded, trusted and dependable. You can count on me always."

After a blissful romance, Bassey agreed he had found in her a virtuous woman of integrity.

Events building up to her inauspicious travel were quite similar. Frequently her overseas travels would always raise some levels of anxiety in her husband and the family. And most often, Bassey wouldn't be happy during such periods, but managed not to interfere but endure as much as possible for the sake of peace.

"For how long this time?" Bassey asked his wife in the lounge, as he slumped into upholstery on his return home from a very busy day in office. Esitima took a look at him and turned to unbutton his shirt after he pulled off his jacket

"One week at most" she replied with a smile and welcome kiss"

"Mmmh" Bassey groaned holding his face in disapproval, then got up into his bedroom.
"Just that?"
"Just that" Bassey responded grudgingly.

Esitima was uncomfortable; she wasn't at ease with the situation hence quickly rushed in to ease his mind before it escalated into a full-blown family tussle which might have a serious negative impact not only on her planned trip but family life and marriage.

"Kpan Eka, it seems you don't believe me. We have gone through many times, I know you'll be missing me greatly, but is only one week please"

"That's okay" he responded not particularly interested.

"I have to arrange a few things for my travel tomorrow, please. And this might perhaps be the last trip in a long while" Esitima prophetic utterance brought to conclusion her aged long undaunted marital loyalty.

It was this particular trip abroad that ended the long years of bliss and harmony that characterised their union. But for this shopping trip for her celebrated 45th birthday anniversary, things wouldn't be the way they were. It had turned her into a celebrated paramour, unfortunately.

If she had listened to her husband's frequent concerns or shared her birthday tips with him, perhaps her long years of marital faithfulness, and commitment to preserving her virginity until marriage, would still remain novelty and honourable. But now that single impulsive and stupid act had turned the table against her, Esitima was devastated.

CHAPTER 40

'WHY IS LIFELIKE THIS; THOSE who flirt around, those who make it a hobby of jumping from one man to another even in marriage, still preserved and enjoy the privacy and sanctity of their marriage and they're happy.

"But people like me," she reasoned, "who made unflinching sacrifices to remain faithful have received the greatest dose of embarrassment. Why, why and why?" She was hysterical.

"Esitima, I know you're a very honest person. The problem with sincere people is that they do not know how to keep a secret. Once they commit a sin they rush to the priest. Honestly, this might perhaps be the reason why you are where you are today"

She calmed down reflecting on that prompting carefully. And busted suddenly into an audible voice like she was talking to herself.

"Oh yes o, I can see" nodding her head in dismay. Eh-eh! ...Had I kept the Vegas ordeal to myself without telling anyone, not even Joyce, perhaps I wouldn't have been so disgraced, and perhaps my marriage and family would have been saved from these contemptuous embarrassments"

She laid the blame of the rumour at Joyce's feet and wandered when Joyce did turn a squealer. With enormous confidence reposed on her, why would she do such an unspeakable thing? If indeed is true that she is the reason for her current pain, it's absolutely unfortunate and disgusting. Such betrayal of trust wouldn't be forgiven. Esitima continued in her depressive symptoms remaining indoors without going to her shop.

There was evidence of self-care deficit, low mood, hopelessness, and feeling of tearfulness. She also experienced profound guilt especially that of Las Vegas ordeal. And found it difficult to make a decision including going out to her boutique with complete loss of interest in life, so she remained indoors.

As Esitima continued brooding in her shame, her wares and customers dwindled. Children finances reduced drastically until Etimbuk found it almost impossible to continue with his Education or mingle with friends as before. Even though with Patrick, life went on as usual. No worries indeed as he was less concern with education or any happening around him. And Uduak, continued on her concerns as a child. She spent most of her time with her auntie, Aritie either at home or at work.

Esitima was still brooding in her shame in her room when there was a hard knock on the door. She refused to stand to open the door or answer the caller. She had resolved in her mind to spend another day indoor as she had clung to it tenaciously with a convincing resolution in her heart to stay in or stay out forever. That meant, if the worse comes, Esitima had decided to end it all and leave this unfriendly world with all its unfair treatments.

"Look mummy, if you don't open this door, I'll tear it down in shreds" Etimbuk ordered her outside the door.

And she suddenly became alert with fear.

"Hang on, Etimbuk. I am coming" Then came a voice from within.

"Better" Etimbuk said.

Esitima quickly dried up her eyes. She put on her gown and flips the latch, turned the key and opened the door.

"Come in"

She invited her son who has just come in from school after being away for two weeks of study tours.

Etimbuk sluggishly moved into the room and was about to sit down on a chair when he noticed the room was so unkempt. Everything was out of order and scattered all over the room. From all indication, broom hadn't touched it for weeks when he was away.

The stench of the unpleasant odour of decayed food was emanating from the corner of the room, and flies gathered in their numbers to feast on them. Etimbuk hurriedly left the room only to re-emerge again with a bundle of broom in his hand.

"Mummy what are these" pointing to nothing in particular. "You mean you could stay in this stinky environment? I am surprised, what's the matter with you. Meaning you probably has been indoors for two weeks now while I have been away? Something is definitely wrong, mummy. What about UD, where is she?" He ended almost at the verge of tears.

His mother didn't answer a word but looked at him silently.

"Mum, I am asking about UD, where is she"

"She's with your aunt. I've not seen them for ages, gone away"

"Gone away where?"

"Far"

She was back in herself once again.

Etimbuk spent time meticulously sweeping through all rooms including all nooks and crannies and dusting everywhere then keeping them in good order as much as he could.

"Thanks, my son I really appreciate this." She spoke.

"You are welcome" he responded.

"Etimbuk, I am not very well the reason I decide to remain indoors."

"You are not well; you have refused to take the medication prescribed for you. Could leave your room so unkempt? Mummy, I know you to be a lover of decency; I am so worried anyway, have you been to see a doctor again?"

"No"

"Why, did Joyce come to see you?"

"I don't need the company of anyone, I am fine"

"Not even Joyce Mummy?" Etimbuk was aghast! He turned around looking at her with dismay.

"What has she done?

Esitima had considered Etimbuk still a minor to share in the adult world and wouldn't bring herself down to the level of discussing anything relating to Joyce with Etimbuk, hence remained silent.

"Mummy, it baffles me that things are this way in this family. I am surprised once revered family in this community is sinking so fast so deep into the abyss of nothingness. From the sudden death of the family head to a shameful scandal, I wonder what the future holds for us?"

At the mention of the word scandal Esitima was startled in her heart but carefully shielded that fear from her son. This had been her real fear. It was her intention never to drag him into this problem.

'He is too young to share in this trouble' She had reasoned. Although, Esitima was aware Etimbuk was conversant with the scandal as it had become current news in Mkpasang and the environs for months now, Esitima didn't need to be reminded of this malady which had bogged up her mind severely.

She had no need of a reminder especially from close relatives, the reason at the mention of the word 'scandal' she was intimidated and suffered post-traumatic shock.

Esitima continuous sobbing, groaning and moaning in the room indicated her vulnerability to the whole saga. For over a year, she stayed home scarcely got to her shop, or travel on a business trip anymore.

"Well, mum I know your sickness is purely psychological, doesn't need a consultation with a physician, but a psychologist, and maybe a psychiatrist. In any case, I might be of help mum"

Esitima was awakened to the reality of the situation. Her mind made a mental twist, giving enough reason to ponder.

"Etimbuk, I've told you there's nothing to worry about. The present problem is simply not too big for me to handle. It's one of those moments when you're left alone by loved ones helpless in solving those minutest problems of life."

"Mummy I am here for you. I can do anything for you in helping. If there is what I should do to help you in any way, I will. If I don't do, who else will mummy?"

"Thanks, my son, I appreciate your concern, but I think…" She held back and remained silent for a while, Etimbuk observed her gesture carefully. After a while he questioned.

"You think what?

"Never mind" she finished up staring at her son with the look of concern in her eyes. She was thinking of how innocent he was, so caring with a sense of compassion in him.

"Well, mum maybe you still consider this your son a little baby of yesterday, inexperienced and incapable of making any meaningful contribution into the adult world. Make no mistakes mum; my limited knowledge could be just enough to help get you out of the present whatever-it-is."

"Really?"

"Of course, Mummy"

She was so surprised Etimbuk had grown up and could be reasonable. Much more so, bold enough to engage in what she thought a meaningful conversation with her.

"Thanks, my son. I never knew you could be such a good helper. Maybe we shall talk about this later, but for now, let me have a bath and after getting something into my stomach first then, the dialogue."

At the mention of food, Etimbuk was so excited and saw the situation a welcoming one. He was profoundly delighted to hear his mother talked about food

"In that case" he asseverated "I'll prepare something for you to eat mum."

"Thanks, that's so kind of you my son."

"You're welcome" Etimbuk left the room rushing into the kitchen to see what he could put together as lunch for both of them. But in his mind, he was worried about her sister, Uduak.

CHAPTER 41

Family house of late Bassey Mbede was a duplex property. It's comprised of a massive lounge with 36 inches Television Set on a golden stand situated in one corner of the well-furnished property. Two sets of identical upholsteries spread across the huge lounge, with a giant size wedding portrait superimposed on top of a golden cabinet comfortably situated in the room.

The portrait appeared so real at first sight but on close view, one would adjudge the golden coloured edifice to be a delicate artistry masterpiece of real royalty taste only known with Mbede in this part of the world for decades. In general term, it was a tastily furnished and cosy home; with superb Elizabethan oaks, panel-to-size Mahogany woods of Tropical African forest spread across the wall casting a clinquant glistering vault as one opened into the massive lounge. A large dinner apartment is enough to seat ten guests at a time.

Other combinations and varieties of harmonic wood carvings, pottery; graphics, ceramics and collage by world-renowned artists, took strategic positions of importance in the room. These decorations clearly depicted great artistic taste which for nearly three decades, defined Esitima as the enigma of beauty in a class of her own.

"I always owe the artistic mastery of my home to the delicate skills and ingenuity of my dear wife" Professor Mbede once joked with a guest who was so fascinated by the mastery furnishing of his home.

"This is simply amazing and the combination of various designs so breath-taking; Prof. with this, home is a resort that you'll always long for" the visitor had said.

So, every time any visitors had come into the home of Mbede, he would leave with the impression of a loving wife-the absolute respect for Esitima's artistry essence and an enormous sense of beauty which was simply impeccable.

The balcony, a private sit-out, was located at the top floor of the property enough to host six guests at a time. A small bar sat at the left-wing of the well laid out property, with Italian size upholstery taking their strategic places of importance in the well-laid edifice.

It is here that the Mbedes usually socialise at mealtimes and other family engagements.

The most distinguishing feature about this balcony is that it is located at the back of the property and completely unobtrusive. Because of how the balcony is designed, any first-time visitor to the home would be unaware of the existence of such a huge structure.

Etimbuk was so concerned about his mother's health and while he was preparing the renaissance meal, he thought of taking her to the hospital again to see a doctor. He will try to persuade her to go with him immediately and perhaps Joyce can also be convinced to come along with them.

Contacting her again to accompany them on the trip appeared a good idea but first; let them finish with the meal.

He finished cooking the food and took it to the balcony. His intention here was to give her a treat. He wished to help her recapture that glorious past when all of them would often come together to relish at ease in social interaction.

For him, this had been one of the fundamental threads that solidly knitted the bond of unity of the family members. He was trying to see if this could recapture her past and bring her back to normalcy.

"I've finished your favourite Mum, come let's eat together, please" Etimbuk spoke outside his mum's door while making his way briskly across the lounge into the balcony. He waited in the balcony for a couple of minutes without any answer. He continued to wait patiently for her mother to emerge from her room for this historic renascence meal. But to his surprise, nothing came out of it.

"Mum, I'm still waiting, hurry up please the food will go cold"

There was still no answer, no movement and everywhere was dead still. Etimbuk listened without hearing, looked but couldn't see anything. The whole vicinity was dead still-no movement of any kind.

"Perhaps she is still in the bath," he thought. Etimbuk exercised patience a bit more. As time went pass, he became agitated, jittery, and uneasy. A sudden weird fear came over him. Stealthily, he moved to the door that was kept ajar, tapped and listened, and yet no sound came through!

With trembling fear, Etimbuk pushed the door open and walked into the room. Alas! Esitima was nowhere to be found. But on top of the table was a hurriedly scribbled note with just a single sentence on it:

"I am sorry to leave this wicked world with all its sorrows"

"What's the meaning of this?" he questioned throwing back the paper on the table. The young man searched everywhere in the building including the garage downstairs and under the staircase, but she was nowhere to be found.

"What's happening here; oh my God, is this a James Bond movie with all intrigues built-in, could it be true?" Etimbuk was agitated, lacking in a clear and precise idea of what to do.

While he was preparing the meal, his mother summed up courage and left the building unnoticed. Her purpose was to ensure that she did inconceivable-commit suicide.

"Why should there be this pronounced gang up against them just in the society; no one is infallible, therefore no matter how good you're, you'll still make mistakes. And when there is no forgiveness, then something terrible is wrong.

Why should those who are trying fervently hard to be good be punished severely in a little mistake they make, while the very bad-those the society know as evil, are given the red-carpet treatment, why and why?" She moaned.

During her self-imprisonment, Esitima was severely depressed losing a sense of decency. She refused to go back to the hospital after the last visit which she considered as inappropriate and never liked. Psychologist's prescriptions did very little to lift her mood.

Esitima was brooding through and licking the traumatic wounds of her flashbacks into her guiltiness. When she remembered her glorious youth, the happiness of preserving her virginity until marriage; she increasingly wished to be dead at every passing moment.

She recalled her faithfulness in marriage the past years despite her frequent travel engagements, and how men have constantly harassed her severally.

Above all, when Esitima reflected on the wrong impressions of promiscuity people always made of her because of the nature of her business, she just couldn't hold back her emotion.

Outrageous rumours and scandal going around in the community had become her greatest worry which broke her nerves down; indeed, she was in a serious state of crisis.

Going to The Taverns on that fateful day was just a normal way to unwind as a couple, nothing extraordinary about it. The unfolded event was quite unfortunate following the recounting of her ordeal at Las Vegas; she still managed to put up a brave face.

'Could that be the real crux of the matter?' she thought carefully. "But that should not be used against me as if I deliberately caused the death of my husband."

Esitima moaned, she muffled her mouth inarticulately.

Continuous drinking of alcohol and strong wine as a new hobby further deepened her fragile state of mind. But little did she know that 'anyone who drinks to drown the problems of life wakes up to swim along with them.'

Alcohol had reduced the great Esitima to a mere goof and she cannot stop but continued to booze. She experienced delusional ideation, hallucinations and eminent psychotic symptoms in a higher scale.

Constant flashbacks into that atrocious and shameful act at Las Vegas and that insult from Uyai in her office had left her with a perpetual bleeding heart. The rumours going around in the community of her being the person that actually killed her husband which she suspected Joyce may perhaps be the person peddling it was the greatest cause of her worries.

The impulsive nature of Esitima made her so intractably depressed leading to her condition becoming untreatable, subsequently, her world come to a sudden end. Everything about her had been in disarray with emotions, feelings and thoughts directed toward taking the easy way out. Anxiety, agitation and fear gripped her world with dead wish lurking around her constantly.

She had no nerve to contain the psychological taunts, disappointments, frustrations, and a tremendous sense of guilt enveloping her world. Her coping mechanism, the only psychological aid left for her had gone haywire.

In her mind, Esitima had programmed taking the next available exit out. And that she must do, do it as quickly as possible if she indeed must save herself from imminent embarrassment and shame.

She wouldn't afford to put any more distance between her suicidal ideation and the real act itself. Now is the right time to execute that monstrous judgement. No more delays. If she has to wait, perhaps Etimbuk would talk her out of her ever-pressing wish, and she might be the loser.

"Go on quickly there's no procrastination; go on baby you don't have any more time to waste! No more delays. It would be cowardice to do otherwise. Act now and act quickly!"

Her sinking mind kept urging her onto this highway to dooms. A course to bring to a final stage in her well-envisaged game plan.

When Etimbuk offered to cook instead of her, Esitima saw that offer as a veritable roadmap to her outrageous plan-an opportunity she mustn't allow to slip away. It spurred her courage towards taking up the weapon of death against her own life!

"No, I can't stand to look him on the face; he is too young for me to start explaining anything. Better to die than live to the account of anything to him!" Esitima had said

"Look, it's obligatory that parents be open and honest to discuss issues of life with their children, except on matters of unfaithfulness which they may find very hard to dabble into." Esitima once told her friend Joyce.

"But you know, Ima, once that mutual bond is broken, marital secrecy becomes open to all, no more privacy seal guarding the door" Joyce had replied.

And for Joyce deceitfulness and unfaithfulness are the threats that easily open the marital door so attacks. In her case, fighting tooth and nail to ensure security is the only remedy. Always she had no doubt her friend is above board in this regard.

"That's true, and the reason I fight hard to keep my door securely sealed-impenetrable and sacred, in spite of what otherwise impression people make of me" Esitima had told Joyce.

"I trust you my queen, people of your stock are hard to find. And your husband is exceptionally lucky to have you for himself."

Joyce had finished as they rose to their feet at the end of their outing at a famous The Taverns.

"Well, we return all glory to God the creator." Esitima summarised

. Surreptitiously, Esitima sneaked out of the compound in a Toyota Jeep her husband bought just before his sudden illness and eventual death. Like James Bond, impetuously, she wrecked the vehicle into the rushing waters of Ubenefa, a massive river that separated Mkpasang from Ubenefa village.

This is the River from where the village of Ubenefa derives its name. Instantly, the vehicle sank deep down and disappeared from sight.

CHAPTER 42

UBENEFA RIVER WAS A BODY of water covering a considerable distance. It runs from Obuatuman district cutting across Mkpasang and emptying directly into the Atlantic Ocean at the easternmost part of the Bight of Biafra. Ubenefa River goes for a distance of approximately 28 kilometres in length, and its depth deepens more as the river approached the ocean. With Ubenefa taking the deepest depth as it bounded directly with the sea.

Across Ubenefa River was an aged-long centenarian bridge. An archaic and old-fashioned architectural structure that hung in the air like a trap set up to catch some bush rats as one approached the river from its descending hills.

At the point of insertion, the ground had so much given way making it almost impossible and impassable to drive across the bridge even with extreme caution. In fact, it was extremely risky, and the suicide mission to use this route for any journey with a vehicle. Even those on foot still dreaded the idea of going through attenuated Ubenefa Bridge.

Although driving through Ubenefa community would be the shortest route into the city, but because of the risk of using Ubenefa Bridge, many preferred going extra mile for the sake of the safety of their lives and vehicles. And as the years passed by, it further told the extent of negligence the community had suffered from succeeding governments in Idiaimah.

Over the years, water had gone deep beyond the edge of the bridge, bye-passing the supporting pillars, etching and swaying significantly through into the banks. Major access road through the village was almost submerged into parts of the muddy surrounding which became impassable as a result.

On each side of the river too, the muddy water was about 15 meters in depth. Considerable parts of its banks were overgrown with seaweeds that created aerie scenery without clear demarcation of the edge of the bridge.

This was compounded by clear lack of access routes through the bridge which made it difficult to use it either with vehicle or just walking across the bridge on foot.

The myths of the mermaid, UBENEFA, purported to live in the river to protect the village from any invasion by enemies, had confounded the villagers with profound negative influence on the use of the bridge.

This god was venerated by the people of the land and given supreme importance by the community. Annual sacrifices were brought to seek her continual communal protection.

Ubenefa village was a warring community and praised for her gallantry, courage, and heroic bravery by surrounding villages around. Continued veneration, devotion and fidelity to

UBENEFA blinded the people so that they wouldn't dare to extract numerous aquatic resources that abounded in their number in the river. This superstition was so strong among the people.

Persistence requests over the years by the community for Idiaimah Government to rebuild the bridge had fallen on deaf ears. But politicians would come during the campaign period to deceive people with their sugar-coated tongues. And of recent, the community had lost so much faith and confidence in the Government of the day to help.

This had been one of the many projects in and around Mkpasang that Bassey undertook upon himself to convince the Government to embark upon. Arrangements had started, and signs of commencement were seen just weeks before his sudden demise. There were heaps of sand and gravel around the vicinity and construction work was expected to commence soon before he took ill.

Esitima capitalised on this negligence by the government to execute her well-rehearsed monstrous game plan. She had used this route lately and had a thorough knowledge of the Achilles feet of her mission. Particularly on the day of her shameful meeting with Uyai, her initial intention was to do it right away but was only served by sheer happenstance.

Many dignitaries were around the river, they came for inspection for possible commencement of the project. So, this stalled her plan. On this fateful evening, therefore, approaching the river from the narrow portion which hardly received anybody by day, Esitima swerved instantly off the road plunging the vehicle directly into the depth of the deep. And almost instantaneously, it sang down into the muddy waters with the rushing current pushing it through the Bight of Biafra, a few metres away.

The banging noise echoed and re-echoed sending several decibels of sound miles away from the vicinity of the river and beyond. These drew the attention of many to the scene for first-hand information.

"Oh, no it cannot be true!" A man on top of the palm tree in the creeks who had recognised the black jeep as that of the late Dr Mbede before it plunged into the sea, screamed and quickly rushed down to see what had happened.

"Oh Esitima, our dear Esitima! The bone and soul of Mkpasang is gone" he was distressed "Disaster strikes the very heart of her who always brings us joy"

Etim was aghast as he stood at the sight of the vanishing vehicle extremely astonished. That echoing and re-echoing sound brought many into the river who came to see things for themselves. There were great mourning and outrageous expression of tears that flowed effortlessly.

CHAPTER 43

WE HAD A DUTY OF care to alert Esitima as those privileged to have first-hand and horrific information about her death. We were terrified therefore hurriedly set out to her compound in order to intimate her of the impending danger to her dear life. But unfortunately, before we arrived, Esitima had taken the plunge to her death, she left the compound for the last time and never to return.

We met Etimbuk alone in the compound very anxious and scared. He was shouting with the suicide note in his hand. Devastated! Etimbuk seemed like an actor in a thrilling movie scene, and yet it was a true-life story!

"What's the matter?" Enametti asked in desperation, we were really confused.

Etimbuk couldn't hear although he had seen us even before we pulled the car to a stop. We had to physically hold Etimbuk in hands before he could get a sense of what was going on.

"Come on boy, are you alright?" Enametti said.

"I am finished, my world has come to a sudden end" He had shown us the note, we took a quick look at it asking again.

"Is your mother alright, Etimbuk?" We held him in his hands, squatting in front. "Where's she, we came to see her on a very important issue" Etimbuk was devastated. He continued shouting, writhing and squirming around.

"Come on boy, pull yourself together. Talk to us… we're your friends. Where are mummy and your sibling?" We insisted.

"My mother was at home; I was cooking in the kitchen only to come out and find this crab" He showed us the not again "on the table in her room. Meaning her life is in danger"

"Ooh my God" we looked at ourselves, "we need to do something fast else, she might be in serious danger, Enametti"

We couldn't hold our tears but held Etimbuk tightly consoling him as friends and those present who can offer some consolation and hope in a depressing time of extreme anguish.

"We had only come to the compound to alert Esitima of an imminent threat to her life but regrettably, we couldn't be early enough to stop her from taking her own life" Enametti lamented.

Although death was the inevitable route for all, something that we all can't avoid, Esitima's cup and the mission were indisputably full to the brim. The reason while it was still being plotted at Ebosom Restaurant, it was happening in real life in her own house.

Hurriedly, we left the compound with Etimbuk in the car we came with. And as we drove along, we came to a group of people streaming toward Ubenefa village. We joined the trail of these spectators and mourners hurrying to and from Ubenefa and managed to keep Etimbuk out of danger as much as we could.

Etimbuk couldn't hold the loss. He was completely devastated out of form. For him, he was at the end of his world. What he was praying for initially; he was seeing the naked reality, hard to believe.

"Oh my God, my world is in shamble. What sort of darkness in the afternoon? God, I am finished"

He sat down quietly shrugging his shoulder with indifference and staring into the air.

"Could this be possibly true?" Etimbuk contemplated, "Two years ago I mourned for my father, and look at me now for yet another tear for my mother. When shall my sorrow come to an end? What have I done to deserve this o o"

He burst out into vent of hysterical frenzy. Enametti got him home into their compound where many sympathizers were already gathered, and Joyce was one of them with tears in her eyes. She quickly rushed down to embrace Etimbuk pressing him to her bosom with entwined brokenness.

Etimbuk had spent up emotion released abruptly with his eyes full of tears that poured out freely. He remained there weeping, shouting and screaming. To him, it seemed no end in sight. And he could hardly be consoled.

Attempting to run away, an elderly man intoned from a close distance.

"Hold that boy" It took reinforcement of three able-bodied men to restrain Etimbuk.

"While none of us can change the past, let us with all certainty resolved to manage the future at our hands. This is a devastating blow to Mkpasang"

"A big rain has fallen in Mkpasang" another man intoned from the crowd that gathered in the compound "we need no umbrellas to shield us away from this thunderstorm but ever-increasing love and unity of mind in the face of this horrible weather"

There was confusion in Mkpasang once more, and many were running helter-skelter in all directions. Some people hurriedly got to the Mbede residence to confirm the breaking news and others to the river to see things for themselves while jet some groups headed to the boutique. There was a real sense of pandemonium in the whole of the community.

Residents gathered in groups for jet another tongue-wagging. Real confusion has broken off and many were astounded. Etimbuk was extremely saddened and aggrieved so were the kith and kin, and indeed the whole of Mkpasang community.

"Grief is a very perplexing process that makes the logical expression of ideas difficult to the grieving person" A woman intoned from the crowd of mourners who gathered outside the compound.

"This grieve, our grieves was least unexpected in Mkpasang again, no! not this time…"

"Mmm, what do we do when it has happened? As it appears none of us can prevent it. Only God knows what the terrible thing means" another woman asseverated.

Pain and anguish that accompanied this second death in two years increased Etimbuk stress level considerably. He was overwhelmed with tiredness and exhaustion as he continued to put himself in a great amount of sorrow, fatigue, sleep difficulty and outright anxiety.

Certainly, this grieving moment for the family had been a time of tremendous heartbreak and others were handy to give them much needed support and comfort.

A time everyone rallied around with warmth and affection to ease their minds. The atmosphere of understanding and affection were created to ease their thoughts, fears and emotions. And none attempted to stifle the expression of tears which flowed easily unrestricted.

Doing otherwise would have hindered the healing process that tears and anger brought to the children in the long run.

Bassey's mother, strolled in with her head covered in her wrapper quite unrecognisable only when she collapsed at the veranda near the verge of the eave sobbing, did some elderly women noticed and quickly rushed down to her rescue. Everyone pitied her for the loss so great to bear.

The death of Esitima grieved and anguished Mkpasang community paralysing every community engagement. Few individuals had expressed genuineness of the situation while the majority evaluated it in the light of the rumours and jet; others were very confused asking many unanswered questions why and how it should be Mbede again.

Life was in a standstill for weeks in Mkpasang.

Everyone mourned the loss in their unique ways expressing anger, some denials while others confusion as to why this calamity continued to berserk this family repeatedly. Indeed, the community of Mkpasang was prostrate with one heart in a mourning mood.

Dark night dominated Mkpasang. Trepidation and anguish like never before made everyone sorrowful. Some were genuinely expressing their deep sympathy and condolences for the family that had affected the community positively for decades.

Patrick arrived and alighted from his vehicle; he looked drained, he was very surprised to witness so many people in a mourning mood and crying in their compound.

"What's happening here?" he questioned.

None gave him any serious attention. He moved into the house-to his mother's bedroom quickly and to his greatest amazement, some women were there soaked in tears, and some holding their faces to the ground. He had then realised something terrible thing had happened.

Patrick saw Joyce her mother's friend sitting in the corner of the room, falling down in front of her, he held her wailing loudly.

"Auntie Joyce what has happened, where is mummy. Oh my God I am finished o oh"

The intensity of the sad news made Patrick rushed out with outbursts of tears, ranting and shouting with tears and tearing his clothing apart while running around the compound. He was completely devastated losing the sense of direction.

His world had suddenly come to an end. Patrick could only earn the attention of very few sympathizers around who helped to console him.

"A truant child sleeps in his mother's house only when unwell" a man intoned from the crowd. "This is perhaps the only thing that will teach him some lessons about life" he murmured.

And some were there staring at him with bewilderment and asking many unanswered questions.

"Look at this one, what is he shouting, so he could be humble?" Many had thought.

Some were quite unsure of the reaction on getting close to a boy with an enormous sense of pride, so they stay aloof.

"Sometimes it takes heartbreak and disappointment to attend maturity in life. However, truancy is the brokenness of youth which might be amended by the brokenness of hearts as we grow up meeting terrible situations such as the death of a loved one" Etebong intoned.

"See how he is completely turned apart losing a sense of what had happened. He was quite sure of his mother's illness wouldn't lead to death, but for her to commit suicide was a horrific tragedy, a thing many were still trying to comprehend" his friend Mfon articulated.

"It horrific, such an act was strange to this part of the world, no one had ever died this way before in our recent memory" Eteobong responded.

Patrick was so heartbroken with grief that he broke loose of those who were trying to restrain him doing something quite bizarre-he almost want naked. The pain and chaotic emotions that accompany the death of his mother was so great that Patrick tore everything on him in shreds wriggling and running around shouting about in the compound.

Feeling of anger, emptiness, despair and sadness were quite sickening becoming unbearable for Patrick as he continued imagining the depth of his loss.

After several hours of crying and shouting, Patrick appeared very drenched with emotional turmoil. He suddenly woke up to find himself standing alone and, he had to learn to grow up and leave that childish behaviour, those puerile attitudes that rule his life; time to leave them behind was up.

Etimbuk and Patrick were nevertheless supported, encouraged and comforted by friends and family members during the duration of their grief. And Uduak was their major concern, she had been taken care of by their grandparents.

Able-bodied young men, expert swimmers were launched to undergo a search for Esitima's remains. The group started streaming from every angle of the river tributaries in canoes spreading tentacles as far as Mbembe River, about twelve kilometres away. And for three days running, they traversed the length and breadth of the massive body of water without success.

Finally, the mangled body of great Esitima was discovered in Itonuneke, six kilometres away from Mkpasang. She was still embedded in the car with which she had travelled. And as custom demanded; she mustn't be brought out to the open, she was buried at the bank where she was discovered.

The calamity that befell Mkpasang community was batter imagined than felt. For weeks everyone mourned for the Mbede family and no one could be consoled. Deacon Mbede's health and wellbeing were matters of concern for all. And everyone rallied around him in this moment of grief.

Truly, the death of Esitima brought jets another untold pain to the community of Mkpasang. Etimbuk sobbed and moaned expressing outright grief for the loss so great to bear. Patrick on his part was confronted with the reality of things as they truly were as they joined the rank of orphans with all the problems that this offer. Above all, they faced the reality of managing day to day life on their own. Family members and friends attended as they could, but that was only temporary. As they dispersed, the children came to realise what it meant to leave without someone to learn from, a father or mother.

Aritie received the news of Esitima's suicide act on the way while going home from Uyai's office. he was absolutely distraught. Her mind was empty, running helter-skelter, in a haphazard manner in all directions; she panicked and couldn't control her anxiety.

"Oh, for heaven's sake, pray it's not true"

Aritie was in a state of dilemma as she skedaddled home hurriedly. She was seeing the result of her horrendous and weird action too horrific to be true. But before she left the premises, she put a call out to Enobong.

"Hello, Enobong have you heard the breaking news"

"What?"

"Esitima is dead!!!"

"How do you mean Esit..." Enobong questioned.

Before she could pronounce the last word, Aritie dropped the phone down, she couldn't control her emotion. Emotional outburst occasioned with the dropping of her phone on the floor drew attention of people nearby to her. They rushed down to console her. "Hello Hello Hello" Enobong kept repeating without any answer. She left driving recklessly, as fast as she could to see Aritie.

CHAPTER 44

WHEN THE NEWS WAS PUBLISHED everyone was in a sombre mood. Those who knew her and those who knew only the boutique, both were faced with enormous sadness for missing such a fashionista in Mkpasang.

The fashion world was prostrate in sadness too, it was as part of the business had been ripped off. Darkness enveloped everywhere; some shops shut their doors as a mark of solidarity to the departure of a star.

Customers thronged the Boutique to pay their last respect to the one who had made a meaningful impact in the lives of Mkpasang and fashion for decades. Friends and foes alike, all eulogised the departure of such an indefatigable icon of fashion splendour.

Etimbuk opened a condolence register in the boutique and family home to registers, one in the family house and another in the boutique support to evergreen memories of his mother.

"There would never be a replacement, the very best is gone, and gone forever. This day marks the beginning of an end for Ndiokko de Vogue to the world" Dr Essien registered regrettably as the first signatory on the register at home. Many more such condolences were pencilled down by numerous personalities that came to the funeral.

The indispensability of Esitima Mbede was unravelled on the day of her official burial. Condolences poured in from far and near. Above all, one received from the famous fashion house, DE Cousins in the United States of America.

All in all, Aritie secretly wished it didn't happen. Her cynical attitude towards Esitima's death swings like a pendulum. She had been full of death wishes with condescending arrogance and now, sober with impulsive desire for her dear life. Aritie was frightened with fear as to the departure of Esitima and counts with pride her numerous achievements for Mkpasang.

For how long shall the community continue to mourn for the Mbede family; what wrong have they committed to be subjected to this stormy calamity year in year out? The very thought of it sent nagging fear down the spine of everyone. Surely, the memories of Mbede shone brightly in their souls.

Epitaph

Mkpasang, the euphoria of Mbedes is gone
Harbinger of light for us in darkness
Gone with the tides of ages past
Leaving us with grief to mourn at last

City once impregnated with awesome pride
Amidst academic and fashion splendour ride
young and old in fullness bliss reside
Enthralled in Mbede's treasures without a price

Bassey a boffin with the strength of iron steel
And Esitima, fashion splendour with zeal
Years of life stood so richly supplied
But all gone too soon in their prime of life

Ndiokko de Vogue, your knell is toll today
Of doom and gloom and rod never unfold
In Mkpasang and all its surroundings be
Oh! Bassey and Esitima Mbede,
Mkpasang mourns for you in grief.

Oh death, our death disaster trails
Wherever you strike you leave tales
Of loss and calamity in a scale so great to bear
Bassey and Esitima, Mkpasang forgets not your care

Sleep on dear, Jewels of inestimable value
Your death is not the end
We all shall sleep
Sleep, and sleep and sleep
To an unending peace!

These words of devastation dotted Mkpasang for weeks and none could hold their peace. It was like the life of the community had suddenly come to an end or was ripped off everyone mourn; none could be consoled.

The great Esitima was laid to rest beside her beloved husband figuratively and a tombstone erected to commemorate the fact that in Mkpasang once lived a genius who treated everyone, including fashion, with much respect and care.

CHAPTER
45

THE TRIO OF ARITIE, UYAI and Enobong were arrested within days following their infamous meeting at Ebosom Restaurant. They were arraigned before a competent jurisdiction charged with the murder of Esitima. They planned this poisonous attack on that innocent lady, and they must dance to the music they all had played.

Although they pleaded not guilty, the evidence we presented, however, stood tall against their liberties. Therefore, the trio was subsequently sentenced to imprisonment for life with a minimum term of fifteen long years without the option of a fine.

Speaking before sentencing, Honourable Justice Etokudoh stated,

"The trio planned and executed their nefarious judgement on their victim far beyond the capabilities of women. Their actions were evil, atrocious and flagitious especially coming from three women, who should be tender-hearted and caring. This court absolutely has no mercy for them because they too didn't show any kindness for their victim"

Many came to understand the conspiracy to peddled by the trio in the community as untrue. This thick smokescreen of hatred that billowed around Mkpasang with intensity, suffocating the people was condemned by every standard.

Aghast by this despicable show of hatred to the family that had positively affected the lives of many in Mkpasang community for decades, majority of the community demonstrated overt condemnation and dislike for the culprits' action.

Aritie who had been earning her living from Esitima's purse to turn around and be the very one that manipulated circumstances surrounding her death was appalling evil. And she deserved no mercy at all.

Her action further heightened Etimbuk's lack of trust and confidence in people. As the only person who was close to him, and whom he could ever develop some level of trusting relationship and confidence, to turn out to be the very person who plotted and actually resulted in the death of his mother, was detestable and painful.

Aritie escalated her ruthlessness and scandalous rumour around the whole of Mkpasang and the environs just to ensure that she got Esitima out of the way. This is another Pharaoh who kept terrorising her victim and inflicting her with the pains and sorrows of mental illness.

Etimbuk reasoned that his mother suffered from severe depressive symptoms as a direct result from Aritie's intimidation and bullying every day. This was a woman who had been brimming with good health even after the death of her husband when suddenly; she developed devastating and debilitating clinical symptoms of depression. Leaving her with the agony, and she perceived life as hostile, not worth living.

Etimbuk may not have come closer to an understanding of the cause of his father's death, but the evidence provided clearly revealed the brewer of the rumours, Aritie and her cohorts. They intimidated the Mbedes with their rumours just to ensure his mother was dead. They're the most appalling and wicket human being on earth.

Esitima was anxious, tearful and sadly most of the time, a condition that impacted seriously on her desires and skills to manage life well including her business. Therefore, Ndiokko de Vogue experienced marked holes on its walls as there was a complete cessation of regular foreign products which were key to its sustenance, leading to its death.

Incidence of her illness and inability to cope with life had exposed Esitima to suicidal ideation. Self-inflicted death is despicable, a thing strange to our cultural heritage. Look at her level of distrust for her youthful friend, Joyce, and increasing wish to be left alone. Above all perception of herself as a victim of hatred by those who should care.

"All these were calculated attempts by my very cousin, Aritie to ensure she's is dead". Etimbuk's thoughts got his entire being as he remained reflecting on this tragic incident six months after his mother's burial.

"Aunty Aritie is maliciously wicked and heartless. Who could have imagined her of all people could do such a terrible thing. Crushing the very finger that house her, feed and clothe her daily? Human being needs to be feared.

They had joined forces with Enametti and Etido in the execution of that remarkable landmark court proceeding leading to their imprisonment. Even with that imprisonment, the children never laid off the rancour that Aritie had caused them to bear.

Her kindred, brother, sisters and parents were sceptical in relating with other family members. Especially the father who saw the situation as shameful and outrageous, as opposed to Mbedes.

However, Imprisonment of the duo raised the level of awareness in the community far beyond and recognising how bad things really were. For many, moral was slipping away fast into the trash can in the community. Although few individuals denied this fact that something was terribly wrong in what they had done.

For them, actions of Aritie, Uyai and Enobong shouldn't have been called to question in the court of law in the first place. What they did, if at all they had actually done so was normal gossips as far as Idiaimah was concerned. It shouldn't have been a matter for the Court of Law to decide.

Yet the majority was appalled by their wicked action which clearly became a reference for good moral conduct and practices for everyone in Mkpasang and beyond. Such reason prompted well-meaning individuals in the community to contribute finances towards the project of upholding the moral decorum.

For us it was a landmark development, a feat achieved for Esitima and Mkpasang people at large. This demonstrated defeat of injustice over justice, prejudice over love for Esitima and of evil over good.

We ensured that this project stood as an indelible icon of immortality for Bassey and Esitima Mbede, the drivers of Mkpasang unity and prosperity.

CHAPTER
46

Aᴇᴀʀ ʜᴀᴅ ᴘᴀssᴇᴅ sɪɴᴄᴇ ᴛʜᴇ three villains were prosecuted, the four of us, Enametti, Etimbuk, Animah and I were working on a plan to change the behaviour of Mkpasang people. We were seriously touched by the morality of the people ebbing into the trash can. This had not been pleasing to us. Therefore, looking for a way to resurrect that fire that defined Mkpasang as people with strong liberal values.

We met to finalise plans and programs to kickstart the campaign for the emancipation of the moral framework of Mkpasang on a full scale. Enametti stood rejected his sonorous voice tapered as he lowered himself on the iron rail on the foyer. He mumbled and could hardly be heard. Seriously frustrated and saddened by the situations which he blamed on the Idiaimah government inability to exert a grasp on the governance of the people.

Corruption raised its ugly head to heist us of resources located to the project we hoped to reshape the moral compass of Mkpasang. What saddened us most was that some government functionaries delayed releasing of money for the implementation of the plans. They sort gratifications before giving us finances to use into the lifeline of the project. This was absolutely unacceptable by a modern standard.

Enametti was not convinced of the success of the behaviour change project going by the rate of corruption found in government. Frightened that although necessary legislation had been enacted on the project, no fund was released two months after. Those sitting on the finances were asking for a bribe before they set the ball rolling. He now came to understand vividly the frustration and sense of paranoia Etimbuk expressed in his desire to get a scholarship award.

"This is not the winning attitude we want, Etido. Focusing on passion and committed to the goals and ambition without making excuses had been our desires. Not the negative way of killing the passion and enthusiasm of the people by stifling funds that should accrue to the project. That means some people are not true to themselves. Under this, how can we grow, why would people behave that way quite contrary to acceptable standard and practice?" Enametti expressed his frustration with Idiaimah policymakers in government.

I looked at him with interest, his lack of experience in the policies of Idiaimah civil service was the problem.

"This is laughable." He continued "This laudable project is about to end because of lack of funds, Etido. We shouldn't have any barrier along the way. We should be sailing smoothly without any hindrances. It's a project meant for all."

"I know, but we need to understand that this is Idiaimah, the antics we're familiar with.

Journeys may be long and arduous like I said, the hiccups and breaks are normal in any project destined for success in Idiaimah, especially those that concern the public. Finally, we'll get there as we press on stepping on big toes in the desire to offset the norms of the society." I told him.

"What do you mean by 'offset' Even on a project like free education meant for all?"

"Of course, the reason things are not working in their order. Why morals decadence is thriving in our community is this culture of corruption. You'll dismantle so many roadblocks and fortresses even with those you wouldn't expect could be involved with corruption."

"Is it that bad?"

"Absolutely, that's the experience I was talking about. What you'll witness in the office as you are building a career in the public service in this country in exactly staring you on the face right now. Probably you have seen or have been forced against your will to involve with things out of your character. Things that are obviously not in conformity with the norms of a civil society"

"In another word, I'll be infected by the virus of corruption. Is that what you mean?"

I looked at him approvingly.

"How did we come to this, Etido. I feel betrayed when people sit on my right or rights of others"

"I never meant that Enametti, betrayal has long been embedded in the lexicon of Idiaimahi. We're so used to it. Mine you, it's no more referred to as corruption, disloyal or perfidy but *'Idiaimah way'*. The culture of conducting business in the public even in the private people are still bent on finding a short cut to their advantage."

He took a gulp of his beer and remained infuriated, feeling the heat, disappointment and frustration. But I was indignant of the whole thing, it had become the norm and that was quite sad.

"Etido, are we justified in taking on the project?"

"Yes, Why?"

"Because this is the very behaviour that we're trying to prevent, the same which confronts us, about to disrupt our good intentions. Sad enough, this is coming from policymakers in government. We should rather start with the officers first"

I burst into a good-humoured laugh reeling off sitting on the sofa.

"This isn't funny Etido, is it?"

"Not at all" Still laughing "I'm amused by your statement. Idiaimah question shouldn't be a problem any longer to you. Everyone does it, it's not new. We're familiar with it my friend"

"Uh, are you corrupt, Etido. You said that everyone does it?"

I looked at my friend and shook my head imagining myself found on any messy deals in the office which I am paid the taxpayers' money to occupied.

"I am not corrupt, Enametti. You know I do my own business; I don't work for anyone. Even if I were to work in the civil service, I think I would not be involved in any shoddy deals. You are away I was not comfortable in fraudulent activities in my secondary days the reason I was appointed disciplinary prefect. Corruption is not a part of me."

"I feel anyone that involved with corruption should be formally prosecuted"

"Prosecution; did you mean prosecution, who will be the prosecutor; do you think the police can arrest the offender? That may be in the office, only to be led off the hook when he gets his own share of the loots. This is why people do not bother reporting such to law enforcement- if we have any. Even Judges in the Court of Law do not help matters, they like everyone else are neck-deep in the business of corruption, not to talk about the Executives or Legislature. All are there to loot, steal and kill anyone who stands in their way.

"But shall we succeed when the seat of governance is laden with corruption? How can those to whom the law is entrusted to be dishonest?"

"Certainly. I know it will be an uphill task. Changing people's behaviour is daunting in this country, even those in government. It's demands tact and the will power to get out of our comfort zone. We have to be bold in pacifying the officials into changing their behaviour too. You know everything is a journey, and we're starting a long and arduous journey right now. There may be loops and bumps along the way, but if we press hard enough, we shall succeed. You know change is difficult at the start, becomes quite messy as it progresses but absolutely gorgeous at the end. Don't worry, Enametti let us press on till the end."

But my friend was not still quite convinced of the success of the behaviour change project. He remained silent thinking if this kind of behaviour can be found in the seat of government.

"It's been long since I left the village Etido, the message will go down well with someone like,

Animah, you and Etimbuk whom the people can trust. I can only follow from the side-line, just being an auxiliary"

At that instance, Animah walked in and greeted us. He has been appointed to take charge of the project as its own Director-General (DG) after a year in the university reading for journalism, the program he so much wanted.

"Hello, folks, how is your day?"

"Hi, AniBaba, how are you? The day is not bad except for the bad news of corruption in Idiaimah."

Enametti responded with sadness in his heart. Etido regarded him with a note of optimism as he was expecting Animah urgently.

"You are welcome the DG. How far is the project going on in Awat Street, did you meet with Eteidung as discussed?

"Yes, I met with him and he surprised us with a very handsome contribution into the treasury, so, pleased with this magnanimity. Subsequently, I have written letters expressing our appreciation to him and other donors. Good news, Mrs Okon called this afternoon to invite me to meet with her by 04.00 pm tomorrow as she has some money to give to us. I am so thrilled, mates"

"Very thoughtful of you AniBaba, we are putting our heads together to see how to increase funds into the project. I am surprised that there is so much waywardness in the polity in Idiaimah, AniBaba. We have not been able to get the money as expected up till now despite approval being received about two months ago."

"Ah! Animah gave a chuckle. That's Idiaimah for you, no problems. We have to press on harder and be optimistic. It is not yet time to give up."

Animah responded accessing them with a note of disappointment.

The DG was not surprised they have not collected the money; in fact, he did not expect it without payment being made to the officials. Although a letter inviting them to the

Treasury but they had not gone prepared in the usual '*Idiaimah Way'* to get the money.

Animah joined them on the table sharing in the lager the were dinking. He gave them the report he needed to ask permission to be aware of for a week to enable him to submit the course work he was currently handling. His compatriot did not raise any objection.

"As I have said Enametti," Etido went back to what Enametti said before Animah walked in.

"you need not worry about being involved wholeheartedly in the project. You're the son of the soil, the need to play an active role, not supplementary. You have lived in the community for over a year now, people like and trust you, my friend, you have to play an active part in our resolve to bringing sanity into the polity. If you of all people don't, who will?

"However, I've spent most of my life in the past decade in this community, people do know who I am. Animah is the Mkpasang personified, he is widely known and even beyond the boundary of Mkpasang. Let's leave Etimbuk out of the question, for now, he is still very traumatised to be involved at the moment, at least in this early part of the campaign"

"Well, you're right" He reluctantly agreed. "But obviously, I am very scared by what I see this one year in government." He shook his head as he finished the sentence.

With that, we got into the real business of the day. We were set to design a valid and reliable interventions scheme for the project. The necessary billboards that we were to use in passing on the messages of behaviour change to the people were delivered by the artist that afternoon. This was to ensure our programmes were connected and communicated with the people through the consistency of the messages throughout the duration of the campaign.

"A piece of overwhelming evidence indicates that changing people's attitude and behaviour can have a major impact on how they relate with one another in society, folks. This can have a profound positive impact on long-term social position and access to information, services and resources.

"We need to make education the target problem and key to the change we need. With this majority of Mkpasang people will be easily disposed to be a part of the project. The current abhorrent situation in Mkpasang provided a good reason for us to kickstart the project." Animah counselled.

"You are right, AniBaba" Enametti concurred with Animah. "For the programme to succeed, we must bring the army of youth into it. This is to engage with individuals, household, and all within the community using personal and face to face contact and talking to the majority of the population about behaviour change. Social media like Facebook, Instagram, LinkedIn, TikTok and YouTube should be used widely.

"We need to emphasise continuous control of the life of those who do not benefit from the four walls of education or learn a trade. Their own life and circumstances left at the mercy of educated ones. Emphasising the need to allow their children to benefit from the beauty which education has to offer.

"Brainstorming seminars and workshops sessions are the methods to bring about this behaviour change, and we are set to deliver. Before the commencement of the project, we need to go into men groups, women and youth organisations, different Church organisation and marketplaces and find out their needs and fears. Spread the message everywhere. Of course, the University has to be involved.

"So Animah, issue a letter to the University intimating them of our mission. Tell the Vice-Chancellor of our activities and request a forum with him. This is a serious mission, all hands in the community must be on deck and contribute to its success. We need to draw input from various perspectives into the creation of a campaign that we thought would be compelling and appealing to all."

Enametti offered his expertise to the project.

"I agree totally with you Enametti, The University will play a major role in this direction Comrades, I hope the printer will deliver the posters as promised, Enametti."

Enametti nodded in agreement.

"As we want to use education as a veritable tool to accomplish our aim, don't we think identifying the benefits of education will be appropriate? I think we should start identifying its benefits first as inevitable.

"And not forgetting to dispel the fear that the three young women involved in the crime each had acquired formal education beyond the secondary level. Those women were using their skills in a negative way to accomplish their callous desire. And education is necessary to keep the community save." I said as part of my contribution to keeping the conversation going.

"Absolutely," Said Enametti.

Therefore, we sat down to delve into the process of identifying the benefits of education. First on the list was that education terms crime and criminals by providing and preparing an educated person to lead a happy life and enjoy the good things of life. People with enable skills are those that have gone through the education process, and they come out enjoying the good thing that is in store in the world for them. Such individuals position themselves to have good jobs and earn better salaries.

Social interaction and reputation including the better interpersonal relationship with others are those basic skills that those with good learning acquires through education. Also, we bring to the understanding that education is a must feasible accomplishment for a promising an enduring future and a stable lifestyle.

In fact, the educated individual is a useful member of society. His character is moulded, and mind illuminated, and he encourages himself and others to understand the basic tenets of a fulfilled life. Certainly, he has a greater chance to contribute to his community effort through. becoming an active member of society. Brings about participation in the ongoing changes and developments that his social needs. This is an aspect that can only be made possible through education.

Not only that, but any educated mind also broadens his understanding of society making him able to integrate with what is ideal and useful to him and the society. Opening a world of opportunities for the poor so that they may have an equal right to well-paying jobs. Rising up to call for women right to vote and be voted for was very significant. They would not have been able to do this without education, subsequently, we find women included in the process of choosing those who govern over them and to whom they can govern over. Educated minds are bold, their voice respected in matters that affect the community.

When people are educated, they are assertive in defending their right and bringing this to have a greater impact on the lives of others. Talk of women in any profession like engineering, medicine, aviation industry, nursing etc, which they have shared with men. It is empowerment in education that plays a major role in their understanding of their roles in the industry that makes them able to ensure equality in salary and wages, same that place them in the same positions of authority with men.

Indeed, education exposes people to know the difference between right and wrong. Makes your personality stands out and you lead a matured and purposeful life. In fact, the benefit of education is limitless.

Animah said.

"This shall provide us with the compass to work with. We shall be able to accomplish what we have to do with the blueprint in hand. He went further to state that the accomplishment of everything through the delivery of workshops on behaviour change will give us good opportunities to bring diverse insight into the project. Quite a lot of Mkpasang people will understand the proposals and engage well in it."

We worked on the initiatives of short and long-termed literary education programmes. The wheel to stop moral rot and massive unemployment abounding in Idiaimah and Mkpasang.

The disadvantage of not being educated is the challenge in household income, although this may not be the case always. Often too, people left in the low-income bracket are seen in every household giving a clear message on how education can change lives and get families out of the poverty line.

People with low-income bracket give the message that had they embrace training or been educated their earning would reflect the status of educated ones. They would not have earned far less than one dollar a day to sustain their vulnerability in material and finances for survival. Animah went ahead to say that.

"The struggle to eke out a living, doing menial jobs that taxed the health and wellbeing of the people to the brink could be quite painful. (He had been there before and knows what, he is talking about)

"A situation whereby few better-placed individuals exploit the vulnerabilities of the people was appalling and not acceptable in this community. This has caused the people great pain to their gain. The only solution is finding a workable solution to this mess, is for people to get behind the campaign for literary and vocational education. We have to get people seriously involve in the process wholeheartedly."

With massive poverty resulting from illiteracy and the majority incapable of participating in any meaningful social, economic and political discourse, they will continue to remain on the last prong of the ladder. The only solution remains compulsory education of the masses, preventing people from being robbed of their future.

"The vision of the elders in the community must burn alive in their heart. And the famous *"Mkpasang five"* acronym must not die," Enametti said

"The legacies which defined Mkpasang as a community with love and care must burn with intensity for the generation yet unborn. And this, through the campaign for massive education for behaviour change. It should become clearer with the vision, to illuminate the minds of the Mkpasang people."

Certainly, our elders knew the value of education, they pursued with energy and eagerness in their heart. We made it clear not to rest on our oases until a suitable remedy is found to change the behaviour of our people so that they can contribute their own quota to this noble inheritance and that of the future yet unborn.

One of the cardinal points of the programme was using the right words in daily conversations. Words of respect that has a greater positive impact on the way people think, behave and relate with one another. We know the key to changing behaviour is to try new techniques and find ways for people to stay engaged and motivated.

The other was inculcating the culture of fairness and justice along with evidence of positive and acceptable moral values which impacted the entire population of Mkpasang people. Those norms, beliefs and values which made Mkpasang proud were what we focused attention and mind seriously on.

Using persuasions, we got people to listen to our messages, especially the youth and women who they very first to gradually embrace the change we needed with zeal. Yes, "*the only permanent thing is change*", was the official slogan that we used to carry the change in our messages. And, in fact, we were set to sweep under the carpet those repulsive and retrogressive behaviour foreign to Mkpasang and brought to bear, messages of love, brotherhood and fairness.

These were compelling messages that the change team propagated with love and togetherness.

Organising people well to evidence such attributes was really magnificent as a majority of the people evident these through awakening interests in the project of behaviour change. It set priorities to identify target resources, problems and solutions that promoted sustainable development far above our expectation.

As a way of maintaining that tempo, we set up what we called the '*Mkpasang Champion Award*' something meant to encourage and arouse interest in the envisaged project. The award came with various cash prizes, and with this, a healthy sense of competition was created deeply engrained in the life of the community. And many, especially the youth and anyone in the community was willing to sign up for it.

Next, we created the community tabloid, which we christened, *Mkpasang Chronicle*, we highlighted the message of behaviour change. Posters and billboards were judiciously used and any available spaces within the community to spread the message of education on behaviour change. Also, the use of town cries in the process of intensifying our campaigns.

These created much-needed awareness motivated the people toward acceptance for the project. And Mkpasang Champions award earned credibility generated massive followership which we used to harness resources for the project. The financial contribution was staggering by well-meaning individuals and groups, home and abroad. And we worked tirelessly assessing the target groups through planning, delivery and evaluation of a programme of activities.

Overall, it was a huge success.

And we saw change drawn from the profound heritage and culture of goodwill portrayed by our progenitors. Something precious they left for us continuing to be at the forefront. The majority saw the programme as the need to open to change by rejecting negative instincts brought about by Aritie and her cohorts that kill rather than build us as one united people.

Through this programme, the majority of the people did the right thing and live right in attitude and behaviour as they welcomed change with open arms. They also allow these changes to permeate the very fabric of Mkpasang society through their good conducts and practices. Through this, we witnessed many children enrolling in Community Secondary School, Mkpasang. Our joy knew no bound. Also, many parent and ward withdrew their children from the street into classrooms as the legal framework that established this emphasised jail term for those who flaunt the order.

Before now, we witnessed the abuse of children denied their future by allowing them to roam the street hawking food and other good around Mkpasang. Such children usually become recalcitrant and not obedient to the authority and hard to manage. The campaign for behaviour changed really turned the table for our good.

At the end of the programme, Enametti who was very sceptical due to the magnitude of corruption he witnessed turned around to give a very encouraging testimonial.

"The reason bad things are a triumph in the society is that good men are lip tied. Had we kept silent and allow the rot to continue, perhaps Aritie and co would have gone scot-free. And perhaps, many with such tendencies would have sprung up in the society to encourage such crimes of killing, abuse and such behaviours that is absurd to our cooperate existence.

"Our contributary efforts may not go for any patriotism or nationalism folks, but the little we do has certainly gone miles out to make a difference, keeping most of the vices out of Mkpasang.

"The level of participation in the project was phenomenal, I was blown away by the way people took ownership of the campaign. I can see the few caring individuals can change the world for good, and education programmes that drive a gamut of changes are worth waiting for. It is good how we identified and use the skills and knowledge of those few individuals available to achieve this remarkable success"

"Look at the willingness to cooperate and work together, indeed, this was phenomenal! The enthusiasm of the people had been one value that we so much like with the people of Mkpasang. Our coordination and partnership with change-minded people in the community who were willing and ready to take ownership of the project really paid off. I was absolutely blown away personally."

Just as the problem of illiteracy and moral decadence is not peculiar or isolated to Mkpasang alone, it's a widespread phenomenon amongst the rural and urban population in Idiaimah. We intended this project will see the light of the day in the whole the State of Mkpasang so that it could be adorned with liberal values.

Our campaign for literal education made the impoverished people awaken from their slumber and take up the responsibilities they had with society in their hands. It made them see that their capabilities of attaining greater heights was solely in their hands and had been undermined for years. They started to find themselves in the constant evaluation as people capable of meaningful achievements to humanity.

We witnessed how the programme empowered people with knowledge and ameliorated their conditions. These were possible because they were provided with enough reasons and need to understand essential and basic information which change their lives and circumstances for the better.

This programme, behaviour change, really curbed illiteracy as the main virus eating deeper into the attitude of Mkpasang people. We pursued it with zeal and enthusiasm working closely with members of the State Assembly and government in pursuance of the enabling law that made it mandatory for the prosecution of anyone that flaunts the order.

Promotion of aggressive, stronger and exhaustive effort toward free and compulsory literary education for children between the ages of 03 and 15 years old in the state was our aim. Although education at all level was an impossible venture, we were proud the little we fought for had rewarded.

As a long-term project, we set up informed feedback right from the inception of the campaign.

We wanted this to be a veritable way of removing barriers and allowing all to take ownership of the project. This also triggers memories and emotions of the past that acted as a motivation of the majority, especially elders to ever connect with the project.

Animah was in charge of the day-to-day running, review and intervention of the project. He gave us regular reports and insight into the project as an ongoing programme. This gave us ideas on how to allocate resources on a monthly or yearly basis. He worked tirelessly helping people to develop accurate knowledge about good behaviour and the consequences of bad behaviours to society.

This really enhanced Mkpasang to belief in their ability for change. Eventually, Mkpasang was seen as the epitome of achievement in this direction. The enabling political will and strong determination on the part of the people was the force that made the project to succeed in spite of the problem of corruption in government.

"For me winning attitude had been what matters most. It draws people around helping to accomplish things that matter in life which otherwise wouldn't be possible to achieve."

Etido stated that the majority of our ancestors never acquired any formal education; jet they left us with sagacious and intimidating catalogues of profound wisdom-heritage evidenced in our a culture which he found both incomprehensible and incontestable, one of which had been the an acronym, '*Mkpasang five*'.

"No, such heritage cannot go into recession. We must fight and fight with all our might to preserve the integrity they held so dear to hearts which they handed over to us.

It was incumbent on us to bring these desirable psychological changes into the behaviour and attitude of the Mkpasang people. Better habits that will portray her as heritage capable of demonstrating a standard of trust, value and integrity in dealing with others.

In the end, the campaign turned into a charity forum that sponsors youth in their educational pursuits and many were beneficiaries of this magnanimous project. *Mkpasang five* turned into *Mkpasang for all*. The concept our progenitors fought for.

Aminah joined the rank of this elite group. And when he graduated from the University, the level of integration which he used his journalistic skills to coordinate into a harmonious whole was second to none.

Animah helped, along with others, to foster unity, leadership and expected behaviour change in a massive scale. Mkpasang as people were portrayed with high regards to moral responsibility in character and behaviour. There was the outright demonstration of the virtue of love and care in the eyes of the world, especially our neighbours, they were jealous saw Mkpasang as a true harbinger of growth and prosperity

The Project Director-General, Animah, good leadership, honesty and accountability in this the direction was highly appreciated and adored by all in Mkpasang.

ABOUT THE AUTHOR

Gregory Effiong was born in 1960 in Idoro Uyo, Akwa Ibom state Nigeria. A Registered Mental Health Nurse, he moved to the United Kingdom in February 2008, and continued practicing the profession. Writing happens to be one hobby he cherishes with a deep passion and *Esitima (The Beloved)* is his first published book.

Gregory Effiong is married to Veronica; they have two sons Elisha and Emediong. He had had another son, Anietie, in his earlier relationship.

Printed in the United States
by Baker & Taylor Publisher Services